Praise for the *Diagnosis Murder* novels

"*Diagnosis Murder: The Past Tense* is the latest—and arguably the best—original mystery based on the popular Dick Van Dyke TV series, which Goldberg wrote and produced. What makes it more than just another spin-off is the way Goldberg takes the reader—and his hero, Dr. Mark Sloan—through forty years of Los Angeles history, a journey that captures the unique flavor of the city so many of us used to call home." —*Chicago Tribune*

"All the elements of a fine mystery novel: good characters, interesting plot, surprising twists and, above all, crisp and enjoyable writing. With books this good, who needs TV?" —*Chicago Sun-Times*

"[*The Past Tense*] is Lee Goldberg's best *Diagnosis Murder* novel yet. He can plot and write with the best of them." —*Mystery Scene*

"A whodunit thrill ride that captures all the charm, mystery, and fun of the TV series . . . and then some. . . . Goldberg wrote the very best *Diagnosis Murder* episodes, so it's no surprise that this book delivers everything you'd expect from the show. . . . A clever, high-octane mystery that moves like a bullet-train. Dr. Mark Sloan, the deceptively eccentric deductive genius, is destined to join the pantheon of great literary sleuths. . . . You'll finish this book breathless. Don't blink or you'll miss a clue. A brilliant debut for a brilliant detective. Long live Dr. Mark Sloan!" —*New York Times* bestselling author Janet Evanovich

"Can books be better than television? You bet they can—when Lee Goldberg's writing them. Get aboard right now for a thrill ride." —*New York Times* bestselling author Lee Child

continued . . .

DIAGNOSIS MURDER

THE DOUBLE LIFE

Lee Goldberg

BASED ON THE TELEVISION SERIES CREATED BY

Joyce Burditt

A SIGNET BOOK

SIGNET
Published by New American Library, a division of
Penguin Group (USA) Inc., 375 Hudson Street,
New York, New York 10014, USA
Penguin Group (Canada), 90 Eglinton Avenue East, Suite 700, Toronto,
Ontario M4P 2Y3, Canada (a division of Pearson Penguin Canada Inc.)
Penguin Books Ltd., 80 Strand, London WC2R 0RL, England
Penguin Ireland, 25 St. Stephen's Green, Dublin 2,
Ireland (a division of Penguin Books Ltd.)
Penguin Group (Australia), 250 Camberwell Road, Camberwell, Victoria 3124,
Australia (a division of Pearson Australia Group Pty. Ltd.)
Penguin Books India Pvt. Ltd., 11 Community Centre, Panchsheel Park,
New Delhi - 110 017, India
Penguin Group (NZ), cnr Airborne and Rosedale Roads, Albany,
Auckland 1310, New Zealand (a division of Pearson New Zealand Ltd.)
Penguin Books (South Africa) (Pty.) Ltd., 24 Sturdee Avenue,
Rosebank, Johannesburg 2196, South Africa

Penguin Books Ltd., Registered Offices:
80 Strand, London WC2R 0RL, England

First published by Signet, an imprint of New American Library,
a division of Penguin Group (USA) Inc.

First Printing, November 2006
10   9   8   7   6   5   4   3   2   1

To Gina Maccoby and Mitchel Stein,
for making my double lives possible

ACKNOWLEDGMENTS

I would like to thank Dr. D. P. Lyle for his friendship and his invaluable medical advice and Jack R. Parker for sharing his experience on autopsy practices.

This book would not have been possible without the enthusiasm and support of William Rabkin, Tod Goldberg, Kerry Donovan, and, most of all, my wife, Valerie, and my daughter, Madison.

I look forward to hearing from you about this book, or any of the previous novels in the series, at www.diagnosis-murder.com.

CHAPTER ONE

Dr. Mark Sloan believed in ghosts. Not as disembodied spirits of the dead haunting the mortal world, but as shadows of the living that linger in the places we go and the things we do.

He never saw the ghosts, but in his role as a special consultant to the Los Angeles Police Department, there came a point in every homicide investigation when he sensed their presence.

They lurked at the edges of his awareness, as if he were sitting in a dark room, his back to the door, but with the creeping certainty that someone was standing behind him. There was always a palpable change in the air, a displacement created not by physical movement but by the tremor of intent and the rumble of imminent death.

The ghosts that haunted Dr. Mark Sloan were the murderers he pursued. He rarely felt them while he was working a crime scene or examining a corpse. Observing stark evidence of the murderer's brutality or pleasure, rage or intellect, remorse or glory, wasn't the same as actually feeling his physicality, sensing it all around like a low, barely audible hum.

That came later.

Mark would methodically conduct his investigation, interviewing witnesses and suspects, studying evidence and assembling disparate facts, waiting for that moment of skin-crawling awareness when he finally felt the breath of his adversary on the back of his neck.

In that instant he always felt fear and dread. But he also felt a dark glee—the thrill of the hunt. He knew himself well enough after sixty-some years to admit without guilt that it was this jolt as much as anything else that drove him to do this ugly work, a calling that was as vital to him as his medical career.

Of course, whenever he embarked on a homicide investigation, he knew there was a killer out there even if he hadn't yet *felt* his existence. So when the moment came, it was never a surprise. He expected it. He welcomed it.

This time was different.

His investigation didn't begin with a murder. It began with a coincidence at Community General Hospital in West Los Angeles, where Mark was the chief of internal medicine. He had a nagging instinct that something wasn't right, that somehow the natural course of events was out of balance, tipped by an invisible hand.

The more he had looked into things over the past couple of days, the more his uneasiness had grown, taking on shape and substance. That morning, he awoke fully alert in the predawn darkness of his bedroom, hearing only the gentle lapping of the waves outside his Malibu beach house. But he strained to hear something else, the sound that had awakened him.

The sound wasn't outside. It was the pounding of his heart. It was the rush of blood moving through his veins.

It was fear.

It was the awareness of a subtle shift in his environment. He wasn't alone. There was a presence with him now. A ghost.

A killer.

It was a sensation so visceral that it raised goose bumps on his flesh and left him trembling. He had to fight the childish urge to pull the covers over his head and hide.

But he knew that wouldn't protect him. There was no escaping what haunted him. The killer felt close because he was lurking somewhere deep in Mark's psyche.

The identity of his adversary was hiding in the facts Mark already knew, waiting to be revealed in that instant of astonishing clarity when the thousands of bits of information he'd assembled aligned themselves like pixels to become a sharp image.

The key to making that alignment happen was recognizing some overlooked fact, by looking at what he knew from another perspective. Sometimes all it took was a word, a smell, or a specific image to make it all happen.

Feeling the presence of a killer was one thing, but proving he was there and catching him were quite another. That was Mark's mission today. He was determined to go through everything once more, to find the answers that eluded him.

He got out of bed, took a scalding shower, dressed for work, and was on the road by seven, driving south into the swirls of gray fog that drifted off the ocean and rolled over the Pacific Coast Highway, lapping up against the bluffs of Santa Monica like the surf.

He exited the highway in Santa Monica and climbed the steep California Incline, the aging roadway up to Ocean Avenue that was carved out of the eroding cliff decades ago and reinforced with poured concrete. The California Incline always struck Mark as a grandiose name for something as mundane as a retaining wall with a road on top.

Once he got onto the palm-lined Ocean Avenue, the Champs-Elysées of homelessness, he turned left onto Wilshire Boulevard. The street was choked with traffic as far east as he could see, turning what should have been a straight shot to Community General Hospital into an agonizing crawl. Mark didn't bother taking one of the many elaborate alternate routes on residential streets, knowing they were just as bad, a jittery journey between Stop signs that gave the illusion of faster movement but the reality of motion sickness.

Sitting behind the wheel of his rented Ford Five Hundred, Mark was frustrated and impatient, acutely aware of his hard plastic surroundings. The car also had faux burled walnut trim seemingly designed by someone who'd *heard* about wood but had never actually *seen* any.

The slow-moving cars crowded around him. He could feel their pressure, as if the walls of his car were crushing in on him. He choked on the exhaust fumes that seeped into the cabin despite the closed windows and sealed vents. But most of all, he felt the killer in the car with him, sneering at his discomfort and powerlessness.

Murder gives you power, Mark. There's nothing else like it. You ought to try it sometime. You'll feel great.

He glanced at the empty passenger seat. Was this the ghost of the killer whispering to him or the collected shadows of all the murderers he'd pursued? Or was it some nightmarish aspect of his soul? He wondered then, as he often did, if it was really possible to come face-to-face with so many killers and not be infected, even a little, by their evil.

Not so long ago, Mark was shaken by the discovery that one of his closest friends, a doctor he'd known most of his life, was a serial killer. For decades, Mark's friend had spent his days relieving pain and suffering and his nights inflicting it. The revelation made Mark question many of his basic assumptions about life, about medicine, and about himself.

Over the last forty years, he'd been told many times that he had a gift for solving murders and capturing killers, a unique ability to see patterns and connections where others saw only a blur of information.

But what if his gift was actually a mutated curse? What if he was so good at catching killers because, at some level, he thought the same way they did? Or worse, was driven by the same desires?

Mark shared this fear with his forty-something son,

Steve, an LAPD homicide lieutenant, during an evening walk on the beach.

"Of course you think like them," Steve said. "They're hunters and so are you. You just have different prey. And you don't kill what you catch."

"Several of the murderers I've caught have been executed," Mark said. "I watched them die."

"Only because they asked you to be there so they could enjoy one last act of manipulation, and inflict just a little more misery, before they died. You've never killed anyone."

"Not with my own hand." Mark knew his son had killed in the line of duty, but he'd never summoned the courage to ask Steve what it felt like.

"Did you enjoy watching them die?" Steve asked.

What about you, Steve? Mark thought. His son watched those executions unblinkingly, without the slightest hesitation.

When Steve killed someone in self-defense, those terrible experiences happened quickly, in the heat of battle. But Mark couldn't help wondering if Steve found it exciting, too. Was there just a little thrill involved? Was it the adrenaline rush of survival, or something darker?

Mark shook his head, more to clear his thoughts than to respond to Steve's question. "Witnessing those executions made me sick."

"That's what sets you apart," Steve said. "That's what makes you human and them inhuman. You've spent your career saving lives, not taking them."

Mark often thought about that conversation, about what was said and what wasn't.

His investigations had led to many murderers being imprisoned for life or sentenced to death. He wondered if he would pursue killers with the same zeal if he had to carry out the sentences himself.

He didn't find the answer to that question, or any others, during his commute that morning. When he finally arrived at

Community General, he sped up to the second tier of the parking structure and pulled into his reserved spot, coming up just short of tapping his front bumper against the concrete pillar, the sure sign of a man in a hurry.

But despite his short, tiresome journey and a mild case of claustrophobia, he didn't hurry to get out of his charmless rental car. Instead he sat there for a long moment, disoriented and disturbed, as if he'd just this instant awakened instead of an hour ago.

It's nothing a hot cup of coffee and a surge of caffeine won't cure, he told himself.

Mark emerged from his car just as Dr. Jesse Travis strode out of the ER like a man who'd been released from prison. He was wearing a lab coat over his wrinkled blue scrubs, his hair was askew, and a day's stubble showed on his face. There was a surprising spring in his step, though, considering he probably hadn't slept much in the last twenty-four hours.

Many people were quick to misjudge Jesse, taking his boundless enthusiasm and boyish demeanor as signs of inexperience and immaturity. But in a medical crisis he became a different person, displaying a confidence and calm authority that eluded him in every other aspect of his life.

The two men, the mentor and his apprentice, met in the middle of the steep incline leading up to the next level of the parking garage.

"Good morning, Jesse. Coming off a rough shift?"

"Is it that obvious?"

"I assume every shift is rough," Mark said.

"This was worse than most. I'd be glad to wow you with tales of my medical heroism, but I've got to get home. Susan and I only have a two-hour overlap before she starts her shift, and that doesn't give us much time to—"

Mark interrupted. "I get the picture."

Jesse and his wife, Susan, a nurse at Community General,

were longtime lovers who were still adjusting to becoming husband and wife.

"I'd like to meet the cruel administrator who scheduled us on opposite shifts," Jesse said. "We never see each other lately."

"It makes you two appreciate one another even more."

Jesse narrowed his eyes at Mark. "Spoken like someone in charge of scheduling."

Mark raised his hands, begging off. "It wasn't me."

"But it's worked out for you. There's nothing to get in the way of me devoting all my free time to those files you want me to go through."

"See—there's a positive side to everything."

Jesse still regarded Mark suspiciously. "After I've had a couple hours of sleep, I'll get back to it."

"Let me know when you find something."

"I can't help noticing that you said *when*, not *if*," Jesse said. "You still think there's something there?"

Mark nodded. "I *know* there is."

Jesse studied Mark. "I believe it. You've got that look."

"What look?"

"Like you're staring right through me at the sonofabitch." Jesse gave Mark a smile and glanced at his watch. "Yikes! I've got to go. I'll meet you at Barbeque Bob's for lunch."

"I'm buying," Mark said.

"At the restaurant your son and I own," Jesse said. "Do you really think I'd take your money?"

"You didn't have a problem taking it when you were looking for investors."

Jesse pondered that for a moment. "Come to think of it, you're right. Now that I'm saving up to buy a house, the idea of *you* slowly paying off *my* debt to you makes sound financial sense to me. I'll show up for lunch hungry."

As Jesse hurried towards his car, he caught a movement in his peripheral vision. It was a car coming down from the next floor. The old Camaro glided out of the murk like a shark, picking up speed. The driver was hidden behind deeply tinted glass, which only added to the car's aura of menace.

There was also something unsettlingly deliberate about the way it was rolling forward. It took a second before Jesse realized consciously what he knew instinctively.

The driver was adjusting his steering, keeping Mark dead center in front of him.

Dead center.

At that instant the car shot forward, the engine roaring, the tires squealing, the deafening sounds echoing off the walls of the parking structure.

Jesse shouted Mark's name in warning.

Mark turned and saw the car bearing down on him, the dirty chrome grill like fangs with flesh caught between the teeth, and he knew several truths at once.

This wasn't an accident. There was no time for escape. And he was going to die.

But the impact he felt next wasn't from the car. It came from the side, knocking him off his feet. Mark saw the concrete rushing up to his face and took an instant of solace in the knowledge that he wouldn't hear the sickening, wet smack or feel the excruciating pain. All he would know would be a deep, never-ending night.

And as he was thinking that, his night came.

CHAPTER TWO

The first thing Mark became aware of was the pain. He grabbed it like a rope and used it to climb his way into awareness. The closer he got to consciousness, the greater the pain became, until it felt like an ax was buried in his skull.

He wanted to shrink away from the pain and fall back into the senseless depths from which he'd risen. But he fought the temptation. He kept his grip on the rim of consciousness by trying to recognize other sensations sharing the bandwidth with his pain.

He smelled the aroma of disinfectants, soap, and rubbing alcohol and recognized it as what passed for fresh air within the walls of Community General Hospital. The realization grounded him, strengthening his hold on consciousness. He was in the hospital.

Was he asleep on his office couch?

No, the sounds were wrong. He was hearing electronic hums, clicks, and beeps, the cicadas of the intensive care unit.

Had he fallen asleep in a chair while watching over a patient? Was his head aching from lolling at an uncomfortable angle for too long?

No, he was lying flat. His head was on a pillow.

As the murk in his mind began to clear, he became aware

of other irritations: the catheter, the IV in his left arm, the electrodes on his chest, and the oxygen cannula in his nostrils.

With those sensations came an obvious realization that nonetheless came only gradually to him: He was a patient in the ICU.

How could that be? What had happened to him?

He tried to open his eyes, but it was like bench-pressing weights with his eyelids, an effort that required the full measure of his meager concentration and nearly sent him plummeting back into unconsciousness.

What saved him from slipping back was someone dabbing a wet towel against his brow. He focused on that, the moisture and the relief, and then his eyes opened and he found himself trying to focus his blurry vision on a woman's face.

Mark blinked hard and the image sharpened. It was an ICU nurse that he knew. But he couldn't remember her name; he was having a hard enough time just keeping her face in focus. Seeing her, however, confirmed his conclusions about where he was and his present circumstances.

The nurse was a slender Asian woman in her early thirties with a bright smile and perfect teeth.

"Welcome back, Dr. Sloan."

He tried to speak, but couldn't summon his voice. She placed a hand gently on his chest to soothe him.

"Take it easy. I know you've got lots of questions. I'll get Dr. Noble."

She left before he could try to say anything.

Mark glanced at the machines around the room and studied the readout from the cardiac monitor. There was nothing irregular about his EKG or his blood pressure, and there was no breathing tube down his throat.

That was a good start.

Besides his agonizing headache, which probably accounted for his blurred vision and disorientation, he wasn't aware of any other pain.

He tried flexing his fingers and toes, then lifting his arms and legs. They were stiff, but otherwise normal. No broken limbs or paralysis. He made fists, then rubbed his hands together to test his sense of touch. Everything was okay. In fact, he was even able to reach out, pick up a plastic cup from his bedside table, and take a sip of water.

The headache seemed to be his only ailment. He raised a hand and gingerly explored his head. There were stitches above his brow and some swelling.

He let his gaze drift around his cubbyhole in the ICU. There were several fresh bouquets, the "get well" arrangement from the gift shop downstairs, and two others that were wilting. There were also some gift boxes of candy neatly stacked next to the flowers. Two of the boxes had been opened and freely sampled, suggesting that someone got bored sitting at his bedside. A paperback copy of John Irving's *A Prayer for Owen Meany*, with a deeply creased spine, was on the chair, suggesting that his visitor wasn't Steve. His son would have left some issues of *Sports Illustrated* and *Guns & Ammo*.

"So, what's your diagnosis?" a woman asked as she entered his room. The Community General photo ID clipped to her lab coat identified her as Dr. Emily Noble, but the rest of the print was too small for him to make out with his blurred vision.

Studying her slender nose, her sharp cheekbones, and the gentle curve of her chin, Mark could see exactly what Dr. Noble had looked like as a child, a teenager, and a young woman. Her face was like a painting that stayed the same while the lighting that illuminated it changed. In all phases of her life she must have been beautiful, as she was now.

There was a certain elegance and authority in her eyes, and yet he saw that smiles came easily to her. The laugh lines gently etched at the edges of her mouth revealed her overall contentment and her age, which Mark estimated to be early fifties. She was wearing a black dress under her lab coat, which seemed a little formal for making rounds.

When he tried to speak this time, he was relieved to discover that his voice came easily.

"I've got a whopper of a headache. I'm disoriented, dizzy, and nauseous. I'm suffering from mild photophobia and I've got a nasty contusion on my head," Mark said. "I'd say I've suffered blunt force trauma and a concussion."

He knew that a concussion was simply a catchall description of a blow to the head that causes a brain malfunction, which could be as simple as a headache or as serious as a prolonged coma, and anything in between. The concerns would be internal bleeding and swelling of the brain.

"Judging by the flowers and the candy, I'd say I've been out a few days."

"Three days, off and on. It's nice to know that your deductive skills remain intact."

"What did my CTs and MRIs show?" Mark asked.

"Some mild brain swelling. We've been keeping you on diuretics and Decadron, eight milligrams IV twice a day," she said, holding up the index finger of her right hand. "Follow my finger with your eyes."

He did as he was told as she moved her finger this way and that.

"You can save yourself the trouble of doing any more of those basic tests," Mark said. "I just gave myself a neurological examination and I passed."

"Humor me. As I recall, hospital rules clearly state that the doctors are supposed to do the exams, not the patients."

"I am a doctor," he said.

"Glad you remember. That's a good start. Can you tell me your name?"

"Dr. Mark Sloan. I'm chief of internal medicine at Community General Hospital, where I am now residing in the ICU."

She asked him to move his arms and legs for her and to make fists. He reluctantly complied, a scowl on his face.

"I've already done all this," he said.

"Stop complaining, Mark. After three days of lying around, you can use the exercise."

Her overly familiar manner surprised him, but he let it slide. He would have a serious talk with her about it when he wasn't a patient anymore and was back at work as a hospital administrator.

She tested the strength in his legs by asking him to extend his legs while she pushed against his feet.

"Can we please move on?" Mark said, unable to hide his impatience.

"Not yet. Besides, in your current mood, you'll like this one," she said. "Stick your tongue out at me."

He did.

"I think you liked that so much, you want to grin. Go ahead, indulge yourself."

He did what she asked, giving her an exaggerated grin, knowing she wasn't teasing him but rather testing his cranial nerves. This was a test he'd forgotten in his own quick self-exam. There was another one, too, that he'd overlooked, so before she could ask, he extended his left arm, touched his nose with his finger, and then repeated the exercise with his right arm. The actions tested the functioning of his cerebellum.

"Very good," Dr. Noble said. "You must have smacked your head against concrete before."

"Is that what happened to me?"

She stiffened, as if she regretted the words immediately after she'd spoken them. "What do you remember about how you got hurt?"

Mark searched his mind. "Nothing."

He wasn't concerned by his lapse of memory. Not recalling how the injury occurred was an extremely common symptom among those who'd suffered concussions. The recollection of recent events is wiped away by the trauma, at least temporarily. He often compared it to writing something on your computer just as the system crashes. Whatever fresh information you're in the midst of inputting is lost.

He'd treated more than a few car accident victims who couldn't even remember leaving home. Their last memory was reading the morning paper and enjoying a cup of coffee. In some cases, that was a blessing.

Dr. Noble began to press on his legs, abdomen, and face, asking him repeatedly as she did so if he could feel her touch.

"Yes, yes, and yes," he said irritably. "You can stop these tests now. I'm fine. You haven't answered my question yet."

"There's just one more sensory test I need to perform first," Dr. Noble said, her hands still cupping his face. "Tell me if you can feel this."

He thought she was going to pinch his cheeks. But that wasn't what she did. She leaned down and kissed him gently on the lips, lingering for a moment to look intimately into his eyes.

"Is that always part of your neurological exam, Dr. Noble?" Mark asked.

"Only with my sexiest patients, Dr. Sloan." She smiled coyly.

He didn't know how to deal with this and wasn't in any shape to try. It was time to get rid of her.

"I'd like to see Dr. Travis," Mark said.

She leaned back and hesitated. "Jesse isn't here."

Dr. Noble said Jesse's name as if they knew each other well. If that was the case, why had Mark never heard of her before?

"Then get Amanda," Mark said. "Dr. Amanda Bentley, the staff pathologist."

"I know who she is." Dr. Noble cocked her head at an angle, regarding Mark strangely, her expression bordering on fear.

Was she only now realizing how far over the line she'd gone, how inappropriate her behavior had been? What if she wasn't even a doctor at all but some crazy person pretending to be one?

"Amanda is on her way up. I called her right after I called Steve," Dr. Noble said. "They should both be here soon."

Mark was relieved to hear that, though surprised again by the easy familiarity with which she used his son's first name.

"Thank you," he said.

"What's the last thing you remember, Mark?"

He thought for a moment. "The wedding."

"Whose wedding?"

He wondered if he should say, since Jesse and Susan might not appreciate him spreading the word before they got a chance to announce the news themselves. All it would take was Dr. Noble telling one nurse or doctor and the whole hospital would know about the nuptials within the hour.

"A fellow doctor's, out in Las Vegas. It was sort of a spur-of-the-moment thing."

Jesse and Susan had been in Las Vegas, along with Steve and Amanda, helping Mark in an elaborate plot to trick a murder suspect into confessing. The trick worked, and within moments of solving the case, Jesse asked Susan the big question.

"You're talking about Jesse and Susan's wedding," Dr. Noble said.

"You've heard about it?"

She nodded. The color seemed to drain from her face. Mark wondered if maybe he should squeeze the call button and get a doctor for her.

"An Elvis impersonator performed the service," Dr. Noble said. "Then Jesse serenaded Susan with his own version of 'Love Me Tender.' You started to sing along until Steve nudged you to be quiet."

Word had traveled even faster than he'd expected. Everyone in the hospital already knew. Jesse and Susan must have started calling people from their honeymoon suite at the Côte d'Azur resort casino. Either that, or Amanda had leaked the news after the ceremony. There weren't a lot of other suspects. Mark, Steve, and Amanda were the only guests at the couple's impromptu wedding, though it wasn't as rash a decision as it seemed. Jesse and Susan had been dating for years. The only surprise was the moment Jesse had chosen to ask Susan to marry him and his eagerness to do it right away.

"Did I have an accident on the drive back to Los Angeles?" Mark asked.

He would have been driving an unfamiliar car on the Pearblossom Highway, a notoriously dangerous two-lane stretch of road across the California desert that was lined with makeshift crosses and memorials honoring the scores of people who'd left their blood on the asphalt. If all he'd suffered in a collision was a concussion, he'd been very, very lucky—though trashing two cars—one on the way to Las Vegas and one on the way back—couldn't have made his insurance agent too happy.

But what if he hadn't been in the car alone? Mark felt his heart start pounding and heard his cardiac monitor beeping to the same beat.

"Was anyone else hurt? Was it my fault?"

She shook her head. "That's not what happened."

"Then why do you have that troubled look on your face?" Mark said. "There's obviously something important you're not telling me."

She sighed. "Their wedding was almost two years ago, Mark."

He stared at her, his vision blurring again. He blinked hard and tried to stay calm. Retrograde amnesia was common with head injuries. It could wipe away anything from hours to years, or in some very rare cases, an entire lifetime of memories. In most of the cases Mark had seen, the memories came back, albeit slowly and in maddeningly incomplete bits and pieces.

But not always.

Sometimes the memories never returned.

He was missing two years.

While a lot could happen in that amount of time, he figured it was just a small fraction of his sixty-three years. A mere blip on the time line of his life.

How much could have changed?

Mark hadn't lost his mental capabilities, so it wouldn't take long to adjust to whatever had occurred. He would simply devour the newspapers, magazines, and medical journals that had been published over the last twenty-four months, educating himself on what he'd missed. His life could go on as before—even if his memories of that brief period never returned.

He was alive. His mental capabilities were unimpaired and he wasn't paralyzed.

That was enough.

"Do you know who I am?" she asked softly.

"Dr. Emily Noble."

"If I wasn't wearing this name tag, or if the nurse hadn't mentioned my name before, would you have recognized me?"

Mark studied her. "Have we met?"

She sat down on the edge of the bed and took his hand in hers, giving it a squeeze. This time it wasn't a neurological test.

"Mark," she said, looking into his eyes, "I'm your wife."

CHAPTER THREE

There was an old James Garner movie that Mark liked a lot. Garner played an American major captured and drugged by the Germans, who fooled him into thinking he'd awakened from a coma in an Allied hospital five years after the Nazis were defeated in World War II. The truth, of course, was that it was all a clever Nazi plot to get the major to reveal what he knew about the upcoming D-day invasion.

The TV show *Mission: Impossible* used to pull variations of that same con all the time on dictators and mobsters to manipulate them into revealing their secrets or orchestrating their own doom.

Mark had even mounted a similar con himself by enlisting the aid of a Hollywood producer and using the sets of a TV medical drama to trick a murderer into incriminating himself.

In the movie, the TV series, and Mark's own experience, the key to pulling off the con was isolating the target, limiting his movements to one secure location, and controlling all the information and stimuli that he received.

Like keeping him in bed in a windowless hospital room.

That's the approach Mark took when he ran the con—and what he suspected was happening to him now that he was the target of one.

He had to get on his feet as soon as possible. Once he got

outside of this hospital, if that was really where he was, it would be impossible for anyone to sustain the con. If the con men lose their rigid control of the environment, the deception crumbles.

But why were they doing it? What information or secrets did he have that would justify going to such extremes? He didn't know any military intelligence, security codes, bank vault combinations, or important formulas. He wasn't hiding his own guilt in some terrible crime. He didn't know the location of any hidden treasure.

So what were they after?

When he sent Dr. Noble away, asking for some privacy, she looked genuinely hurt. Her face reddened as if he'd struck her. He had to admit that she gave a convincing performance. It would take an accomplished actress to pull that off—but Los Angeles was full of them, out of work and desperate for cash.

Mark, I'm your wife.

While he was thinking about that, he noticed the gold wedding ring on his left hand. Curious, he wriggled the ring up towards his knuckle. There was a pale band of skin where the ring had been.

A tan line. That's a nice touch, Mark thought. They'd considered everything. He took the ring off and set it on his bedside table.

He wondered if he'd really been out for days or merely an hour or two, helped along by a steady flow of drugs in his IV to help muddle his memory—or loosen his tongue. Perhaps the flowers and candy were simply clever set decoration, like his wedding ring.

Mark was about to test his theory by pulling out his IV tubes when Amanda Bentley walked in. She was dressed in black, her ID clipped to the belt of her slacks. Judging by her formal attire, he guessed she'd just come from testifying in court as part of her duties as an adjunct county medical examiner.

"Tell me you weren't about to yank out your IV," Amanda said as if she were scolding her toddler son.

"I wasn't about to yank out my IV."

"Are you being a surly, difficult patient?" Amanda said.

"I wouldn't dream of it," Mark said.

"Then why did Emily come out of here looking like she'd taken a beating?"

The woman in front of him looked and sounded like Amanda, but he had his doubts. The agents on *Mission: Impossible* wore incredible masks that they could peel right off, like a surface layer of skin. Martin Landau and Barbara Bain did it all the time. Even Tom Cruise did it in the movie version. He narrowed his eyes at her, trying to see if he could spot a seam along the edge of her face.

"You know Dr. Noble?" Mark asked. He couldn't spot any seams. His vision must still be too blurry.

"Of course I do," Amanda said, giving him the same stricken look that Dr. Noble had just a few minutes ago. "She's your wife. You know that, right?"

"Not really."

"Oh Mark, I'm so sorry," she said and sat down on the edge of the bed where Dr. Noble had been.

How do they make those face masks, he wondered. After all, *Mission: Impossible* was a fanciful TV show, a very old one at that, that tested a viewer's incredulity every week. Did such technology even exist?

It had to, because this lady in front of him was wearing an Amanda mask right now.

"I don't believe any of this," Mark said. "I haven't forgotten my wife—I'm not married."

Amanda studied him. "So what do you think is going on, Mark? Some kind of big con?"

"As a matter of fact, yes."

"Like that terrible movie with James Garner."

"It was a *great* movie," Mark said.

"We have this argument every time the reruns come on," Amanda said.

"Maybe if you'd watched it you'd know it's the playbook for what's happening to me now."

Even as Mark said it, he knew how ridiculous he sounded. If she was part of the con, she knew it was a con. What was the point he was trying to make?

Mark closed his eyes. His head was pounding like it was an egg and some enormous creature was anxious to break its way out.

Amanda slid closer to him. "If this is all a big con, how do you explain me?"

He opened his eyes and his vision blurred again. He blinked hard, trying to focus. "A mask."

"Dizziness and disorientation are common side effects of a concussion," Amanda said. "But paranoid delusions could be a sign of something far more serious."

"Let me feel your face," Mark said.

She leaned over him. "Be my guest."

He pulled at her skin and felt around her hairline. Her face was definitely flesh and not a mask. This was Amanda, unless someone had undergone an extreme makeover to replicate her features. It was possible.

No, it's not, he thought. Get a grip on yourself. What is the most likely possibility? That you had a concussion and forgot two years of your life or that someone has mounted a con of such massive proportions that people were willing to have plastic surgery to pull it off?

"Feeling foolish yet?" Amanda asked, as if reading his thoughts.

He dropped his hands and looked at her sheepishly. "Foolish doesn't come close to describing what I feel."

What he felt was numbing shock. The real emotions, whatever they might be, would come later when the enormity of his situation sank in, though one sentence was worming its way into his psyche.

Mark, I'm your wife.

"I'm sorry, Amanda," Mark whispered.

"It's okay. It's a lot of information to process for a guy whose brain is already pretty scrambled."

"Thanks," Mark said. "I think."

"I don't blame you for being skeptical. If you weren't, I'd think something was seriously wrong with you. I might wonder if you were really Mark Sloan."

He smiled. She was definitely Amanda. No one else could make him smile at a time like this, except, perhaps, Jesse, who never let anything get him down.

"It's all going to come back," she said. "You know that. Temporary amnesia is common in cases like this."

"Like what, exactly?" Mark asked. "What happened to me? How did I get hurt?"

"Maybe we ought to wait for Steve to get here. I'm sure he'd like to tell you himself."

"I want to know now."

She pursed her lips, thinking it over, then finally nodded, more to herself than to him. "It happened three days ago, in the parking structure here. You got out of your car and were walking into the hospital when someone tried to run you over. Jesse saw the car coming and tackled you out of the way. You hit your head on the pavement."

"Remind me to thank Jesse for that," Mark said.

"I will."

Mark considered what she had told him. "Are you sure it wasn't an accident?"

Amanda shook her head. "He was heading straight for you. We have it on security camera video."

"Did the driver get away?"

"Yes, but Steve's chasing down some leads," Amanda said.

"Why would someone want to kill me? Was I investigating a case at the time?"

Amanda patted Mark's arm and stood up. "We can talk about it tomorrow, when you're rested."

"I've been resting for three days," he said. "Or so I'm told."

"There will be plenty of time to catch up," she said. "There are more important things you should be concentrating on right now anyway."

She handed him his wedding ring, kissed him on the cheek, and walked out.

Mark looked at the wedding ring for a long time and then slipped it back on his finger.

The nurse served Mark a cheese sandwich, fruit juice, and a chocolate chip cookie that tasted like it was freshly baked on the last day he could remember. He began the task of grounding himself in the present by finding out the date, what day of the week it was, and the current time of day. It was midafternoon on a Thursday.

He asked the nurse to get him a copy of the day's *Los Angeles Times* to see if Earth had tilted off its axis while he was away.

Away.

That's how it felt to him, as if he'd been traveling and some doppelgänger had been living his life for him in the meantime. He believed that everything that Dr. Noble—no, *Emily*—had told him was true, but he still couldn't accept it. He couldn't connect intellectually or emotionally with the startling news she'd shared with him.

Mark searched within himself for some feeling for Emily and came up empty. There was nothing there. He felt no more for her than he would a complete stranger.

Maybe if he saw her face again, heard her voice and felt her hand on his, some twinge of recognition would return. At the same time, the thought of seeing her again filled him with anxiety.

How could he be so deeply in love with someone and not

feel anything for her now? What kind of trauma could cause that?

He still remembered his first wife, Katherine, still felt the pain of her death as if it had happened yesterday instead of years ago.

So how could he have forgotten Emily?

He believed that love was stronger than mere memory, that it was rooted in the soul. Had he lost part of that, too?

Steve came in wearing a black jacket, black slacks, and a black tie. Either he'd been to a funeral or he'd teamed up with Will Smith to fight aliens. He was in his forties, but he hadn't yet been able to shake the tan, the sun-bleached hair, and the casual swagger of his surfer youth.

He leaned down and embraced his father. Mark couldn't remember the last time they'd shared a hug. Although they were close, neither of them had ever been big on physical signs of affection, much to the chagrin of the women in their lives. It had been frustrating for Katherine—and, Mark supposed, for Emily, too.

"It's great to see you awake again, Dad."

"Seeing how you're dressed, it must be a big surprise," Mark said. "Were you expecting to find me in a casket?"

"I had to go to a funeral this morning," Steve said. "I haven't had a chance to change."

Attending funerals was one of the regular and least enjoyable functions of Steve's job as a homicide detective.

"No one likes it when a homicide detective shows up at their door looking like an undertaker," Mark said.

"No one likes it when a homicide detective shows up, *period*."

"Maybe they wouldn't mind so much if you were more avuncular," Mark said. "Like me."

"Maybe I should learn some card tricks, too, just to keep the sociopathic killers entertained on the way to jail."

"I could teach you," Mark said. "Got a deck of cards?"

"You sound perky," Steve said. "How are you feeling?"

"I've got the headache to end all headaches," Mark said. "And I'm a little hazy on some things."

"Like what?"

"The last two years of my life," Mark said. "But I have a feeling you already knew that."

Steve nodded. "Emily is pretty upset. You really don't remember her at all?"

Mark shook his head. "I don't mean to hurt her."

"She knows that," Steve said.

"Do you like her?"

Steve nodded. "She's amazing. You're lucky you got her before I did."

"So are you married with kids now?"

"I know you haven't had a chance to look outside yet, but pigs still don't fly."

"Are you still living at home with your father?"

"Not anymore," Steve said.

"Maybe I *should* take a look outside," Mark said.

"I moved out after you got married," Steve said. "It was my wedding present to you and Emily."

"If I'd known that was what it would take, I would have remarried long ago," Mark said with a grin.

The truth was, he enjoyed sharing a house with Steve and his son knew it. Mark hoped their close relationship had endured despite the marriage and Steve's moving out. If it hadn't, that was something Mark would be sure to fix.

"I found a place near the beach in Marina del Rey," Steve said.

"Obviously, a lot has happened in the last two years. It's going to take a while to fill in all the blanks."

"It will come back," Steve said.

"Let's start with three days ago. Amanda told me someone tried to run me down in the parking garage. Have you got any leads?"

"Not yet."

"What about the case I was working on?"

Steve frowned. "There wasn't one."

"What do you mean? Amanda said I was working on something."

"You may have thought it was something, but no one else did. It had to do with a patient of yours, Grover Dawson."

Grover was a retired landscape architect in his early sixties, a widower who spent his free time fishing, traveling, and helping to raise money for his local church. He suffered from coronary artery disease and had nearly died of a heart attack.

"He's been my patient for twenty years," Mark said. "What happened to him?"

"He died in bed last week from a drug interaction," Steve said. "It was an accident."

"What drugs?"

"His heart meds," Steve said. "And Viagra. It's not the first time I've seen that happen. At least he died happy."

The last time Mark remembered seeing Grover, the man was taking nitroglycerin as well as long-acting nitrates to treat his plugged arteries. Nitrates open up the blood vessels and cause a drop in blood pressure. So does Viagra. The combination of those drugs would have sent Grover's blood pressure crashing to a lethal level.

"Was he still single?" Mark asked.

"He wasn't married to anyone, if that's what you're asking. But he obviously wasn't sleeping alone. Whoever was in bed with him when he died left in a hurry."

"That doesn't make any sense," Mark said. "Grover didn't believe in sex before marriage."

"I guess that makes him either a liar or a hypocrite," Steve said. "Or both."

"How do you know it wasn't murder?"

"I looked into it. Grover didn't have an enemy in the world, and he'd willed everything to the church. Nothing suspicious or unusual happened in his life in the weeks leading up to his death. So that was the end of it for me. But I have a feeling it wasn't for you."

Mark had to agree. He wouldn't have let it go, not until he could prove to himself that Grover had really been engaged in a sexual relationship.

"Where did he get the Viagra?"

"He didn't have a prescription. But there's a big underground market for those little blue pills. It wouldn't have been difficult for him to score a few."

"Grover Dawson wasn't the kind of man who'd buy drugs off the street or on the Internet."

"He would if he didn't want his friends at church or his doctors to know that he was having sex and suffering from erectile dysfunction."

"So if you don't think the attempt on my life was related to me poking into Grover's death, what's the approach you're taking?"

"I'm checking to see if anybody you helped send to prison is out on the street again."

"It's not likely," Mark said. "Most of them got life sentences. Or worse."

"Which means one of their relatives, loved ones, or sicko followers might have tried taking you out as revenge. We're checking out that angle, too. But it's tough. You've got a lot of enemies for such an avuncular guy."

"Amanda said you have a videotape of the car trying to run me down," Mark said. "Have you been able to enhance it to get the license plate or a shot of the driver's face?"

"We didn't get the driver's face, but we got the plates," Steve said. "The car was reported stolen a few days ago. We found it abandoned last night in Chatsworth. There was still blood on the grille. The crime lab is going over it now."

"Blood?" Mark said, his brow furrowed in confusion. "But Amanda said I wasn't hit by the car."

"You weren't."

"Then who was?"

Steve took a deep breath and let it out slowly. "Jesse."

Mark's chest tightened with anxiety, and the pounding in his head increased its agonizing intensity as he had a sudden realization.

Emily and Amanda were wearing black, too.

The answer to his next question was obvious to him before he asked it, but never in his life did he want more to be wrong.

"Is he okay?"

Steve looked at his feet and shook his head. "His funeral was this morning."

CHAPTER FOUR

It was as if he'd lost his own son. The news of Jesse's death was almost too painful to bear. The fact that Jesse was killed while saving Mark made it even more horrible. If given the choice, Mark would gladly have sacrificed his life for Jesse's.

There was nothing more to say to Steve and nothing more he *could* say if he'd wanted to. He was stunned speechless, so overwhelmed by grief that even tears wouldn't come.

Steve may have said more, but if he did, Mark didn't hear it. His ears were ringing from one concussive piece of shocking news after another. It was too much. He didn't want to see or hear anything else. Not now. He didn't have the strength. Fatigue washed over him and he embraced it, sinking into the comforting numbness of sleep.

But it was a cruel trick. There was no escape from his pain. His dreams were all about Jesse, like a loop of home movies of their experiences together over the years. They were happy images set against a deeply mournful sound track.

When Mark awoke later that night, there were tears in his eyes. For a moment it was possible to believe that it had all been a nightmare, that his reality was only beginning now. But when he saw Emily sitting in the chair beside the bed, reading her John Irving paperback and picking at a box of chocolates in her lap, he knew that the nightmare was real.

.The intensity of his grief for Jesse made the emptiness

and lack of emotion he felt for his wife even more stark and disturbing.

Emily glanced over the top of her book at him. "Don't worry. I left you the caramel-filled ones."

"My favorites," he said.

She set the book aside but left the box of chocolates in her lap. "How are you feeling?"

"Physically, pretty good. Emotionally, I'm in critical condition."

"That makes two of us."

They looked at each other in silence for a long moment, their sadness the only bridge between them.

"Could I have a chocolate?" he asked.

"Consider it a prescription from your doctor." She smiled and picked out a caramel for him, placing it in his hand. "I think the proper dosage is two candies every hour."

"Looks to me like you've been doing some self-medicating," Mark said, tipping his head towards the other opened boxes of candy.

"Are you going to rat me out?"

"I don't think a husband can be compelled to testify against his wife."

She seemed to brighten a bit at his casual acknowledgment of their relationship. It was intentional on Mark's part, a peace offering of sorts.

Mark chewed on the candy and was surprised to find that it *did* make him feel better. It was something familiar. Something blissfully unchanged.

He held out his hand for another piece. "How did we meet?"

She searched the box for more caramels, gave him one, then took one for herself. "We collided in the hall."

"Was one of us on roller skates at the time?"

She nodded, smiling at the memory. He envied her that.

"It wasn't me. I never wear my skates to job interviews," she said. "I'd just arrived that morning from Houston to interview for the post of chief of pediatric surgery. We were both late for the meeting with the board. I was running and you were rolling. After I met with the board, you took me to lunch at Barbeque Bob's to make amends. And that's how it started."

"Did you get the job?"

"I got a lot more than that," she said.

"How long have we been married?"

"Almost as long as Jesse and Susan," she said, her voice trembling a bit. Bringing up Jesse was clearly painful for her, too. "This is my second marriage. I've been divorced for fifteen years. I don't have any children. My patients have fulfilled whatever mothering instinct I have and then some. I see so many kids. One of the greatest things about being a pediatric surgeon is that you don't just save a life, you save an entire lifetime."

Emily continued talking about pediatrics, and why she loved the field, but Mark was only half listening. He had hoped that hearing her story would stir something in him, some connection. Instead, all he felt was his grief for Jesse and his anger at the circumstances of the young man's death.

"Did I tell you anything about the case I was investigating when Jesse was killed?" Mark asked abruptly, interrupting her.

If Emily was offended by the interruption, and what it revealed about the scant attention he'd been paying to what she was saying, she didn't show it.

She shook her head. "You kept it from me."

"Why would I do that?"

"Your compulsion to investigate murders isn't something I understand or that I'm comfortable with. So I'm not part of your crime-solving team."

"It didn't stop us from getting married."

"It's not like we're talking about a drinking problem or a gambling addiction. We were both single for a long time and aren't about to change each other. Besides, there are trade-offs in every relationship. You're not too happy with how often I'm away. I'm on call nationwide. In fact, the day you were hurt and Jesse was killed, I was in St. Louis performing emergency fetal surgery on triplets, two of whom were sharing one heart."

No wonder she traveled a lot, Mark thought. There weren't many surgeons qualified to do that kind of risky, experimental surgery.

He knew about the rare disorder known as twin-to-twin transfusion syndrome. In most cases, one of the twins died, killing the other. If both twins died, the third fetus would likely perish as well. To save one or more of the fetuses, Mark knew that Emily would have had to operate in the womb, using a laser to separate the blood vessels between the two fetuses who shared the same heart.

He'd never witnessed a surgery like that—unless, of course, it had happened in the last two years and was one of the many memories he'd lost.

"How did it go?" Mark asked.

"We saved two of the fetuses," she said. "I walked out of ten hours in the OR and got the call about you. I took the next plane back and have been right here ever since."

"I'm okay now," Mark said. "You can go home."

She put her hand on his. "Home is wherever you are."

"I'd feel better if you got some rest," he said, hearing the professional detachment in his voice. The fact was, he felt nothing for her beyond his newfound respect for her surgical abilities. "We're both going to need our strength in the coming days to get through this ordeal."

Emily let go of his hand and rose from her seat.

"No matter what you're feeling now, or *not* feeling, you're still Mark Sloan. You fell in love with me once and you will again."

"I hope so," he said, uncertain whether he really meant it.

"I love you, Mark."

She kissed him on the forehead and walked out.

He watched her go. At that moment, the prospect of resurrecting his love for her seemed like an impossible task. But there was one set of lost memories within his reach, one that was only a few days old: the investigation he was conducting when Jesse was murdered.

Instead of trying to recover two years, he would start by reclaiming the last week, retracing his steps from the moment when he learned about Grover Dawson's death right up until he was nearly hit by a car in the Community General parking structure.

That decision felt right, unlike anything else since he'd regained consciousness. It gave him an immediate, achievable goal instead of the prospect of aimlessly wandering in the vast desert of his lost memories hoping to find a familiar landmark.

He would rediscover what he'd learned before, piece together the clues, and find Jesse's killer. And maybe, along the way, he'd find some of himself again, too.

Mark slept for a few more hours, then awoke before dawn, too keyed up and anxious to lie in bed for another minute. He used his authority as a doctor, and as chief of internal medicine, to intimidate a nurse into helping him remove his IV and catheter.

When he got out of bed, he was a little dizzy and his head throbbed, but he hid his symptoms from the nurse and made his way carefully to the doctors' locker room. He traded his hospital gown for surgical scrubs and a pair of tennis shoes from his locker.

He went to his office, where he put on his lab coat over his scrubs, grabbed a Diet Coke from his icebox, and sat down at his desk. The drink was so cold it was nearly frozen, just the way he liked it. He took a few sips and felt revived.

A wedding photo faced him on his desk. It was taken in Hawaii. Mark and Emily stood side by side on an impossibly green lawn against a backdrop of palm trees, crashing surf, and craggy shoreline. She was beautiful in a white wedding *holoku*, a long, form-fitting *mu'umu'u*, and a Haku lei of white dendrobium orchids, baby's breath, and roses on her head.

Mark studied himself in the photo. He wore a white aloha shirt, white linen pants, and a green-leaf lei around his neck. There was a big smile on his face, broadcasting his happiness and pride.

He didn't recognize anything about the photo except his face. Everything else about it struck him as a convincing forgery. It was as if someone had taken his face from one picture, his clothes from another, and artfully combined the elements, then inserted Emily Noble at his side and a generic Hawaiian backdrop behind them both.

But Mark knew it wasn't the picture that had been altered. It was him.

Jesse is dead. He was killed saving your life. Someone has to pay.

He set the photo aside, facedown, and sorted through the papers on his desk. Most of them dealt with hospital bureaucracy and current patients. He didn't find anything relating to Grover Dawson.

He sifted through a week's worth of phone message slips, discarding anything that seemed to be part of his administrative routine and keeping the rest. Next he turned to the yellow legal pad he kept by the phone. The pad contained random scribbles—names, phone numbers, doodles, lunch orders, and scattered reminders in no particular order. A few caught his eye.

First Fidelity Casualty
Wedding band
Dentures?
Kemper-Carlson Pharmaceuticals
Cal-Star Insurance
Sechrest + Pevney + ?
The glass fish?
The pearl necklace?

He had no idea what the notes meant or if they were even related to the case. They were just scribbles.

There were two lists on the notepad that he'd boxed and doodled around, which suggested to him now that he'd given them lots of thought. They read:

Jesse
Insurance records & hospital admittance forms
Amanda
Deaths/three years

The notations were too general to glean much from them, except that he'd asked Jesse and Amanda to do some research. He would talk to Amanda and find out the details.

He opened his date book and reviewed his schedule for the previous two weeks. The days were filled with administrative meetings and appointments with patients. There were three meetings outside Community General with doctors whose names he didn't recognize: Dr. Richard Barnes, Dr. Tanya Hudson, and Dr. Bernard Dalton.

Mark looked up the three doctors on the Internet and discovered that Dr. Barnes was an epidemiologist, Dr. Hudson was a sociologist, and Dr. Dalton was a cardiologist.

What had he wanted to talk to them about? Were they related to his investigation into Grover Dawson's death? Or were they people he was consulting as part of his day-to-day medical routine? Perhaps they were new friends he'd made in the last two years and he was seeing them simply for the pleasure of their company. He would need Amanda and Emily to help him figure out the answers to those questions.

There was nothing more he could do in his office. His next stop was the morgue.

CHAPTER FIVE

Too many people died every day in Los Angeles, resulting in more corpses than the county morgue could handle. Not only that, but the morgue downtown was a tiring commute from Community General Hospital.

So several years ago, Mark had come up with a way to relieve some of the county's burden and, at the same time, make it easier for him to examine the victims of the homicides he investigated.

He brokered an arrangement between the county and the hospital, establishing a satellite county morgue at Community General. The county gained more space and additional manpower at a fraction of the cost of a new, stand-alone facility. The hospital gained a new revenue stream and publicity points for supporting the community in a tangible way.

Dr. Amanda Bentley, the hospital's staff pathologist, was hired as an adjunct county medical examiner to oversee the new morgue and to roll to crime scenes as needed. Somehow she managed to effortlessly balance her dual responsibilities, becoming as comfortable at a crime scene as she was at an autopsy table.

Mark was sitting at one of those tables, files spread out in front of him, when Amanda arrived, holding a paper plate with an enormous cinnamon roll slathered in frosting.

"Busted," she said.

He looked up at her. "This isn't the first time you've caught me going through your files."

"But it's the first time you've caught me eating a ten-thousand-calorie cinnamon roll."

"I'll let you off on one condition," he said.

"What's that?"

"You split it with me."

She grabbed a clean scalpel, slid a stool over to the autopsy table, and sat down across from Mark.

"I'm having such a feeling of déjà vu," Amanda said, cutting the roll in half.

"Why?" Mark asked, picking up his piece and taking a bite.

"Because I had this exact same conversation with you last week," she said. "You were even reading Grover Dawson's file."

Mark set down the roll and licked the frosting off his fingers. "That would explain why the file is sticky. You must have shared a cinnamon roll with me that morning, too. You just lied to me. This isn't the first time I've caught you with one of those pastries."

"Busted again," she said. "See? You're back to rooting out dishonesty wherever it lurks."

"What did I have to say about Grover Dawson's file?"

"You were convinced something wasn't right about the man's death," Amanda said, "but you didn't find anything unusual in the file."

"I don't know what I was expecting to find anyway. Your report simply confirms what Steve already told me," Mark said. "What else did we talk about?"

"That was it," she said, carefully dissecting her roll with the scalpel to reveal the cinnamon filling between the layers.

"Tell me about the deaths I asked you to look into," Mark said.

"What does it matter now, Mark? Seems to me you

should be at home with Emily, trying to put your life back together."

She cut off a bite-sized strip of the cinnamon roll, speared it with the scalpel, and popped the morsel into her mouth. Mark guessed she was probably one of those people who separated Oreos before eating them, too.

"I can't do that until I find whoever was driving that car," Mark said.

"Leave it to Steve," she said.

"Jesse didn't get killed saving Steve's life. He got killed saving mine," Mark said. "I need to do this. For him and for me."

Amanda sighed. "Three days after I found you here, you showed up one morning with another one of these." She held up the plate with the cinnamon roll on it. "We were splitting it when I mentioned how sad it is when someone barely survives a life-threatening experience only to die later in an accident or from some other ailment."

Mark raised an eyebrow. She tipped her head towards him.

"That's exactly the expression you gave me then, too," she said.

"So what provoked you to share that unusual observation with me?"

"There was this twenty-two-year-old woman named Sandy Sechrest who tried to kill herself by drinking a lethal cocktail of vodka mixed with handfuls of opiates and benzodiazepines. She came into the ER at Northridge Hospital flatlined, but they managed to save her. Three months later, she cleaned herself up, got into a counseling program, and even found a job. And what happens? She's taking a bath one night, her hair dryer falls into the tub and *zap*, she gets electrocuted and drowns."

Amanda took another bite of her cinnamon roll and licked the frosting off her lips with the tip of her tongue before continuing her story.

"That was the case I was coming from when I saw you that morning," she said. "You thought it was odd and I said no, it's simply ironic, those kinds of things happen all the time. I gave you another example, too. A woman named Leila Pevney survived a quadruple bypass only to die from the common cold. She took too many decongestants. The amphetamines in the medicine caused a fatal change in her cardiac rhythm."

"So let me guess," Mark said. "I challenged you to prove to me that cases like that 'happen all the time' by putting together a list of people who died, accidentally or otherwise, shortly after near-death experiences. I asked you to go back, say, three years."

"Yes, you did," Amanda said. "And dutiful fool that I am, I fell for it."

"Fell for what?"

"You getting me to do a load of research. There I was, thinking I was doing it for myself to prove a point to you, when in fact I was doing it for *you* to satisfy *your* idle curiosity."

"I'm not that manipulative." Mark took another bite of his roll and licked his fingers again afterwards.

"Sure you are," she said. "You hide it by being avuncular. That's your charm."

"And did you do it?"

"The list was the size of a phone book. There are roughly fifty-seven thousand deaths, excluding homicides and suicides, in Los Angeles County every year. Of those, about seven hundred eighty people survive life-threatening conditions requiring hospitalization within a year preceding their deaths. Of those people, about thirty-four die within ninety days of their release from the hospital."

"And those figures have stayed pretty constant over the last three years?"

"More or less, except for the people who've died within

three months of a life-threatening episode. That's up from thirty-three last year to forty-eight so far this year."

Mark did the math. "That's a forty-five percent increase. That can't be normal."

Amanda shrugged. "There's no telling what's responsible for the uptick. It's probably just bad luck."

"What about the autopsy reports on those forty-eight deaths? Did I ask for them?"

"Of course you did, as if you hadn't already given me enough work to do. But most of the patients died of natural causes and weren't autopsied. Their deaths were certified by their family physician, which, in at least two of the cases, was you."

"Which two?" Mark said.

Amanda got up, went to her desk, and scrounged around until she found the files she was looking for. "Hammond McNutchin and Joyce Kling. Their deaths were sad, but not unexpected."

Mark browsed through the files while Amanda returned her attention to eating her cinnamon roll.

Hammond McNutchin was a seventy-three-year-old man who, when Mark last saw him, was brought in by paramedics with a collapsed lung, congestive heart failure, and prostate cancer. Mark managed to save his life. He died peacefully in his sleep of a heart attack not long afterwards. At least it was in the comfort of his own home, Mark thought, instead of in a hospital bed.

Joyce Kling was a fifty-six-year-old lupus patient who came into the ER with chest pains. It turned out her pericardium was filling with fluid and Mark had to drain it. She nearly died on the table, but she pulled through, thanks to his valiant efforts, only to die of respiratory failure two months later while sitting in her recliner, watching women-in-jeopardy movies on Lifetime.

Both of the patients were very sick and died naturally. There was nothing about the circumstances of their passing to suggest otherwise. If there had been, his suspicions certainly would have been raised at the time. And yet he felt that familiar tingle at the back of his neck, that shiver of uneasiness.

He set the files down. From what he could gather so far, a week ago he'd been stumbling in the dark, driven by a vague discomfort and blindly trying to find the cause. Steve was right. There wasn't a case here. Not yet.

Mark started picking at his pastry again. "This isn't going to be easy."

"You know I'll help any way I can," Amanda said. "But can I give you some advice?"

"Of course."

"Don't forget about Emily."

"That's the problem. I already have."

"I know why you have to get back to your investigation. I respect that. But please don't use Jesse as an excuse to avoid dealing with Emily," Amanda said. "He didn't save your life just so you could throw it away. If you can't get back your memories of Emily, start working on some new ones. She's the best thing that's happened to you in a very long time."

Mark nodded. "So I've been told."

"You'll see," Amanda said. "She's a strong woman, and she won't let you push her around any more than I do."

"I thought you just got done telling me how I shrewdly manipulated you with my avuncular charm."

"She's immune to all that," Amanda said.

"Not entirely," Mark said. "She married me, didn't she?"

"How do you know you weren't the one charmed into it?"

"Good point," Mark said.

They were silent for a moment while he worked up the courage to ask her something that had been on his mind since last night.

"What was Jesse's funeral like?"

She took a deep breath and let it out slowly. "It was very nice, an intimate little service held on the beach at sunrise."

"Which beach?"

"The one in front of your house," she said.

Mark was taken aback. "Why there?"

"His parents split up when he was very young and he was never close to them. You, Steve, and I were his family. Your house was the family home. It was where we gathered to hash out cases, celebrate holidays, and where we went to find safety and comfort. Of course that was where he wanted the funeral to be."

"Who was at the service?"

"Susan, Steve, Emily, and I. That was all. No priest or rabbi. Those were his wishes. Steve gave a wonderful eulogy, full of humor and affection. He said he'd lost his little brother. I feel the same way. Susan was so grief-stricken that all she could do was whisper good-bye and cry."

Amanda's eyes started to tear up. She wiped her eyes before the tears could fall.

"I'll find whoever did this to him," Mark said. "That's a promise."

"You're not doing this alone," Amanda said.

"I know."

Mark got up, gave her shoulder a squeeze, and walked out into the corridor, where he found Emily waiting for him, a wheelchair in front of her.

"I knew I'd find you here, already on your feet and investigating Jesse's death."

"It's what I have to do," Mark said, unapologetic.

"I know that, but not until you've been checked out by your doctor first to make sure you're okay."

"I've taken care of that."

"The hell you have," Emily said. "Now sit down in this chair."

"Don't be ridiculous, I need to go—"

Emily interrupted him. "You're not going anywhere

without your wallet and your keys. And if you want them back, you will do what I tell you. I have your durable power of attorney and I can have you committed, in case you've forgotten."

"As a matter of fact, I have." Mark sighed and reluctantly dropped into the wheelchair, and let Emily wheel him down the corridor.

Chapter Six

Dr. Heidi Mack was technically the physician handling Mark's case and, as such, she gave her patient a thorough examination, though she'd previously ceded much of her authority and responsibility to Dr. Noble. Mark's injuries weren't serious and Dr. Mack pronounced him completely recovered. She gave Mark some painkillers and told him to take it easy for the next few days, but she knew her patient well enough to assume that her advice would be ignored.

Emily wheeled Mark out to the parking lot, where her Mercedes SLK convertible was parked next to his Ford Five Hundred sedan.

"I'll follow you," Mark said.

"I'm driving," she said. "You can come back for your car tomorrow."

"You heard Dr. Mack. She said I was fine."

"Yesterday at this time you were unconscious with your head split open," she said. "And I know you lied to Heidi about your vision. You probably see three of me right now. You'll drive when *I'm* convinced you're okay."

"You're one tough lady." Mark grimaced and headed towards the passenger side of her car.

"I'll take that as a compliment," she said, climbing into the driver's seat.

"How's your driving?" Mark asked.

"Fast and nimble," she said. "Where to?"

"You're not taking me home?"

"I am if that's where you want to go, but I'm sure you have other plans."

"I thought you weren't part of my crime-solving team," Mark said.

"I am now," she said. "Besides, I want to keep my eye on you."

"You're that worried about my concussion?"

She shook her head and smiled. "I just like the view."

Mark wasn't used to someone flirting with him, at least not that he remembered. He liked it.

The top of the SLK retracted into the trunk with the touch of a button. Twenty-eight seconds later, the car was zipping along residential streets to Santa Monica, staying off the major thoroughfares.

Mark had forgotten how much he enjoyed driving with the sun on his skin and the wind whipping his hair. He'd forgotten lots of things, but this memory pre-dated his amnesia.

Until two years ago—four years if he counted the two erased by his head injury—he drove a Saab convertible. The Saab met a nasty fate. Mark was carjacked and the car got totaled. His next car, a Mini Cooper, suffered a similar fate. He'd barely owned the car for a month when an RV collided with it and knocked it off a cliff about a hundred miles from Las Vegas.

Mark decided his next car would be another convertible, assuming he could find a company that would insure him again without charging exorbitant premiums. Perhaps, he thought, he'd married a wealthy surgeon just so he could afford his auto insurance payments.

Emily pulled up to the curb in front of a tiny Spanish Revival bungalow with white stucco walls, arched windows, and a flat roof, the parapet lined with decorative red tiles.

"I thought we were going to Jesse and Susan's place," Mark said.

"This is it," Emily said.

Mark remembered Jesse and Susan living together in what had been Jesse's apartment in Venice. Obviously, they had moved in the last two years.

The house was small, no larger than twelve hundred square feet, and it incorporated motifs from several Spanish architectural styles. It boasted an arched entryway with a gabled, red-tiled roof and a triple-arched living room window covered with a decorative wrought-iron grille.

Mark and Emily walked up to the front door and rang the bell. Susan opened the door, and before Mark could speak, she embraced him, wrapping her arms around him, which wasn't easy given her enormous belly.

"It's so good to see you," she said. "Nobody told me you'd regained consciousness."

"I'm sorry," Emily said. "That's my fault. You were going through so much yesterday, I didn't want to intrude."

"I sat here alone, crying. I would have welcomed any intrusion at all."

"But you sent us all away," Emily said. "You said you wanted to be left alone."

"Dumb move on my part," Susan said.

Mark took a big step back from her and looked her over.

"You're pregnant," he said in astonishment.

"How did you notice?" She smiled and motioned them inside. "Sometimes I feel like all I am is a belly with legs and blond hair."

The house was decorated with an eclectic mix of comfortable-looking furniture in traditional styles and of varying ages. None of the pieces matched, which indicated to Mark that the couple had bought each item one by one, getting what they needed when they could afford it.

"I had no idea," he said, shaking his head and looking at her belly again.

Her smile waned as she realized he wasn't joking. "You were the first person we told."

He nodded, reading her expression. "The blow to my head has caused some amnesia. I don't remember anything that's happened for the last two years."

Susan gasped, glanced at Emily, then looked back to Mark. "Not even your wife?"

"We're working on that," Mark said.

"I hope so," Susan said, waddling over to an easy chair and taking a seat.

"So do I," Emily said.

"In the meantime, I'm working on something more immediate," Mark said as he and Emily sat down on the couch opposite Susan. "I'm going to find Jesse's killer."

Susan swallowed hard. "I'd prefer that Steve did that."

Mark furrowed his brow. "You know what I can do. If you've lost confidence in me because of my injury, I can assure you that although I've misplaced a few years, I'm still as sharp mentally as before and—"

Susan held up her hand, stopping him. "I haven't lost any confidence in you, Mark. You're probably the best detective in the country."

"Then I don't understand."

"You don't carry a gun," Susan said.

"I'll watch out for myself," he said.

"No, *I'll* watch out for you," Emily said.

"I want Steve to catch him," Susan said. "And I want the miserable sonofabitch to try to escape. Steve will kill him. You won't."

"I know how you feel, Susan. But I don't believe in revenge and neither does Steve. We both want justice."

"Call it what you want, revenge or justice, just as long as it ends up with Jesse's killer planted in the ground."

Mark wasn't going to argue with her. There was no point. Her anger and pain were justified. She was a pregnant widow whose husband had been murdered while saving the life of another man.

"I didn't come here to upset you," Mark said. "I want to tell you how sorry I am about Jesse and that I won't rest until his killer is caught. You know how much he meant to me."

"I know what you meant to him," Susan said. "All he wanted was your love and respect, to be a part of your family."

"He had all of that. So do you. You are family, Susan. So is your baby. My home—" Mark glanced at Emily. "*Our* home is your home."

"Then I need to ask you something." Susan took Mark's hand and put it on her swollen belly. "It's a boy. His name was going to be Mark. That's what Jesse and I both decided. But after—after what happened to his father, I'd like to name him Jesse. Do you think that's wrong?"

Mark shook his head. "It's wonderful."

"But it's not what Jesse wanted." Susan looked at Emily. "What do you think?"

Emily smiled. "I think Jesse would understand. And I think Jesse Junior will, too."

Susan nodded, her decision made. "Thank you."

She struggled to her feet. "I suppose you want the boxes."

"The boxes?" Mark said, rising.

"All the stuff you had Jesse working on," she said, hobbling over to the kitchen, shifting her weight from one foot to the other as she went. "You asked him to go through insurance company records and hospital admittance forms to see if all those people who died might have shared the same insurer, insurance agent, admittance clerk, nurse, doctor, whatever."

Mark and Emily followed Susan. "That was a pretty tall order."

"You were going to help him with it once he gathered it all together," Susan said, stopping beside the kitchen table, which was covered with papers. "I haven't touched the stuff."

"Do you know if he found anything?"

She shook her head. "He was waiting for some direction from you. He said you were real close to something."

"How did Jesse know that?" Emily asked.

"He always knew." Susan smiled and looked at Mark. "He said you get a sparkle in your eyes when things are about to fall into place. And they were."

Jesse wasn't the only one who knew it. So did whoever was driving the car that ran him down.

To fit the boxes in the trunk, Emily had to create some space by putting the top back up. Mark felt cramped now in the tiny car. Perhaps he wouldn't have felt that way if he hadn't known that the top could come down. Feelings, he decided, depend a great deal on what you know and what you don't. Feelings can't exist without a foundation of previous experience. If he didn't know he'd loved Emily Noble, would he be attracted to her now? Would he even be making the effort?

"What?" Emily said, taking her eyes off the road to give him a quick, appraising glance.

"Nothing."

"You're staring at me."

"Sorry," he said.

"It's okay. You're wondering if you can love me again," she said, returning her gaze to the traffic on the Pacific Coast Highway.

It was his turn to give her an appraising look. "How did you know?"

"I'm wondering it, too," Emily said. "But I have more grounds for hope. I know you better than you know me."

I don't know you at all, Mark thought. But he wanted to get off this subject and he wasn't graceful about how he did it.

"When is Susan's baby due?" he asked.

"Six weeks."

"Those first few weeks after the child is born are going to be hard."

"More like the first few months," Emily said.

"I don't see how Susan can do it alone."

"Neither do I."

"I'd like her to stay with us," Mark proposed tentatively.

"I've already ordered the baby furniture," she said.

Maybe, Mark thought, I could love her again after all. She was a remarkable woman, and they were on the same wavelength much of the time. There were worse relationships he could be in.

The beach house where Mark Sloan lived was two stories. The second floor, on the street level, was the main house, with living room, family room, kitchen, and master bedroom. A large deck faced the ocean and had stairs down to the sand. The first floor was on the beach, and for as long as Mark had lived in the house it had been Steve's apartment, with its own private entrance.

With Steve gone, there was more than enough room for Susan and her baby to stay as long as they liked.

Emily parked in front of the house and, after arguing over whether Mark was healthy enough to carry a box, they each lugged in one of Jesse's boxes. They went in the front door, and the moment Mark stepped into the foyer he felt disoriented. It wasn't a symptom of his concussion—at least not directly.

Everything about the house had changed. While the place was still recognizable as his home, all the furnishings were different. He saw some of his artwork on the walls, but in new places and sharing space with paintings and photographs he'd never seen before—at least not that he remembered. The bookshelves in the den had been reorganized and now held a mix of his collection and hers. Judging by the book spines, she enjoyed contemporary fiction as opposed to nonfiction, which was what Mark tended to read.

Emily set her box down on the kitchen table, the only

piece of furniture that was still his and still exactly where he'd left it. It was the table where he, Steve, Amanda, and Jesse had spent so many hours sharing meals, discussing cases, and solving problems. Each scratch and nick on the table was a memory.

He set his box down and ran his hand over the tabletop, feeling the uneven surface of the distressed wood.

"It's a good table," Mark said.

"It was the one piece of furniture you were adamant about keeping."

"What was wrong with everything else?"

"Nothing if you're two men living in a hunting lodge," she said.

"I suppose it's all at Steve's house."

"Most of it," she said.

"Amanda gave me a report of patient deaths," Mark said. "Do you know where it is?"

"You were just released from the hospital after suffering a head injury."

"So?" Mark said.

"So slow down. Don't you want to have some lunch? Maybe relax for a few minutes?"

"I won't be able to rest until I know where the report is."

She sighed. "It's downstairs."

"Downstairs?"

She tipped her head towards the staircase in the entry hall. "Go see for yourself."

He did.

As the staircase curved down, the room below was slowly revealed to him. It seemed that he'd taken over the first floor and made it his investigation command center, where he gathered data and coordinated the efforts of his troops, who were Amanda and Jesse.

The walls were lined with enormous dry-erase boards, which were covered with lists of names and dates, hospitals and doctors, illnesses and accidents, arrows and lines drawn back and forth and all around until it looked like he'd scribbled out what he'd written. It was an unintelligible mess.

The scrawl represented his desperate efforts to reveal a pattern in the data he'd culled from the piles of papers and files that were scattered over his desk, his laptop, and his former living room couch.

The papers were everywhere and looked as if they'd simply been dropped on the room from above. It was pure chaos.

But he knew better. Each section of the room represented a different category. Every paper was where he'd wanted it to be. The disarray was actually an organizational system that only he understood—just not anymore. That knowledge had been lost along with the last two years of his life.

Standing there amidst his notes on the walls and papers on the floor was like being in the center of a diorama of his mind, a graphic representation of exactly what he was thinking three days ago, frozen in time.

The first step towards solving Jesse's murder was solving the mystery of this room. Mark had to discover whatever it was that he knew, whatever knowledge made someone want him dead . . .

Before the killer tried again.

CHAPTER SEVEN

Mark spent the rest of the day in his office, reading each sheet of paper and comparing it to his notes on the boards. He tried to map out the piles on the floor and compare them to the columns of names and dates he'd copied to the boards. He struggled to make sense of the multicolored lines, arrows, and circles he'd drawn in the various columns.

What did it all mean?

He squinted at a board, looking at it from various angles, trying to see any patterns within the scribbling.

Hour after frustrating hour ticked by. Emily came in once with sandwiches and juice and tried to convince Mark to take a break, but he couldn't tear himself away.

All he had to go on was that the death of Grover Dawson by fatal drug interaction had made him suspect foul play. His vague uneasiness was apparently exacerbated by Amanda's casual remark about the tragic irony of fatally ill people rebounding from preexisting medical conditions only to die a short time later from some other cause.

There were so many patient histories, formatted by the same database software, that they all began to blur together. The only differences between the documents were the names and causes of death.

It seemed like a lot of deaths, but these were very sick

and often elderly people. The sad truth was that their deaths were expected.

While there was an increase in those deaths this year, Mark didn't see evidence that anything was criminally amiss. If he had found anything, he wouldn't have had Amanda and Jesse doing such a broad, unfocused search for information.

He'd apparently gone through Amanda's report of patient deaths and organized them by cause of death, whether illness or accident. Then he subdivided those groups by age, race, and sex. Then he divided them again by the doctors who treated them and the hospitals they went to.

Still no pattern emerged.

The only thing Mark could see that the patients had in common was that they all had come close to death at least once before succumbing to natural causes or accidents. But even the accidents were, in most cases, directly related to their afflictions and not surprising.

Over the last three years, one hundred sixteen people had died within three months of a near-death experience. Forty-eight of those deaths had occurred within the last twelve months, representing a forty-five percent increase in the number of such deaths annually.

While this seemed to Mark like an extraordinary surge, when he looked at each case individually, he saw that few of the deaths were unexpected considering the medical conditions of the patients.

There had to be a key to crunching the data, to figuring out if something was truly wrong or if the sense of uneasiness that had sparked his investigation was baseless. Until he found that elusive key, he was lost.

He must have found it once; otherwise nobody would have tried to kill him. There was no question that his instincts were right.

Unless the attempt on his life had nothing to do with his investigation.

No, he didn't believe that. His work in this room and what had happened in the parking garage at Community General were linked.

He could feel it.

Mark slogged through the box of hospital records that Jesse had collected for the forty-eight dead patients. From what Mark could tell, Jesse had dug through the computer systems of Community General Hospital as well as several other LA-area hospitals. Jesse must have called in a lot of favors to gain password access to those other systems. Once inside, though, he wouldn't have had much trouble finding his way around. They all used the same Enable database software.

Strictly speaking, what Jesse had done was illegal and a gross violation of patient privacy—if he'd been caught by any administrator besides Mark, he would have been fired. But the patients were dead. It wasn't as if they had any privacy to lose at this point. That was Mark's rationalization, anyway.

He continued to pick through the forty-eight patient files as the evening wore on. It wasn't until about ten thirty that he finally referred back to the notes he'd taken in his office at Community General. This time, when he looked at the unfamiliar names of those three doctors, he understood what they meant and where at least two copies of Amanda's report had gone.

And if he wasn't mistaken, it was one of those doctors who'd given him the focus his investigation so desperately needed.

He turned to see Emily standing in the doorway.

"Hey, remember me?" she said.

"Is that a trick question?"

"We've barely spoken since you got home. It would be nice if we could talk sometime."

"We will," Mark said.

She nodded, though it seemed to be with defeat rather than agreement.

"It's getting late, and you've had a long day," she said.

"Just a little while longer," Mark said.

"You won't do yourself or your investigation any good by pushing yourself too hard too soon. Come to bed, Mark."

He looked at her. The truth was, there was nothing more he could do here, not until he talked to those two doctors tomorrow. But he wanted to put off the awkwardness of going to bed as long as he could.

It wasn't bashfulness or prudishness. Katherine had died a long time ago. It wasn't as if he'd taken a vow of celibacy over the decades that followed. But he'd never shared his bed with a complete stranger.

Intellectually, he knew Emily Noble was his wife. But emotionally, she was nobody to him, just a skilled doctor and a pleasant person. Even so, he didn't want to hurt her by suggesting they sleep apart until he felt comfortable with her again. It seemed too cruel.

He rose from his chair at the desk and without a word followed her upstairs.

While Emily was in the bathroom, Mark searched for his pajamas and changed. Then he stood at the foot of the unfamiliar bed, uncertain where he was supposed to sleep. He liked the left side, but what if she did, too? What arrangement had they worked out?

He tried to guess on the basis of what was on the nightstands, but there were no easy clues like books or magazines. The phone was on the left side, and since she was more likely to be responding to an emergency call late at night, he thought she might have chosen to sleep within easy reach of the receiver. He opened the nightstand drawer and saw ChapStick, nail clippers, and some paperback novels.

She slept on the left side.

Mark slipped into bed on the right side, lay on his back, and stared up at the ceiling. He felt like he was sleeping in someone else's bed. His eyes blurred and he blinked hard, trying to sharpen the world around him as if it was merely a picture on a TV screen. His vision cleared, but he still felt blurry. Perhaps it was his entire being, not his eyesight, that was out of focus.

You're just tired, he thought. But it was more than fatigue. It was the effort of trying to adjust to how dramatically his life had changed in just three days.

Only that wasn't what had happened. He was experiencing two years' worth of changes all at once, with no memory of the events that had led to them.

It would take more than a day to cope, especially to adjust to the idea that he was married again after decades of life on his own. Although Steve had lived in the same house, they still managed to live mostly separate lives. It was a fine arrangement that he realized now he'd been in no hurry at all to change.

He glanced at the closed bathroom door, heard the sound of water running behind it. Emily had changed all that. He apparently loved her enough to make seismic shifts in his life for her.

At that moment, Emily came out of the bathroom, opening the door as if his gaze had been knocking. She was in a thin nightgown, but she didn't seem any more comfortable in it than he did in the bed. He wondered if she ordinarily slept in the nude and was wearing the nightgown to make him feel more at ease.

She was beautiful. There was no denying that.

"You look like you're lying on broken glass," she said. "I'm not going to hurt you."

"I'm afraid I'm the one who has been inflicting the pain around here."

Emily flicked off the lights and got into bed, turning on her side to face him. He could feel the heat radiating from her and drew his arms closer to his body, afraid to brush against her.

"I know you don't mean to," she said. "So I try instead to imagine what it must be like for you, how lost you must feel."

"Does that help?"

"Not really," she admitted. "Maybe you should tell me."

"Tell you what?"

"How it feels," she said.

Mark shrugged. "I feel like a time traveler who has been yanked into the future. The world has changed, but I haven't."

"It's the other way around."

"Intellectually I know that. But at the same time I feel whole. I don't sense the gap in my memory. When I reach back, everything is there."

"I'm not," she said.

"And you wish I was trying as hard to know you as I am to solve the murder."

"That's our marriage in a nutshell," she said. "You're making progress already."

He couldn't see her smile, but he could hear the levity in her voice. What she said wasn't meant as a reproach—even though it was one.

"The thing is, I remember Jesse. I feel that pain and I have to do something about it."

"But you don't feel anything for me," she said.

Mark winced. He'd hurt her again. "You asked how I felt and I'm telling you. I'm not trying to be cruel. Investigating the mystery behind Jesse's death is familiar to me. I know how to do that. I have no idea how to find you again."

"I'm right here," she said, placing her hand on his chest. "We'll find the way together."

He nodded, took her hand, and gave it a squeeze. "I'm sorry."

She kissed him on the cheek. "Sweet dreams."

Mark let go of her hand and rolled onto his side, his back to her. He doubted his dreams would be sweet and wondered in what disturbing ways his guilt, anxiety, and grief would be dramatized on the stage of his unconscious. And within a moment or two he was asleep, where he found peace. The theater of his mind remained dark.

Medical neighborhoods sprang up and grew in much the same way ethnic neighborhoods did. All it took was one restaurant, grocery store, or church to serve as a social and cultural magnet and like-minded people would gather and stay, taking possession of one block after another, extending the boundaries of their neighborhood.

The same was true with hospitals.

West Hills was in the dry northwest corner of the San Fernando Valley, where housing developments, minimalls, and fast-food outlets were advancing on the few remaining ranches and the little bit of scrubland, the last vestiges of the area's rural heritage. At the leading edge of the steadily growing suburban sprawl was John Muir Hospital.

Within a year after John Muir opened, every building new and old within a mile of the hospital billed itself as a "medical center," renting space exclusively to anyone calling himself a doctor: surgeons, dentists, shrinks, veterinarians, and at least one epidemiologist. The entire neighborhood was now choked with pharmacies and other businesses serving the needs of those doctors.

Even though his office was right across the street, Dr. Richard Barnes had no official affiliation with John Muir Hospital and no reason to visit. He was there because the rents were far below what was being charged in Century City, Beverly Hills, and Santa Monica. The neighborhood may not have had the cachet of those other addresses, but it offered a seductively short commute for medical professionals like him who lived in the affluent gated communities in Bell Canyon and the Santa Susana Pass area.

His office was crisp and austere, more like the workplace

of an accountant or a lawyer. It had no waiting room, no nurse, no exam tables. He wasn't even wearing a lab coat.

Dr. Barnes was an African American man in his thirties, wearing a polo shirt and slacks, his hair cut so short it looked like a shadow on his head. He smiled broadly the moment Mark and Emily stepped into the office.

"Dr. Sloan, it's good to see you again," he said, giving Mark a hearty handshake. The man spoke with a slight British accent.

"You too," Mark said, though he didn't recognize the man at all. He assumed Barnes didn't know Emily, since the epidemiologist didn't greet her with the same enthusiasm. "This is my wife, Dr. Emily Noble."

"A pleasure." Barnes shook her hand, then turned back to Mark. "I didn't expect to see you again so soon. What can I do for you this time?"

"Exactly what you did before."

"I'm always glad to help. Do you have more patient death statistics for me to study?"

"Actually, the same ones."

As they all settled into the plush leather furniture in Barnes's wood-paneled office, Mark quickly explained his unusual plight, the loss of memory, and his effort to recapture the facts of his investigation.

"Fascinating," Barnes said. "I have never personally encountered a situation like yours before. It must be especially hard for you, Dr. Noble."

"Call me Emily, please," she said. "It is hard, but I must admit there's a part of me that shares your fascination. Who knows, perhaps I'll write a paper on this someday."

"If you do, let me know. I'd love to read it."

Mark shifted impatiently in his seat. "Right now, I'm less concerned about my own condition that I am with resuming my investigation. Do you mind going over everything you told me again?"

"Not at all," Barnes said. "You came to me with statistics

on several years' worth of deaths involving patients who'd died within a few months after surviving a life-threatening episode. You asked me if it was simply cruel fate or an epidemic. At first I thought you were joking, but you weren't."

"He wanted you to look at those stats using the principles of applied epidemiology," Emily said. "As you did in your study ten years ago of sudden deaths in the ICUs of several rural Texas hospitals."

Mark looked at her in amazement. "I thought I kept you out of my criminal investigations."

"I read the same medical journals you do," she said. "And I was still working in Houston at the time the study was published. I found it very interesting. Thanks to Dr. Barnes's study, and the statistical impossibility that such a cluster of deaths would occur naturally, authorities were able to discover there was a nurse killing patients. Without his study, the unusual number of deaths might have gone completely undetected."

"I was actually contacted by an administrator I knew who'd worked at two of the hospitals," Barnes said. "He was hoping I might be able to reveal some deficiencies in care that he could correct to reduce the number of patient deaths in rural ICUs. I was as shocked as anybody by what I discovered. It's one of the reasons I'm so outspoken about the need for hospitals to have a full-time epidemiologist on staff to identify rapidly spreading anomalies, natural or otherwise, that might otherwise go unnoticed. That's what I do— I help to find the medical, cultural, institutional, or behavioral causes and their solutions."

"What did you detect, if anything, from the information I gave you?" Mark asked.

Barnes sighed heavily.

"I won't bore you again with all the mathematical formulas I used. Suffice it to say I went back six years instead of three. What I discovered was that patients who'd survived near-death episodes this year were almost fifty percent more likely to die within ninety days than those with similar conditions in the past six years. The probability of such a significant increase in deaths occurring by chance alone is less than one in a trillion. That leads to only one possible explanation for this troubling epidemic."

"Murder," Mark said.

Barnes nodded. "The problem you faced after we met was identifying which of the cases were natural, or truly accidental, and which were homicides."

There were too many variables, too many possible suspects, and still no evidence, beyond statistics, that a crime had occurred. There wasn't enough yet to get Steve involved and, with him, the resources of the LAPD. That was why Mark had assigned Jesse the thankless and tedious job of going through hospital records. Mark was searching for any possible commonalities between the patients in an effort to sort out the natural and accidental deaths from the homicides.

Did the victims have the same medical insurance company? Go to the same hospitals? See the same doctors? Have their prescriptions filled by the same pharmacist? Share the same caregivers, nurses, or lab technicians?

Somewhere there was a point of convergence, but without more to go on, a way to narrow the field, it would take Mark months to find it. And in the meantime more people could be killed.

"Did you have any advice for me?" Mark asked Barnes.

"I'm afraid this is out of my range of expertise," he said. "I'm not well versed in the intricacies of murder."

Emily tipped her head towards Mark. "He is."

CHAPTER EIGHT

Now that Mark's instincts had been confirmed, he faced the daunting task of sifting through the forty-eight deaths, identifying the victims, and determining the pattern that would flush out the killer.

Again.

He was certain that he'd already accomplished the task once before. Now he just had to find a shortcut to reaching the same conclusions, whatever they were, all over again.

One of the two remaining doctors on Mark's list was Dr. Bernard Dalton, a cardiologist who had two patients who'd recently died and whose names showed up on Amanda's report. Dr. Dalton's office happened to be in the building next door, so Mark and Emily went over to see him.

Dalton worked out of the Bell Canyon Cardiology Group, presumably named for the exclusive gated community where most of the partners in the practice lived. The practice took up an entire floor of the building. The vast waiting room was lit by pinpoint halogens and was dominated by two large, flat-screen TVs mounted on the wall, one tuned to CNN, the other showing a computer-generated, and surprisingly lifelike, aquarium full of tropical fish. The patients sat on couches lined with pillows of varying sizes and patterns.

Most of the waiting patients were elderly and seemed, to Mark's experienced eye, to be suffering from more than cardiac problems. Many of them used walkers or canes and were accompanied by caregivers or younger family members.

Mark went to the front desk and presented himself to the nurse, who sent them right in, motioning them to the doctor's office at the end of the hall.

The corner office turned out to be a suite shared by five doctors, each of whom had his own built-in desk that faced a window with a view of John Muir Hospital across the street.

Dr. Dalton was the only doctor present when Mark and Emily came in. He was a large man who seemed well on his way to his own heart attack, his huge gut spilling over his belt.

The cardiologist rose from his seat, its springs squealing in relief from the burden of his tonnage, and vigorously shook hands with his guests. Mark explained his situation and asked the doctor if he would mind repeating whatever he'd said before.

"You asked me about Leila Pevney," Dalton said, dropping back into his seat, which let out a screech and seemed to sink a good six inches under his weight. "She was a seventy-eight-year-old woman with a long history of heart disease who also suffered from cancer and senility."

"You mean Alzheimer's?" Emily said.

"I mean she was forgetful, scatterbrained, and a little dazed. Some of it was from her chemo. The rest?" Dalton shrugged. "I referred her to a neurologist, but he determined she was simply suffering from old age."

"How did she die?" Mark asked.

"That's the really ironic thing. She was a fighter. Over the years she survived two heart attacks, quadruple bypass surgery, and two bouts of lung cancer. Then she died from a common cold."

"Colds aren't usually fatal," Emily said.

"They are when you take too many decongestants," Dr. Dalton said. "I found the cold medication on her nightstand.

The pills were in a foil packet. I counted eight tablets missing. Whether she took them all at once or in close succession, I don't know."

It was obvious to Mark what had happened. Many cold medications contained pseudoephedrine, which is a stimulant. For someone with advanced cardiovascular disease, all it would take was as few as three or four pills to cause a rapid increase in heart rate and blood pressure, producing a deadly cardiac arrhythmia such as ventricular tachycardia or ventricular fibrillation. Death could occur in seconds.

"Didn't she know better than to take pseudoephedrine?" Mark said.

"Like I said, she was forgetful. She probably forgot how many pills she'd taken and when she took them," Dalton said. "All she knew was that her nose was still stuffy and her eyes were watery."

"What were the cold pills even doing in the house?" Emily asked. "That's like keeping rat poison where a child can reach it."

"I don't know. One of her kids or grandkids may have had the sniffles last time they visited and left the pills behind," Dalton said. "Maybe even one of her caregivers."

"She had nursing help?" Mark said.

"Not full-time. They were drop-ins. Because she was living alone, they'd check up on her every day, make sure she was taking her pills, eating and drinking enough, that sort of thing. There was also a food service that stopped by three times a week with home-cooked meals she could stick in her freezer and defrost later."

"Who notified you of her death?"

"The caregiver. I found Leila sitting in her recliner in front of the TV, balls of used Kleenex all over the floor around her. It was obvious to me what had happened, and the toxicology tests proved me correct."

Mark checked his notes. "Tell me about Chadwick Saxelid."

"Chad was thirty-seven years old and had a history of atherosclerosis and angina. The men in his family died young, and he was no exception. His gardener found him dead in the backyard, in his bathing suit, a few feet from the hot tub. The way I heard it, the cops found his nitro pills in the pocket of his bathrobe, which he was clutching when he died, and a couple of empty beer bottles by the hot tub. I'm not a detective, but it was pretty clear to me what happened."

It was clear to Mark, too.

"Chad got in the hot tub and had a couple of beers," Mark said. "The hot water dilated his blood vessels and lowered his blood pressure."

"So did the beers," Emily added.

"The combination of the two lowered the supply of blood to his heart," Mark said. "Giving him a stabbing chest pain that he mistook for angina."

"But the pain wasn't from clogged arteries," Emily said. "It was actually the reverse."

"Chad didn't know that," Dalton said. "He took a nitro tablet and made everything worse."

"He might as well have shot himself in the chest," Emily said.

"The pill caused a massive drop in blood pressure, provoking a fatal myocardial infarction," Mark said.

"I can forgive the guy for mistaking the chest pain for angina," Emily said, "but he should have known better than to get into a hot tub and drink in the first place."

"Chad was young, single, and he liked to party," Dalton said. "He certainly isn't the first person to die because of it."

"Some people are just too stupid to live," Emily said.

"Chad was already living on borrowed time," Dalton said. "Less than a year earlier, he had a massive heart attack at a club. Turns out he'd taken some meth. He would have died, too, but the guy next to him happened to be an off-duty fireman who knew CPR."

There was something about the fates of Leila Pevney and

Chadwick Saxelid that troubled Mark, but he couldn't figure out what it was. The two had several things in common besides being Dr. Dalton's patients: They both had coronary diseases, and their deaths, to some degree, were both the result of fatal reactions to drugs.

But that was a stretch, and neither of those similarities was what was nagging Mark. It was something else. He just couldn't identify it and couldn't think of what to ask Dr. Dalton that might bring it to light.

So he thanked Dr. Dalton for his time and he and Emily left.

Emily drove with the top down, wearing a baseball cap and sunglasses. Mark wore sunglasses but no hat. They were on the southbound San Diego Freeway going over the Sepulveda Pass, leaving the smog-choked San Fernando Valley and heading into the smog-choked Los Angeles Basin.

"You should be wearing a hat," Emily said.

"I don't mind the air," Mark said.

"It's not the air I'm worried about, it's the sun. Have you forgotten about that gash on your head? You're going to have an ugly scar if you don't wear sunscreen and a hat."

"If you're so worried," Mark said, "put up the top."

She glared at him. "What's the matter with you?"

"Besides losing Jesse and two years of my memory?"

"And me," she said. "I'd say 'don't forget that,' but you already have."

Mark reached into the backseat, grabbed the baseball cap that was there, and put it snugly on his head.

"There," he said. "Happy now?"

They were silent for a long moment, making a point of not looking at each other. Finally, Emily sighed.

"I'm sorry. That wasn't fair," she said. "I shouldn't have said that."

"It's okay," Mark said. "You were right about the scar and about the way I am treating you. I'm being very selfish when, in fact, it's you who is suffering the most. My condition is a lot harder on you than it is for me."

"Why do you say that?"

"Because you remember everything," Mark said. "Your love hasn't dimmed a bit, and yet here I sit, treating you like a stranger. I feel awkwardness, but you feel heartbreak."

"So you're saying I'm the one who should be surly," Emily said, giving him a smile.

"I'm frustrated, that's all. I don't like having to play catch-up in this investigation. Not only do I have to figure out who the killer is and what he's thinking, I have to figure out who *I* was and what *I* was thinking. It puts me at a huge disadvantage."

"Talking to Dr. Barnes and Dr. Dalton didn't clarify things?"

"Not really."

"But at least you know there *is* a killer."

"I was already working from that assumption, which was confirmed when someone tried to run me over and got Jesse instead," Mark said. "I still have no idea who or what I'm looking for. But at the same time, I feel this nagging itch in the back of my mind, like there's something I'm missing."

"Two years."

Mark shook his head. "No, it's not that. It's something right in front of my face that I'm not seeing."

She gave him a look. "Maybe it's me."

"It's the case," he said.

"How can you be sure?" she said. "How do you know it's not some memory trying to claw its way back to the surface?"

"Because this feeling is something I've felt before on other cases."

"It's something you *remember* feeling before. It's a memory as much as it is a feeling. It may be a whole bunch of memories rising from the murk."

"That would be nice," Mark said.

"Yes, it would," Emily said. "Where to now?"

"You could drop me off at the hospital and I could pick up my car."

"Why would I want to do that?"

"So you wouldn't have to chauffeur me around," Mark said. "I'm feeling fine. My eyesight is good. It's safe for me to drive."

"Trying to get rid of me?" she said lightly.

"I just thought you might be anxious to get back to your work."

"I want to be with you. I want to help you solve this case and then recover your memory so we can continue our lives together," she said. "Nothing is more important than that to me."

Mark nodded. "Okay. In that case, we're going to West LA."

"What's there?"

"Grover Dawson's place. So far I've been working from the present and going backwards. Let's start from the past and go forward. Probably the first thing I did was visit the scene of the crime to see what I could learn."

"Makes sense," Emily said.

"It's about time something did," he said.

CHAPTER NINE

Grover Dawson's apartment was just a few blocks away from the Tropic Sands, where Mark had lived with his first wife and their infant son forty years ago. The Tropic Sands was a typical example of the space-age modernism that had swept Southern California in the late fifties and early sixties.

The buildings of the era were essentially stucco boxes, bland on three sides but with eye-catching street facades meant to grab a motorist's attention. The Tropic Sands had two palm trees out front and the name of the apartment house written in flowing plywood script over a strip of lava rock and punctuated by a starburst lamp.

The architecture seemed to say that these weren't just places to live—they were a trip to paradise or a rocket to tomorrow. The bright colors and sweeping rooflines were meant to distract tenants from the fact that they were actually living in cheaply made, cramped, assembly-line boxes that wouldn't be standing when the future they promised finally arrived.

The apartments were built around and over the car, the carports literally incorporating the automobile as part of the exterior design. That worked well when cars all looked like rocket ships and ocean liners. The rapid decline and neglect of the buildings came about the same time that cars started looking like the shabby boxes they were parked under.

Only a few years ago, the Tropic Sands and remaining buildings like it had become decaying slum apartments destined for demolition, to be replaced by the block-long condominium monoliths that were reshaping West LA.

But then a miracle happened. Young, successful professionals embraced the exuberant optimism that the buildings represented, restoring the vintage properties to their gaudy grandeur.

Now the Tropic Sands looked even better than it had in Mark's day, so much so that it seemed like a figment of his imagination, a fading memory gussied up by sentiment and wishful thinking.

He wondered if Emily drove by the building on purpose as a way to jog his memory. Then again, perhaps he'd never told her about this place and she was merely taking surface streets to avoid the congestion on Santa Monica Boulevard.

Either way, Mark was glad he'd seen the building. It may not have helped him remember Emily, but it gave him another tether between the past and the present to hold on to, making him feel a little more whole.

Grover Dawson's building wasn't as fortunate as the Tropic Sands. It had been built later and lacked the kitsch appeal. It was just a stucco box, with a brand-new FOR RENT sign taped in the window of Grover's ground-floor apartment.

Mark and Emily walked into the courtyard. The front door of Grover's apartment was open, and there was a woman inside, packing things into moving boxes. She was in her twenties, wearing a sweat-soaked T-shirt and shorts, her long hair pulled back from her face into a ponytail. She had a stud piercing one nostril and another in her left eyebrow. It hurt Mark just to look at them.

"Excuse me," Mark said. "I'm Dr. Mark Sloan."

"I know. We met at Dad's funeral," she said, looking at him quizzically. He was getting used to seeing that expression on people's faces. "I didn't expect to see you again."

Mark didn't feel like telling his story yet again, and he

didn't want to give her the impression that her father had met with foul play, at least not until he actually had some evidence. He assumed he'd been just as careful when they met before.

"I used to live two blocks over, back in the early sixties," Mark said. "I was just showing the place to my wife, and I realized you might be here. I thought I'd drop by and see how you were getting along."

Emily stepped forward, offering the woman her hand. "I'm Emily Noble."

"Mallory Dawson," the woman said.

"How are you holding up?" Emily asked.

"I'm running myself ragged. I have to go back to New York in two days, and there just isn't enough time to do all the things I have to do. I'm trying to sort through all of Dad's stuff and get this place cleaned up so I don't get stuck with next month's rent."

"I know how you feel," Emily said. "I had to do the same thing when my father died."

Mallory sat down on one of the moving boxes and took a sip from a soft drink can. "Most of Dad's stuff is going to the church. They'll give it to needy families or sell it at one of their swap meets."

"You're not keeping anything for yourself?" Mark asked.

"The photo albums, of course, but that's about it. I still haven't found his wedding ring. I've torn the place apart looking for it—not that it matters as much now."

"Why not?" Mark said, wondering if she planned to stick the ring through her nose, too.

"It's a little late to bury him with it like I wanted to. That's why I asked you before the funeral if the medical examiner might have misplaced it when she removed his personal effects."

"Yes, I remember," Mark lied.

"You said you'd look into it for me," Mallory said. "Did you find it?"

"I'm afraid not," Mark said. "Have you heard anything from his girlfriend?"

"Not a peep. If he hadn't died the way he did, I probably never would have known he had one. It's funny, he used to give me such a hard time about my nomadic love life, telling me how wrong it was that I wasn't saving myself for marriage. You'd think I'd resent him now for giving me hell and being such a hypocrite. But the truth is I'm glad he died in someone's arms, that he wasn't alone, and that his last moments were filled with affection and tenderness."

"That's a healthy way of looking at it," Mark said.

She smiled to herself. "I'll tell you a little secret, though. During the funeral, I kept looking at all those tearful church ladies standing at the graveside. I tried to see if I could figure out from their faces which one was his squeeze."

"Do you think you spotted her?" Emily asked.

Mallory shook her head. "Whoever she is, I bet it will be a long time before she has sex again."

The conversation with Grover Dawson's daughter only reinforced Mark's feeling that something wasn't right about the circumstances of the man's death.

"Just because Grover didn't tell his daughter about his girlfriend doesn't mean he didn't have one," Emily said as they drove back to their house in Malibu.

"Now you sound like Steve," Mark said.

"It makes more sense than someone switching Grover's meds with Viagra or forcing him at gunpoint to take the little blue pills."

"You didn't know Grover," Mark said.

"But I know men," she said.

When they got back to the house, Mark and Emily had a late lunch of tuna fish sandwiches and cantaloupe slices.

Mark was clearing the dishes when Emily brought several large photo albums to the table.

"What are those?" he asked.

"I thought you might like to see our wedding album," she said.

"Some other time," Mark said. "I've got work to do."

"You've spent most of the day on your investigation. How about spending a few minutes trying to remember us?"

Mark glanced at the album and saw some pictures of them together on the beach at the Grand Kiahuna Poipu, the resort where he and Steve had stayed once.

"I'll look at all the pictures of us," Mark said, "when Jesse's killer has been caught."

Mark turned before he could see the expression on Emily's face. He knew she was hurt, and that he was being unfair, but he had other priorities that were bigger than himself or his relationship with Emily. His memories could be recovered. Jesse was gone forever. And what about Grover Dawson? How many others had died at the hands of this unknown killer?

His memories could wait. Justice for the dead could not.

He went downstairs to his office. His intention was to go through the files again. And again. And again, until the facts coalesced in his subconscious and he found the common thread.

His gaze fell first on his notes on the dry-erase boards, on the same indiscernible doodling and scribbling he couldn't make sense of the day before.

Now it had changed.

Actually, the notes hadn't changed. He had.

It wasn't a bunch of meaningless scrawls and doodles anymore. He had the facts necessary to put everything into perspective. It was as if he'd put on a pair of glasses and was seeing clearly again.

Looking at the board, he saw now that he'd compared all the other patient deaths to the details of Grover Dawson's demise and discovered something.

A pattern.

It was right there, amidst the lists and circled names and

crisscrossing lines and arrows. The intersecting lines formed a web of murder.

He realized now what it was that had bothered him at Dr. Dalton's office. Not only were Leila Pevney and Chadwick Saxelid people who'd cheated death and later died of fatal drug interactions, but they also lived alone.

So did Grover.

So did Sandy Sechrest, the woman who was electrocuted in her bathtub.

And so did two of Mark's dead patients, Joyce Kling and Hammond McNutchin.

There were other patients on the board whose histories were similar to those of Dawson, Sechrest, Pevney, and Chadwick, but with some inconsistencies. It wasn't a perfect pattern. For instance, some cases matched except for the fact that the patients died from natural causes as opposed to accidents or fatal drug interactions.

Were they part of the pattern or not? Or was his pattern flawed?

He was still no closer to identifying the one deadly point of convergence that would determine who were truly victims and lead him to the killer.

Mark looked at his notes, the ones he'd found at his office at Community General.

First Fidelity Casualty
Wedding band
Dentures?
Kemper-Carlson Pharmaceuticals
Cal-Star Insurance
Sechrest + Pevney + ?
The glass fish?
The pearl necklace?

He assumed that the appearance of insurance and pharmaceutical companies on the list meant that some of the victims might have shared the same insurer or pharmacist. That would be easy enough to check.

But what about the other items? How did dentures or a glass fish figure into things?

Perhaps the wedding band mentioned in his notes referred to the ring Grover's daughter was talking about, the one that had been lost.

A shiver traveled up Mark's spine as he came to a sudden realization. He knew why the glass fish, the dentures, and the pearl necklace were significant.

They were items that belonged to the dead patients. They were items that were missing.

They were trophies.

That was when Mark felt more than just the shiver of realization. He felt the living, breathing, deadly presence of the killer, the monster creeping in the darkness.

The phone rang, startling him. Emily grabbed it on the second ring. He couldn't hear her words, but he could hear the urgent tone in her voice.

There was an emergency.

Mark went with Emily to the hospital. He talked her into taking him along so he could pick up his car and drive it back to Malibu.

All Emily knew about her unborn patient was that the fetus was suffering from a serious atrial septal defect, an abnormal opening between the two upper chambers of the heart. The baby wasn't due for another few weeks and could die without emergency in-utero surgery.

"Why wasn't the defect caught earlier?" Mark asked Emily as she drove.

"I don't know. The only reason it was spotted now was because the mother was in a car accident," Emily said. "The ER doctors were checking to see if the fetus had been injured and they stumbled on the abnormality."

They parked in front of the emergency room entrance and

hurried into the hospital, where they were met by a young doctor who looked so much like Jesse, Mark almost called him by name. But it wasn't Jesse. The doctor's name was Carl Kozak.

"Thanks for coming down so quickly, Dr. Noble," he said, leading them towards the trauma room.

"What are the headlines?"

"The woman is twenty-eight years old and in her late third trimester of pregnancy," the doctor said while on the move, referring to his notes. "She was driving through an intersection when she was struck by a drunk driver who ran the red light. She's suffered massive head injuries."

"Is she brain-dead?" Emily asked.

Dr. Kozak nodded. "We have her on a ventilator. I think there's a strong chance we can keep her alive until the baby comes to term."

"The drunk driver?" Mark asked.

"Dead on arrival," Dr. Kozak said.

It was a sad and horrible situation, but one Mark was painfully familiar with. The last thing Emily needed to deal with going into surgery was having to pass this terrible news on to the woman's family. Mark decided he'd volunteer to handle that burden, one he'd carried far too many times in his career.

"Where's the father?" Mark said.

"He's dead," Dr. Kozak said.

The tragedy kept getting worse.

"Was she killed in the accident?" Emily asked. "Or did he die here?"

"He died here," Dr. Kozak said. "But not in the accident."

"I don't understand," Mark said.

Dr. Kozak turned to him as they reached the trauma room doors and hesitated. "There is no easy way to say this, Dr. Sloan. The father was Jesse."

"No," Mark said, the word coming out as an anguished wail. He pushed open the doors and marched into the trauma room to find Susan on the table, her face so bloodied she was almost unrecognizable, a breathing tube down her throat.

"Please God no," he said.

Emily put her arm around him. "Mark, maybe you should go."

"I can't believe this is happening," he said, closing his eyes.

"Neither can I," she said. "Now we have to concentrate on saving the baby."

His head began to throb, each pulse a blinding stab of agony. He dropped to his knees, clutching his head.

Emily and Dr. Kozak were beside him, but he couldn't see them. He couldn't see anything. He couldn't hear anything except the thunderclaps of pain in his head. It felt like his hands were all that was holding his skull together, that if he let go, it would explode into pieces.

And then it did.

CHAPTER TEN

Steve Sloan rushed into the ER, nearly colliding with Dr. Kozak as he came through the door.

"Where's my father, Carl?" Steve demanded.

"He's on his way to the OR," Dr. Kozak said.

"They're operating on him? Why? What happened?"

"I don't know the details, Steve. You'll have to wait until the attending physician comes down in a few minutes."

"Who is it?" Steve asked.

"It's Jesse," said a nurse, coming up behind him.

Steve turned to see Susan Travis standing behind him in her blue nurse's scrubs, her face etched with concern.

"I thought my father was stable, that all he had was a concussion and that he'd be coming around soon," Steve said. "That's what Jesse told me this morning, right after the attempt on Dad's life."

"There have been some complications," she said, touching him lightly on the arm and gently leading him towards the chairs in the waiting area.

"What kind of complications? Tell me."

"It's better if Jesse does," Susan said. "He hasn't left Mark's side since he tackled him out of the way of that car this morning."

"I would have been with Dad, too," Steve said, "but Jesse told me to go. He told me Dad's injuries weren't serious."

After spending an hour that morning at Mark's bedside, and at Jesse's urging, Steve had decided he wouldn't be helping his father by maintaining a vigil. Mark would want him out on the street, trying to catch the person responsible for his injury. That's what Mark would do if the situation was reversed. In fact, that was exactly what Mark had done when Steve was seriously wounded in a shoot-out.

"That came out all wrong. I didn't mean that as a reproach," Susan said, taking a seat. "I'm just saying that Mark is in good hands."

"I never doubted it," Steve said, sitting down beside her.

It was the truth. Although he often teased Jesse, he had great respect for his medical skills. After all, Jesse had learned from the best.

"You might want to tell Jesse that. He's blaming himself for what happened."

"It's not his fault," Steve said. "Jesse saved Dad's life."

At that moment, paramedics charged through the ER doors, wheeling a bloodied man on a gurney. Susan left Steve and joined the other nurses running alongside the gurney into the trauma room.

Sitting there alone, Steve finally had a moment to rest, to reflect on the chaotic events of the day, which began when he got a frantic early-morning wake-up call from Susan at his girlfriend Lissy's apartment.

"Your father has been hurt," Susan said. "Someone tried to run him over in the parking garage."

Steve drove with his siren wailing, weaving through traffic and blasting through red lights, arriving at the hospital within ten minutes of getting the call. He found Mark unconscious in the ER, an IV in his arm and Jesse tending to him at his bedside.

Jesse told him about tackling Mark out of the path of a car and that it wasn't an accident. There was no doubt in Jesse's mind about the unseen driver's murderous intent.

"But it wasn't the car that hurt Mark," Jesse said. "It was

me. I don't have your experience in tackling people. I'm usually the tackle-ee. I took him by surprise from behind, so he never had a chance to break his fall. His head smacked right against the pavement."

"You knocked him out of the way and didn't get run over yourself. If you ask me, that's a perfect tackle," Steve said. "Is he just out cold or is it more serious than that?"

"Although there's no sign of a cracked skull or internal bleeding, he does have some minor brain swelling."

"Does this mean he has brain damage?" Steve asked.

"No, it's to be expected and nothing to worry about," Jesse said. "He may even be dreaming now."

"So what do we do?"

"We wait. Concussions are unpredictable and vary from person to person and injury to injury. Mark could wake up in a few minutes or a few days. There's no way to tell. But we'll monitor him very closely, and we'll call you if there's any change in his condition."

Steve nodded, chewing nervously on his lower lip. Someone obviously wanted Mark dead, but who? And why?

As far as Steve knew, Mark wasn't working on any active homicide investigations, and none of the murderers he'd put away had been unexpectedly released from prison on appeal or parole. Of course, that didn't mean one of them hadn't arranged a little vengeance from behind bars.

"Did Dad say anything to you before the attempt on his life?"

"He had The Look," Jesse said.

"What look?"

"*The* Look," Jesse said.

Steve knew The Look. It was the intensity in Mark's eyes when he'd reached the point in his investigation that he knew his adversary, if not by name or face, then by evil intent.

Now Steve had to somehow reach that point himself.

"What did Dad have you doing for him?" Steve asked.

"Going through hospital records, searching for anything in common among patients who'd died shortly after leaving the hospital for treatment of critical medical conditions."

"Like Grover Dawson," Steve said. "The guy who died standing at attention."

"So to speak," Jesse said.

"How many patients are we talking about?"

"About eight hundred died within a year, forty-eight within ninety days."

"That's an awfully big job with nothing to go on," Steve said.

"Mark was concentrating on the forty-eight," Jesse said.

"It could still take you weeks to find anything—and that's *if* there's actually anything there to find beyond the occasional coincidence. That's a big *if*."

"Mark loves big *ifs*," Jesse said wearily. "But I got the impression this morning that he might have found the key to narrowing the search."

"I don't suppose he gave you a hint?"

"Just The Look," Jesse said. "And the promise of a free lunch."

Once Steve left Mark's bedside, the first thing he did was to go to the doctors' lounge, commandeer the VCR, and watch the surveillance footage from the parking garage security cameras. If Jesse had waited a fraction of a second longer to make the tackle, Mark probably would have been killed. Even so, Steve winced every time he thought about Mark's head hitting the concrete.

The tinted windows of the Camaro were too dark for him to make out the driver, but the assailant had done nothing to obscure the license plate, which led Steve to assume that the car was probably stolen. He called the plate in and, within thirty seconds, found out he was right. The car was reported stolen the day before in Canoga Park.

He sent officers to interview the owner of the Camaro and canvas the neighborhood where it was stolen to see if anyone might have caught a glimpse of the thief. He also put out an APB on the car.

Meanwhile, crime scene techs were scouring the hospital parking structure for clues, and officers were interviewing everyone in the building, aside from bedridden patients, on the off chance that they'd seen something.

Steve was still watching the tape when Amanda came rushing in, distraught over the news about Mark and anxious to do whatever she could to help. She explained the research Mark had had her do, which made Steve smile. His father loved to put Amanda and Jesse to work beating the bushes for clues. And they gladly did it, not so much because they shared Mark's love of homicide investigation but out of respect and loyalty to him. They would do anything for him.

And Steve was sure they would do anything for him, too, as he hunted for Mark's would-be assassin. He intended to take full advantage of their willingness to help, because he doubted his superiors at the LAPD would authorize him to devote any additional manpower or resources to the case. He'd probably catch hell for the legwork he'd already assigned to uniformed officers.

It wasn't just because the chief of police wasn't fond of Mark and resented his intrusions into areas of LAPD responsibility. The case wasn't really big enough to merit the kind of effort Steve wanted to put into it. At least not yet.

It was clear to Steve that Mark was investigating Grover Dawson's accidental death and others like it, despite the fact that there wasn't a shred of evidence indicating foul play. A visit to Mark's office and a peek at his appointments and the notes on his desk confirmed that was what his dad was up to.

Steve couldn't make sense of the notes, but he tracked down the three doctors whose names were written on Mark's calendar: a cardiologist, an epidemiologist, and a sociologist.

He was most intrigued by Dr. Tanya Hudson, the sociologist.

What did his father want from her? Steve went to see her at UCLA to find out.

Dr. Hudson was a tall, thin redhead in her thirties who was trying hard to dim her beauty and look more academic. But the glasses, prim suit, and plain hairstyle failed to hide her perfect figure and angular features. She looked to Steve like a *Baywatch* lifeguard trying to go undercover as a psychiatrist.

Her campus office in Franz Hall was tiny, cramped, and choked with books and papers, so she suggested that they talk in the plaza outside.

They took a seat on the brick bench around an inverted fountain, where students sat studying, chattering on cell phones, and dangling their bare feet in the water cascading down into a burbling hole.

"I don't get the point of inverted fountains," Steve said. "They remind me of gigantic toilet bowls that never stop flushing."

She laughed, and Steve was pleased with himself.

"I've never thought of it that way. Now, I fear, I'll have that image in my head every time I see this fountain," she said. "Which is daily. So thanks a lot."

"My pleasure," he said.

"You said on the phone that you urgently needed to talk to me about your father," she said.

He told her briefly about the attempt on Mark's life. "I'm trying to retrace my father's steps and figure out what he was onto. That's why I need to know why he met with you and what you told him."

"I hope he's going to be okay."

"He's probably out of bed already, examining the tread marks the car left behind," Steve said, though he knew it wasn't true—Jesse would have called if Mark had regained consciousness. But Steve wanted to put Dr. Hudson at ease.

"Dr. Sloan was interested in my research. For the last three years I've been hanging out in prisons and mental institutions interviewing doctors, nurses, and other caregivers who've murdered their patients."

"Is this for a book?"

She shook her head. "It's for a study, but I'm also trying to create a profile of these mercy killers, angels of death, and murderers with stethoscopes. Your dad has been very supportive of that effort. I want to help hospitals recognize the warning signs in certain individuals *before* they strike."

"You think you can screen for killers on an employment application?"

She smiled. "You're a very cynical man, Lieutenant."

"It's a requirement of my profession."

"I think there are certain patterns of behavior typical of these kinds of individuals."

"For instance?"

"It would take me three hundred forty-seven pages to answer that question," she said. "Or you could just read my study."

"I'd prefer to listen to the abridged audiobook version."

"First, you need to know that there are several kinds of medical murderers. There are, of course, the ones who give patients fatal injections or smother them out of a misguided sense of compassion."

"Mercy killers," Steve said.

"But it's never really about easing anyone's suffering," she said. "It's about their own pleasure and neediness. Some do it because they get off on a godlike sense of power."

"The more they kill, the more invincible they feel."

"Exactly. Others do it for the attention, a disorder known as Munchausen syndrome by proxy. They like to be at the center of a medical crisis of their own creation."

"Why don't they just make themselves sick instead of some innocent victim?"

"They want attention," she said. "They don't want to die. Some don't intend to kill. They just want to set up a medical emergency so they can save the patient's life and be a hero."

"But they're better at the emergency than the saving."

"Sadly, yes. Others kill out of disgust—they actually resent the vulnerability and weakness of their patients. But they're really acting out their own self-loathing."

"I hate myself so I'll kill you?"

"It's the only time they feel superior to anyone else," she said. "And, of course, there are those who kill simply because they enjoy it. Some even get sexual satisfaction from it."

"And you think you can spot these murderers?"

"I think they often reveal themselves if you know what to look for. I advise hospitals to keep track of who dies and who is the last person with the patient. If Nurse Ratched always seems to be the one around when people die, it may not be a coincidence. Watch the numbers. If there's a jump in death rates, go back and see if that occurred during certain shifts, then see if there's one doctor, nurse, or orderly who is always on that shift."

"Nurse Ratched again," Steve said.

"Or it may be the nicest, most giving nurse on the ward, the one who always shows up to help once the crisis occurs."

"Because she gets off, one way or another, on the rush of excitement and the race against death."

"You're catching on," Dr. Hudson said.

"I'm a quick study when it comes to murder."

"Watch nurses or doctors who receive complaints from patients for being rude, abusive, or uncaring. Pay close attention to inexplicable shortages of epinephrine or other drugs in the hospital. It could mean someone is hoarding them to inject into patients."

"Those seem like pretty obvious signals."

"You'd be surprised how often they are ignored. When it comes to missing drugs, the assumption is they were stolen for sale or recreational use. Rarely do people consider that the drugs were taken to kill patients," she said. "But there are more subtle indications, too. I warn hospital administrators to be suspicious of anyone who has frequently moved from one hospital to another, is overly interested in death, or has a very difficult time with personal relationships."

"Based on those last two criteria, I could be a medical murderer."

"You don't strike me as someone who has difficulty with personal relationships."

"Ask my ex-girlfriends," Steve said.

She met his gaze and smiled. "Maybe I will."

He was pretty sure she was flirting with him, but he was terrible at judging women. Still, he made a mental note to give her a call if his current relationship fizzled.

Or *when*, given his romantic history.

Steve thanked Dr. Hudson for her help and gave her his card, asking her to call him if she thought of anything else that might be helpful.

"I'll do that," she said, in a way that sounded full of erotic possibility to him. Then again, he could read erotic possibility into just about anything any woman said to him.

She gave him her card and returned to her office, but Steve remained at the inverted fountain.

He called Dr. Barnes, the epidemiologist, and discovered after talking to him that Mark might have been onto something after all. Statistically speaking, too many patients were dying for it to be simply bad luck.

Someone was killing people. A *lot* of people.

But Steve didn't have enough evidence to convince his superiors to assign a task force. At least not yet.

He marveled at his father's instincts and wished, not for the first time, that he shared the trait. Steve knew he was a good detective, but it was a learned skill and he worked hard to get results. He didn't have his father's gift for deduction or his sixth sense for murder.

Once Mark's instincts were confirmed by the epidemiologist, his dad had taken a crash course in profiling medical murderers from Dr. Hudson and set out to unmask a serial killer.

Now Steve would do the same. But he was troubled by something else.

How did the killer find out that Mark was on the case?

Steve was pondering that question, and many others, when he got the page from Community General, where he now sat in the waiting room, worrying about his father and trying to figure out what to do next.

He was making an investigative To Do list in his little leather-bound notebook when the elevator doors opened and Jesse came out.

CHAPTER ELEVEN

Jesse limped over, looking beaten and exhausted. There were dark circles under his bloodshot eyes and he winced with each step, trying to keep weight off his left knee, which he'd hurt while tackling Mark.

Steve rose to meet him. "How bad is it?"

Jesse stumbled past Steve and took a seat. Steve remained standing.

"Mark is going to be fine," Jesse said. "He'll be out of surgery in about an hour."

"What happened?"

"He had a seizure. We ran an MRI and discovered subdural bleeding."

"What does that mean?" Steve asked impatiently, a tinge of anger in his voice.

"It's an accumulation of blood beneath the protective membrane around the brain. The skull is rigid bone and it can't expand, so bleeding exerts pressure on the brain, essentially squeezing it into the opening at the base of the skull. If left untreated, the pressure will compress the brain stem, stopping respiration and leading to immediate death. We had to relieve the pressure, and there's only one way to do that."

"You cracked open his skull," Steve said.

"It's not that extreme. We're drilling a hole about the size of a quarter to drain the fluid," Jesse said. "Later, we'll seal it with a bone graft or a metal plate."

"That still sounds pretty extreme to me," Steve said. "Though I suppose there isn't any choice. What are the dangers?"

"Brain damage, infection, more bleeding," Jesse said. "But I don't think that will happen."

"You didn't think *this* would happen either," Steve snapped, then caught himself. "I'm sorry. This is the second time you've saved Dad's life today. What I should be saying is thank you."

"Don't worry, Steve. I won't leave him until he's conscious and out of danger."

"The hell you won't," Susan said, approaching them now. "You haven't slept in over twenty-four hours and you need to get that knee looked at."

"She's right," Steve said. "I'll stay with him."

"That won't do Mark or you any good," Susan said. "I have a better idea. I'll keep an eye on Mark while Jesse gets some sleep and you catch whoever did this. Besides, it's my job and I'm pretty darn good at it."

Jesse looked at Steve. "She has a point."

"But I'm the only family he has," Steve said.

"No, you're not," Susan said, without a trace of anger or hurt feelings.

She was simply stating a fact that, in his worry, he'd overlooked. Mark had always considered Jesse, Susan, and Amanda his family, too.

"You're right. I'm sorry," Steve said. "I keep saying stupid things that I don't mean."

"It's okay. You're allowed when a loved one is hurt and you're afraid of what might happen," Susan said. "Saying stupid things is entirely normal in this situation."

"Thank you." Steve smiled and gave Susan a kiss on the cheek before turning to Jesse. "I'll need those files that Dad gave you."

Jesse tossed him a set of keys. "They're on the kitchen table."

Steve nodded and headed out the door, Susan and Jesse looking after him.

"That's the first time he's ever kissed me," Susan said.

"That's good to know," Jesse said, rising painfully to his feet and limping past her. "He's never kissed me."

"Jealous?" she teased.

Jesse grinned. "A man can dream."

Steve picked up Jesse's files on the way back to the beach house and brought them into the kitchen, setting the box on the table. He took a bottle of root beer out of the refrigerator, twisted off the cap, and began looking for Mark's copy of Amanda's report.

He found the report, and a legal pad full of notes, on the nightstand in Mark's bedroom. From what he could gather, Mark had begun sorting the patients based on their cause of death. A lot of the names were circled and connected with arrows to other names. Steve didn't know what the arrows meant.

It would have been helpful, Steve thought, if his father had included a key to the symbols. What does a circled name mean? How is it different from an underlined name? What do the arrows mean? And what about the lists of names without any heading? What are they lists of?

Steve set Mark's report and notes on the table, then went to the garage and brought in the dry-erase board and easel. He liked to see things in black and white, organized and clear. The way Steve solved cases was through dogged investigation, which often meant hours of research, sorting through facts and figures, interviews and autopsy reports, crime scene photos and physical evidence. The cliché goes that the devil is in the details. He often found that murderers were in the details, too.

He referred to his notebook and the To Do list he had begun writing in the hospital waiting room.

Sort patients by age.
Sort patients by sex.
Sort patients by race.
Sort patients by cause of death.
Sort patients by doctors, hospitals, and caregivers
    shared in common.
Sort patients by geographic location.

It looked like his father had already started doing the same thing. But there were other notations, about glass fish and dentures, that made no sense to Steve. Perhaps they would become clear once Steve began his own lists.

With at least forty-eight names to go through, and possibly as many as eight hundred, he was going to need a lot more dry-erase boards. And some extra manpower.

As if on cue, there was a knock at the door. He opened it to find Amanda and Jesse standing outside. She was holding a pizza and carrying a grocery bag full of soda and cookies. Jesse was wearing a Velcro splint on his knee and leaning on a cane, a laptop computer bag over his shoulder.

"The surgery was a success. We've relieved the pressure," Jesse said. "Mark is still unconscious, but he's out of danger. Susan is keeping a close eye on him anyway."

"That's a relief," Steve said. "But you didn't have to come all the way down here to tell me. You need to get some sleep."

Jesse waved off his concern. "I napped while Dr. Kozak examined me and x-rayed my knee."

"Is it broken?"

"Just a bad bruise," Jesse said.

"Don't you have work to do?" Amanda asked Steve impatiently.

"More than I can handle," he replied with a sigh.

"So what are we doing standing out here letting the pizza get cold? Let's get started," Amanda said as she stepped past him and into the house, Jesse hobbling in after her.

Steve closed the door and smiled to himself.

Four hours later, night had fallen, the pizza was finished, Jesse was asleep on the couch, and the dry-erase board was covered with Amanda's neat handwriting. Two laptops were open on the kitchen table, which was strewn with files, papers, and pizza crusts.

Steve and Amanda sat across from each other, inputting data into their laptops and sorting through files. It was tedious work, and the fatigue showed in their sagging posture and weary expressions. As hard as they were working, Steve didn't feel as if they'd accomplished anything. He wasn't alone.

Amanda groaned, leaned back in her chair, and sighed. "Do you have any idea how many different doctors, nurses, and technicians a patient sees? And not all of them are mentioned in patient records. To do this right, we'd have to see who was working on the floor every time the patient went in to see the doctor. But we don't even know which of these patients are victims and which aren't."

Steve got up and stretched. "In other words, we're getting nowhere slowly."

"What we need is more facts, something that will help us narrow our focus, or we'll be doing this for months."

"Maybe Dad will wake up tonight and just tell us who the killer is," Steve said.

"I doubt it."

"He's surprised us before."

"It's possible that Mark found some organizing principle to wrestle all this data down to size, but I doubt he was much further along than we are, or you would have heard about it."

Steve searched through the papers on the table and finally found the yellow legal pad he was looking for. "But what about his notes? The glass fish and the dentures? What was he talking about?"

"I don't know," she said.

"He had something," Steve said.

"How do you know?"

"Jesse told me that he had The Look."

"It doesn't take much to give him The Look," Amanda said. "You and I would have to see the killer over the body or find a written confession to get The Look in our eyes."

Steve's cell phone rang, playing a ring-tone version of the *Dragnet* theme.

"That means it's the office," Steve said, flipping open the phone.

"Cute," Amanda said.

"Sloan here," he answered. It was another detective, informing him that the Camaro had been found. He listened to the details, then thanked the detective for the call and hung up.

Steve smiled at Amanda. "We've had a break. The car was found abandoned in Van Nuys."

"Why's that a break?" Amanda asked. "Odds are that whoever was driving it wiped it down pretty good."

"Even if we don't retrieve any forensic evidence, we can still get a lot from the car. We know it was stolen in Canoga Park yesterday, used in West Los Angeles this morning, and abandoned in Van Nuys. Why steal it in Canoga Park and not, say, Wilmington or Long Beach? Why drop it back in the San Fernando Valley again? Why not in Commerce or Redlands? Or anywhere else?"

"You think the driver lives or works in the Valley."

Steve nodded. "I'm going to make some other guesses, too. The driver was in a hurry to get the hell away from Community General. I'll bet he took the freeway into Van Nuys."

"So?"

"We have traffic cameras," Steve said. "I'll pull the

footage from this morning. Maybe we'll get lucky and see what exit he took."

"What good will that do you? You already have video of the car, and the windows were too tinted to see anything."

"It's not the Camaro I'm interested in," Steve said. "I'm looking for the car that was following him."

"You think he had an accomplice?"

"I don't think he left his own car parked where he dumped the stolen Camaro," Steve said. "He wouldn't take the chance that someone might notice him or the car."

"Was the Camaro dumped near Van Nuys Boulevard or Ventura Boulevard?"

"Yeah, on Kester, a few blocks south of Ventura and a couple blocks west of Van Nuys Boulevard."

"Maybe he parked the car and then walked to a bus stop or called a taxi," Amanda said.

"Too risky. If he's careful, he'll figure we'll check the bus lines and taxi services, which I'm gonna do anyway, of course," Steve said. "Plus there are cameras in most buses and in taxis, and we know this guy isn't eager to have his picture taken."

"So besides looking at traffic footage, what's your next move?"

"I'm going to find all the hospitals in the Canoga Park and Van Nuys area and get personnel lists from them going back a year. We can cross-reference the hospitals and their employees with the patients in your report and see what hits we get."

"Oh, good, more information to crunch."

"We have a name for that in my business," Steve said.

"What's that?" Amanda asked.

"We call it detective work."

CHAPTER TWELVE

The two of them kept working on the files until nearly ten o'clock, when Amanda finally gave up. She had to get home and relieve her babysitter, who had early classes the next morning. Amanda offered to drop Jesse off at his place on her way, but Steve said he'd do it instead. He roused Jesse from his deep slumber, helped him limp half asleep to the car, and drove him to his apartment. Once they got there, Steve practically had to carry Jesse up the stairs to his front door.

Instead of heading straight back to Malibu, Steve decided to stop by the hospital to check on his father and let Susan know that Jesse was finally in bed. He was halfway to Community General when his cell rang. The ring tone was Donna Summer's "Hot Stuff," which meant it was Steve's girlfriend, Lissy, calling.

Steve hesitated for a moment, ashamed of himself. He'd just realized that he hadn't talked to her since he'd hurried out of her apartment that morning. He tried to think of a way to wriggle out of the misery to come, but avoiding her now would only make things worse. He flipped open the phone.

"Hey, Lissy. I was just thinking about you."

"How's Mark?" she asked, her voice flat and unemotional.

"He's got a concussion. He's been unconscious since this morning, but the doctors tell me not to worry, so I'm not."

"I'm glad to hear that," she said. "Finally."

The last word stung like a slap. And he knew it was meant to. He wasn't going to defend himself. He would admit his mistake and hope they could move past it.

"I'm sorry I didn't get a chance to call you. I've been busy chasing the sonofabitch who tried to run my father down."

"I thought we were building a relationship together."

He groaned softly and hoped she couldn't hear it. They'd been dating for months, and the R-word had never come up once. He was a firm believer that the strongest relationships were the unspoken ones. Once you had to talk about a relationship, it was over. If he could put this conversation off, maybe what they had could still be saved.

"Look, Lissy, this really isn't a good time."

"I know. It's a terrible time. That's when you need the people you care about most. But you don't need me. You didn't even think to call."

"I told you, I was tied up. It's got nothing to do with you."

He wished he could take the words back the moment they'd escaped his lips. How many stupid, hurtful things could a man say in one day?

"That's the problem, Steve. You shut me out. You didn't even think of me. You were in my bed, *in my arms*, when the hospital called about Mark. You wouldn't let me go to the hospital with you, and I didn't hear from you all day. It never once occurred to you that I'd be worried about you and your father."

"I was going to call," he said, sounding insincere and whiny even to himself.

"I would have wanted you with me if my father was hurt," she said. "And if you couldn't be there, I would have called you a dozen times."

Steve let out a deep breath. He didn't know what to do

besides plead guilty—not that it would help. He knew what was coming next. It would be the speech about how he always shut her out, he never told her what he was feeling, and he was insensitive to her emotional needs. He'd heard it a hundred times. Not from her, but from every other woman he'd ever dated.

Why were women so damn needy?

"I'm sorry," he said and braced himself for the speech. But much to his surprise, it didn't come.

"Good-bye, Steve," she said and hung up.

Steve almost wished he'd gotten the speech instead. There was a finality to the way she said "Good-bye" that left no doubt in his mind that he'd been dumped.

He pocketed the phone, and as he did so his fingers brushed the edge of Dr. Hudson's business card. It looked like he might be calling her sooner than he had thought.

Steve parked in the spot reserved for police and sheriff's department vehicles in front of the Community General ER entrance and went inside.

It was a slow night in the ER, and the place was unusually quiet. Doctors and nurses were filling out paperwork, and some orderlies were watching an episode of *CSI*. Steve was a familiar face there, so nobody seemed to notice or care as he walked past the admittance desk.

Steve went up to the ICU, where there was a treatment area made up of several beds, separated from one another by curtains on tracks along the ceiling. Mark was in one of those beds, but the curtain was open enough for Steve to see as he approached that his father was still unconscious and that Susan was changing the bandage around the tube draining the fluid from Mark's brain.

The thought of the hole in Mark's skull made Steve shiver, not with revulsion but with fear. It was the first time Steve had ever seen his father appear so weak and fragile, and it frightened him. For a moment, Steve felt as if he was a child again.

"How's he doing?" Steve whispered to Susan as he stepped up beside her.

"He's stable and doing fine. You don't need to whisper. He's not asleep. Besides, we want him to wake up, remember?"

Steve nodded. "Jesse is home in bed, finally getting some sleep. Is it okay if I sit here for a while?"

"You can stay as long as you like," she said. "Would you like me to bring you some coffee or something?"

"No, thanks," Steve said.

"Buzz me if you need anything." She motioned to the buzzer on the bed and left, dragging the curtain shut behind her.

Steve took a seat beside his father's bed. The chair was uncomfortable and the light was too harsh. The air smelled of rubbing alcohol. He wanted to be anywhere but here.

He looked at all the tubes going in and out of Mark's body and watched the saline drip into the IV line.

He listened to the steady beep of the heart monitor and the hum of the other machinery.

He heard a woman sobbing on the other side of the curtain and a man telling her it was going to be all right. Steve wondered which one of them was the patient and who needed the comfort more.

He wished his father could tell him that everything was going to be all right. Because Steve wouldn't believe it if he heard it from anyone else.

Steve was back at his desk in the West Los Angeles station at 8:00 A.M. sharp. He'd found four hospitals near Canoga Park and Van Nuys—John Muir Hospital, Reseda Medical Center, Woodland Hospital, and West Valley Presbyterian—and a dozen retirement homes. There were probably hundreds of individual medical practices and clinics in the area, too, but contacting them all wasn't practical—at least not yet.

He started calling the hospitals and rest homes, requesting lists of all their employees going back two years. By ten thirty he'd finished with the hospitals and was working his way through his list of retirement homes when Lieutenant Tanis Archer showed up and dropped a DVD on his cluttered desk.

The DVD was labeled "405/134 Traffic Cam Footage" with the previous day's date written below. The "405" was the San Diego Freeway; the "134" was the Ventura Freeway.

Steve hurriedly finished his call and regarded Tanis. "Are you working in parking and traffic enforcement now?"

It wouldn't have surprised him if she was.

She'd worked her way up the department ladder by getting the job done, whatever the cost. She fell down the ladder the same way. Her fatal mistake was apprehending the woman-beating son of a prominent politician and, when he resisted arrest, giving him a taste of what it was like for his victims. When Tanis was told not to press the case, she refused. Firing her would only have made the scandal worse, so she was transferred from one miserable job to another, the powers-that-be hoping she'd finally quit.

They should have known better. "Quit" was a word that wasn't in Tanis Archer's vocabulary.

The last Steve had heard, Tanis was in the basement at Parker Center working cold cases. There, with his father, she'd helped solve the Silent Partner killings. Even so, that wasn't enough to redeem her in the corridors of power.

"I'm on the Anti-Terrorism Strike Force," she said. "I'm the liaison with other law enforcement agencies."

"Sounds exciting," Steve said.

"It's so thrilling that I'd consider a transfer to traffic a step up."

"Oh," Steve said.

"I'm sitting at a desk, Steve. I relay requests from one agency to another. I made an Eiffel Tower out of paper clips the other day."

"So how did you come by this?" Steve asked, picking up the DVD.

"You'd be surprised how many cameras there are in LA now. It's recordings from cameras like the ones on the 405 that made it possible for Scotland Yard to nail the subway bombers within days of the attacks. Among my exciting duties is logging the recordings, which are stored digitally for six months. I snagged your request and expanded on it a bit."

She reached into her leather jacket and tossed him another DVD. "This is footage from our Ventura Boulevard and Van Nuys Boulevard cameras."

He nodded, impressed. "So you're Big Brother."

"In the flesh," she said.

"I always imagined Big Brother being a lot less attractive."

She stared at him, unblinking, her eyes cold and merciless.

"What?" he said.

"Did you just get dumped?"

Now it was his turn to stare at her. "Why do you say that?"

"Because that's the only time you think that flirting with me is worth risking a broken jaw."

"I seem to recall that we dated once."

"I thought we both agreed to forget that ever happened," she said.

"We were perfect for each other. You never accused me of being insensitive to your needs or got upset that I wasn't sharing my feelings."

"I can take care of my own needs," she said. "And why the hell would I want to know your feelings?"

Truer words were never spoken, Steve thought. Not once when they were dating did she ever use the R-word. He was insane not to have stayed with her. So why hadn't he? He couldn't remember.

"Why did we ever break up?"

"We didn't."

"Of course we did," he said.

"We were never together. We did what we did and life went on. Neither one of us was needy enough to need each other."

"Which is why we are both alone."

"Speak for yourself," she said. "I've got somebody."

"You do?"

"Don't sound so damn surprised, like it's some kind of miracle."

"Who is he?"

"His name is Buck," she said. "He's a bounty hunter."

"What's he got that I don't?"

"A twelve-gauge shotgun he calls Betsy, for starters, and a red Mercury Montego."

"These are pluses?"

"He doesn't play by the rules. You're a Boy Scout and a daddy's boy."

"No, I'm not."

"You still live at home," Tanis said.

"I live on the beach in Malibu. Tell me you wouldn't want to live there."

"Not if my dad was in the same house."

"What about your mom?" Steve asked.

"I've never met her."

"*What?*" Steve said.

"It wasn't easy getting that DVD for you," she said irritably. "Are you going to look at it or not?"

"Sure." He was afraid that if he pressed her any more, she might shoot him.

He got up and went to the conference room to use the TV/VCR/DVD combo the homicide officers shared. The detectives had pooled their money and bought the unit at Costco rather than wait for the department to get them one.

Tanis closed the door and Steve slipped the DVD into the machine. Keeping an eye on the time code, he skipped ahead to the hour of the attack.

Impatient, she snatched the remote from him and sped up the scan. "Here's where your Camaro shows up."

She paused the playback on the image of the Camaro coming up the Wilshire ramp onto the northbound San Diego Freeway, five minutes after the attempt on Mark's life in the Community General parking structure.

Steve took out his notebook. "Okay, step it forward. I want to see the next three or four cars that follow him."

"It's the blue Honda Accord," she said, hitting PLAY. "It stays three cars behind him, matching his lane changes, all the way into the Valley."

"You really are desperate for some honest-to-God police work, aren't you?"

"It's that or play with paper clips. Besides, I like Mark, and I resent it when people try to run over my friends. The Camaro transitions to the eastbound Ventura Freeway and gets off at the Van Nuys exit. So does the Honda. In fact, she follows him up Van Nuys Boulevard and then they make a left on Addison, presumably headed to Kester, where the car was dumped."

Steve gave Tanis a look. "She?"

"Her windows weren't tinted." Tanis handed him back the remote and reached into her leather jacket again, pulling out a manila envelope that was folded down the middle to fit in her pocket. She gave the envelope to him. "I made a still and blew it up."

Steve opened the envelope and looked at the picture. It was blurry and had a crease down the middle, but he could see she was a white woman in her twenties, with short blond hair, smoking a cigarette.

"I suppose you ran her plates," Steve said.

Tanis reached into her back pocket for her notebook, flipped it open, and read aloud: "Her name is Wendy Duren, age twenty-seven, lives in Encino. No arrests, no outstanding warrants, no prints in the system."

"I'm surprised you didn't arrest her."

"Can I?" Tanis asked.

"There's no evidence that she's committed any crime," Steve said.

"That hasn't stopped me before."

"I know. That's why you're liaising instead of detecting."

"I detect," she said. "Look at all I just detected for you."

"Now that you mention it, how do the folks in Anti-Terrorism feel about you doing all this work for me?" Steve asked.

"I push paper. They don't know, or care, what paper I'm pushing."

"Good, because I'm pressed for manpower," Steve said. "Do you think you could use that computer of yours to crunch some data for me?"

"That lady in the Honda looks like a terrorist to me. What do you think?"

"Definitely Al Qaeda," Steve agreed.

Chapter Thirteen

After Tanis left, Steve called the hospital to check on his father. Jesse told him that although Mark was still unconscious, he was stable. There appeared to be no further swelling or subdural bleeding.

"So when is he going to wake up?" Steve asked.

"It could be in the next five minutes or five days from now. I can't say."

"And when he does wake up, I assume he's going to have some headaches, dizziness, disorientation, that kind of thing."

"Of course," Jesse said.

"Will there be any lasting injury?"

"He might not remember the accident or even what he was doing that morning," Jesse said. "Some degree of amnesia is common in head traumas like this."

"How bad can it be?"

"Why do you always want to know the worst-case scenario?"

"I like to be prepared."

"The amnesia may go back a few minutes or all the way to day one. He could wake up and have no idea who he is or who you are. Whatever memories he's lost could eventually come back or not at all."

"Wonderful," Steve said.

"You asked," Jesse said. "Is there anything I can do to help with the investigation?"

"Thanks, but you did plenty last night."

"I ate three slices of pizza and fell asleep," Jesse said.

"That was good work. Some of your best."

"C'mon, I really want to do something."

Steve was concerned about getting Jesse into trouble. If any hospital officials ever discovered that he'd been foraging through confidential patient records, his career could be ruined. But Steve needed more information and he knew Jesse could get it for him.

"You could get fired if you're caught," Steve said.

"And the secretary will disavow any knowledge of my actions."

"What secretary?" Steve asked.

"Didn't you ever watch *Mission: Impossible* when you were a kid?" Jesse said. "Look, whatever it is you want me to do, it's worth the risk if it means catching some doctor who is killing people entrusted to his care."

"You think that argument will save your ass if you get caught?"

"Hell no," Jesse said. "So it's a good thing I'm also in the restaurant business."

That was exactly what Steve told himself every time he bent the rules or made one of his typical political blunders. He might lose his badge and his gun, but at least there was an apron with his name on it waiting for him at Barbeque Bob's.

"Can you get into the computerized patient records at John Muir, Reseda Medical Center, Woodland Hospital, and West Valley Presbyterian?"

"Can Ashlee Simpson sing?" Jesse asked.

"Nope."

"Yes, I can get into their databases," Jesse said. "What do you need?"

"See if any of the seven hundred eighty names on our list

of people who nearly died within a year of their eventual deaths were ever patients at one of those hospitals."

"I bet you can't say that three times fast."

Jesse hung up and Steve went back to calling retirement homes in the Valley and requesting their personnel records. In the meantime, the information he'd requested in his calls earlier that morning started to come in, most of it via e-mail. That meant he had more names to cross-check against the nearly eight hundred patients they were already sorting through. He was drowning in names and starving for clues.

Starving.

Steve suddenly realized how hungry he was. It was a few minutes after one, and he hadn't eaten since seven that morning. So he got up and grabbed a vending-machine lunch, consciously selecting healthy entrées from the major food groups—vegetable, dairy, and meat. He took his potato chips, cheese doodles, and pork rinds back to his desk so he could eat while he worked.

He called Amanda and told her he would e-mail her the names of hospital and retirement home employees as they came in.

"You want me to cross-check these names with the medical records of the dead people on our list," Amanda surmised.

"At least that should narrow things down a little," Steve said.

"Not enough," she said.

"I'm working on that," he said, telling her about Wendy Duren, the woman the traffic cameras captured following the Camaro. "We're running a complete background check on her."

"So you think she'll lead us to whoever stole that car and tried to run over Mark."

Amanda's comment gave Steve an idea. "Maybe I'm going at this backwards."

"Excuse me?"

"I'm just thinking out loud," Steve said. "Give me a call when you've got something."

"Considering how much work is involved, I wouldn't wait by the phone if I were you," she said. "You could end up missing a few holidays."

Steve thanked her for her efforts, then turned to his computer and copied Tanis Archer on all the personnel information he'd e-mailed to Amanda. He finished off the crumbs of his cheese doodles and headed out to see Tanis.

He found her downtown in the sub-basement of Parker Center in a windowless concrete room with exposed pipes running along the ceiling. There was an old trash chute in the corner, and a wheeled linen hamper sat below the mouth to catch whatever papers and files dropped down from the floors above.

Tanis, dressed in a tank top and cargo pants, was sitting at her dented and scratched gunmetal gray desk. She had a surprisingly sleek and expensive computer setup on the desktop, surrounded by teetering stacks of bulging files. Wires connecting the computer to the network were strapped together with plastic clasps and dangled from the clutter of pipes on the ceiling. A large paper shredder and a bulging collection bag containing the classified confetti sat beside her desk.

The air smelled like an old library that was being used as a gymnasium locker room.

"Somehow I imagined the headquarters of the LAPD Anti-Terrorism Strike Force would be a little bit more impressive," Steve said as he came in. "I figured it would be a slick, high-tech war room with flat-screen monitors everywhere streaming data and images from around the world. I thought it would be filled with people racing the clock to prevent disasters."

"I'm sure it is all those things and in a bat cave too. I've never been there. This is the liaison's office. Very low tech. Requests come in"—she tipped her head towards the trash chute—"I route them through the proper channels and shred the correspondence."

"Someone upstairs doesn't want to leave a paper trail," he said.

"Somebody upstairs doesn't want to be hauled in front of a Senate subcommittee someday."

"So, where's the Eiffel Tower?" Steve asked.

"Is that what you came all the way down here to see?"

"I don't get to Paris much," Steve said with a shrug.

Tanis opened her lower desk drawer and lifted out a pile of interconnected paper clips shaped in a lopsided triangle that came to a sharp point.

He supposed it could be the Eiffel Tower. It could also be one of the great pyramids of Egypt or a Hershey's Kiss.

"It's nice. Very French," he said. "Why do you keep it in a drawer?"

"So I won't be tempted to throw myself on it in a fit of suicidal boredom." Tanis put her Eiffel Tower away, kicked the drawer closed, and snatched a paper out of the laser printer. "I ran that background check for you on Wendy Duren."

"Is she a member of Al Qaeda or Hamas?"

"Appleby Nursing Services," Tanis said.

Steve felt an immediate charge, so sharp he could almost hear the snap and crackle. It was the first solid lead, the kind that can break a case wide open.

Tanis regarded the expression on Steve's face. "Yeah, I thought you'd like that. Appleby is a hiring agency that provides in-home nurses, caregivers, physical therapists, and household assistants for medical care, errands, whatever. They work part-time or full-time, live-in and live-out, or even just by the hour."

"Can you find out if any of the patients Duren saw are on our list?"

"I'm already working with Amanda on that," Tanis said.

"We also need to find out who else works at Appleby

Nursing Services and if they had any contact with those same patients."

"Way ahead of you," she said, stroking the computer monitor as if it were an obedient pet. "I've already starting inputting the names."

"I know I've asked you to do a lot already, but I have another favor to ask."

"Don't worry about it. You're doing me a favor," Tanis said. "It's either help you or feed myself to the shredder."

"You may be feeding your career to it by helping me," he said.

"Don't flatter yourself," she said. "I'm perfectly capable of destroying my life on my own. I've been working diligently at it for a while now."

"I think there's another way to ID the driver of that Camaro. It's not easy to steal a car without some previous experience at it. Can you see if any of the hospital, retirement home, or nursing service employees have any grand theft auto convictions in their past?"

"That's no biggie," she said. "You can do that from your desk."

"Yes, but I can't get into sealed juvenile records," Steve said. "Can you?"

She smiled. "Anti-Terrorism is an all-purpose pass to violate privacy and civil rights. It's patriotic, even. Why do you think we call it the Patriot Act?"

"Is that a yes?"

"Give me a few hours."

Steve glanced at his watch. "Meet me at the beach house at seven thirty. I'll order some Chinese food and you, me, Amanda, and Jesse can compare notes."

"Where are you off to?"

"My father is getting out of the hospital soon," Steve said. "And he's going to need a nurse to take care of him."

*   *   *

The logo for Appleby Nursing Services was an apple shaped like a heart. Steve wasn't a graphic arts designer or an expert in advertising, but he thought it was a mistake that the apple had a bite taken out of it.

The apple theme was carried over into their Santa Monica offices, where a big bowl of Washington Red Delicious apples was the centerpiece of the table in the waiting room. The place was decorated with paintings of apples, photos of apples, ceramic apples, crystal apples, apple-shaped pillows, and empty vintage bottles of apple cider.

An apple-shaped man with red cheeks came out to greet Steve. He had a handlebar mustache, a gray pin-striped suit, and a black bow tie.

"Mr. Sloan, I'm Sheldon Mitford, manager of personnel services. How may I help you today?"

"I'm interested in hiring a nurse to care for my father," Steve said. "He'll be released from the hospital soon, and a friend recommended you to me."

Mitford beamed. "We pride ourselves on client satisfaction. The majority of our business is based on referrals. Would you like an apple?"

Steve wondered if he'd ever be able to look at an apple again, much less eat one. "No, thank you."

Mitford led Steve into his corner office, which, to Steve's relief, appeared to be an apple-free zone.

Steve took a seat in a guest chair across the desk from Mitford, who sat in a large leather chair and launched into a lengthy explanation of Appleby's services.

Nurses, certified nursing assistants, and caregivers who are looking for work register with Appleby, which checks their references and interviews them, he told Steve. When clients come looking for help caring for their sick, elderly, or handicapped loved ones, Appleby tries to match them with the best possible nurse or caregiver.

"It's almost like matchmaking," Mitford said. "We do personality profiles of our staff and our patients. We then assign our staff to compatible individuals. For instance, if the patient is a writer, we might pair him with a nurse who is an avid reader."

Appleby provided live-in caregivers as well as people who would visit from time to time to make sure the client was comfortable, taking his medications, and had everything he needed.

"I've heard great things about one of your nurses," Steve said. "Her name is Wendy Duren. What can you tell me about her?"

"She's a firecracker," Mitford said. "She's one of our most energetic and enthusiastic nurses. But I'm afraid she isn't available for long-term care."

"Why not?"

"Nurse Duren prefers to be a utility player. When other nurses are sick, or go on vacation, or simply need an extra hand for a day or two with a difficult situation, she's the one we send. She's up for anything and always with a smile."

That could make it harder to connect her with individual patients, Steve thought.

"Maybe I could convince her to settle down with one patient," Steve said. "My father is a very avuncular fellow."

"You could certainly try, though you'd make a lot of nurses very upset. They just love Wendy to death, and so do the patients."

"I'm sure that's true," Steve said. "May I review her history and references?"

"Of course." Mitford turned to his computer and tapped a few keys. His printer started spitting out pages.

Mitford explained how the nurses were paid and other details that Steve didn't really care about but listened to anyway. Steve assured Mitford that he would call with any questions. The meeting ended with a hearty handshake from Mitford, who wouldn't let him leave without a bag of apples.

Steve went back to his car and reviewed Duren's résumé. The first thing he noticed was that she'd moved from hospital to hospital, never staying anywhere for more than two years, which gave him a chill. That innocuous fact matched one of Dr. Hudson's early-warning signals for medical murderers.

Either Duren was a restless spirit, or didn't get along well with others, or was running from something. He was going to find out the answer.

CHAPTER FOURTEEN

Hospitals make a lot of people uncomfortable, but not Steve Sloan. He'd spent time visiting his father at Community General for most of his life. The hospital was almost like a second home.

Although he'd never been to Beckman Hospital in Torrance, Steve felt completely at ease there. More so, it seemed, than Conrad Napp, the vice president of operations.

Napp was a bone-thin man in his fifties who, in his youth, had probably been called lanky. He broke into a flop sweat the instant Steve flashed his badge, identified himself, and said he wanted to talk about Wendy Duren.

"Have you killed anybody, Mr. Napp?" Steve asked. "Maybe your wife or a lover? Or perhaps you ran over someone on your way to work this morning?"

"No, of course not," Napp said, practically collapsing into a seat opposite Steve, who sat on a couch in the administrator's austere office and held his bag of apples in his lap.

The office was so clean, Steve wondered if they performed surgeries on the man's desk when they ran out of operating rooms.

"Why do you ask?" Napp sputtered.

"Because you almost had a heart attack when you saw my badge," Steve said. "I'm still wondering if I should call the cardiac unit."

"I was startled, that's all," Napp said.

"It looked more like terror to me." Steve set the bag of apples on the table between them. "Relax, have an apple. I'm not here to arrest you or tell you that a loved one has died."

Napp removed an apple from the bag and took a bite. It actually seemed to calm him down.

"To be honest, Detective, I've been dreading this day for years. I always knew it would come to this."

"What do you mean?"

"Wendy Duren killed a patient, didn't she?"

Steve gave him a hard look. "Why do you say that?"

Napp bit into his apple with a loud crunch. He chewed for a moment before speaking.

"During the fifteen months she was with us, working in our critical-care ward, there was an unusually high number of deaths," Napp said. "We suspected something was very, very wrong."

"Did you report it to the police?"

"Report what, Detective? These people were critically ill to begin with, so their deaths were not entirely unexpected. Not only that, but several years ago we fired a nurse we thought might be negligent in her care. She sued us for dismissing her without sufficient evidence, and she won a seven-figure settlement. We couldn't afford another costly and embarrassing situation like that."

"But you could afford to let people die."

Napp took another bite of his apple. Steve was beginning to regret giving it to him. In fact, he was tempted to shove the apple down the man's throat.

"We didn't know anything was truly wrong until after Nurse Duren left. The family of one of the deceased patients had an autopsy conducted, and it found lethal levels of digoxin in the dead man's body. We immediately launched an exhaustive internal investigation. The report determined that her presence at the time of all the patient deaths could be coincidental."

If Steve mentally ticked off each item on Dr. Hudson's list of behavioral warning signs of a medical murderer, Wendy Duren matched just about all of them. But what was her motive? Attention? Excitement? Self-loathing? Sexual satisfaction? Playing God? Or was it the pure, unadulterated pleasure of killing?

"On the other hand," Napp continued, "the report determined that negligence or intentional acts of wrongdoing couldn't be ruled out."

"I'm sure that will be a great comfort to the families of all the people she's killed since."

"How do you think I feel? But the fact is, we couldn't prove a thing. There was no definitive evidence of her culpability. It could have been her or any of the other nurses in the ward who were responsible, if, indeed, negligence was involved. We ended up reassigning the entire critical-care staff to other duties in other units. Most of them resented it and ended up leaving the hospital and seeking employment elsewhere."

"Did you warn those other employers?"

"In the absence of any proof, our lawyers advised us not to. They said Duren would sue us and would most certainly prevail, winning damages that would make the other settlement seem like a bargain. We gave them all positive references."

"In other words, you knew she was a killer and you did nothing."

Napp got up, dropped the apple core into his garbage can, and wiped the sweat from his face with some Kleenex.

"My hands were tied."

Steve tried to control his rising anger. "I'm going to need the names of the other nurses on the ward during the period she was working here."

"We'll cooperate any way we can," Napp said. "After consulting with our lawyers, of course."

"Of course."

Steve would have liked to have the names of the lawyers who advised Napp to cover up the patient deaths. He would have liked to arrest them all, and Napp too.

But on what charge?

As infuriating and inhumane as their conduct was, Steve knew that legally the lawyers hadn't done anything wrong. From a financial standpoint, they were probably right. Their conduct was morally reprehensible, but most lawyers, bureaucrats, and corporations could live with that.

"Do you know how she committed the murders?" Steve asked.

"We have a theory," Napp said, "but we couldn't prove it."

"So you keep saying." And if you say it again, Steve thought, I'll shoot you where you stand.

"We think she was getting the drugs by manipulating our computerized disbursement system. She would order drugs for a patient, and then, after receiving the drugs from a motorized dispensing cart, she'd go back into the computer and erase the initial request."

"Then how were you able to figure it out?"

"We noticed a discrepancy between the amount of some drugs stocked in the machine, like procainamide and sodium nitroprusside, and the amount of drugs dispensed to patients. Those drugs, improperly administered, would account for the sudden deaths of some of the patients."

"But to prove it you'd have to notify the families and exhume the bodies for autopsy. You haven't done that."

Napp shook his head. "At that point we didn't see what good it would do to put those families through the pain."

"It would have saved lives."

"No one can be sure of that," Napp said.

"I can," Steve said.

The case was solved.

Steve didn't know who all the suspects were, and he

couldn't name a single victim, but that didn't change what he knew in his heart to be true.

The case was solved.

Everything he needed to know was within the information they'd already amassed. All they had to do was sort it out.

It wasn't as insurmountable a problem as it had seemed only twenty-four hours ago. He believed they'd found at least one element around which everything else revolved.

Wendy Duren.

They would start with her and work outward from there. She was the center of the universe in this investigation. And that was what Steve told Amanda, Jesse, and Tanis when they gathered at the beach house that night and began devouring the Chinese food as if they hadn't eaten in weeks. They'd all been so intent on their work that none of them had eaten much during the day, and what they did consume hardly qualified as nourishment.

After dinner, Amanda, Jesse, and Tanis each moved to one of the four dry-erase boards that Steve had propped up on chairs around the living room and began writing up what had been uncovered.

Jesse listed all the dead patients who had been treated at one of the four Valley hospitals within a year of their deaths.

Amanda prepared a list of the doctors, nurses, and technicians the dead patients had in common.

And Tanis made a list of nurses and caregivers who had worked in Beckman Hospital's critical-care unit during the period when the suspicious deaths occurred. She also listed all the personnel employed in the last twelve months through Appleby Nursing Services.

While they worked, Steve stayed out of their way, clearing the dishes and bringing out fresh coffee, cookies, and a bowl of M&M's. When they were done, they joined him at the kitchen table, and everyone regarded the boards in silence.

Some connections were immediately obvious to Steve, but he waited before voicing his thoughts. There was one more fact he wanted to hear first. He turned to Tanis.

"Do any of the nurses or caregivers have a history of car theft?"

"Nope," she said.

"Not even as juveniles?"

"Nope."

"Damn," Steve said.

"But one of them had a brother who did time for stealing cars, stripping them into a pile of parts and shipping them to Mexico."

"Why didn't you say so to start with?"

"A girl has to have some fun," Tanis said with a grin. "And it gets even better."

She walked up to the list of nurses who worked at Beckman Hospital and circled one of the names.

Paul Guyot.

"Gives you shivers, doesn't it?" Tanis stepped back and took a handful of M&M's.

"So who was killing patients?" Jesse asked. "Was it Guyot or Duren?"

"Or was it both of them?" Steve said. "And what the hell are they up to now?"

He picked up a red dry-erase marker and started circling all the places where Paul Guyot's name came up on the other boards.

Jesse followed Steve's lead, grabbed a blue marker, and began boxing all the places where Wendy Duren's name appeared.

Amanda sat down at a laptop and began noting all the interconnections that were appearing on the boards.

When Steve and Jesse were done, the boards were a multicolored mess of lines, circles, and boxes that wouldn't have made sense to anyone else.

Amanda printed out a page, went up to the one empty

dry-erase board, and drew a line down the center. She began copying information from the sheet of paper to the board, writing the information in either column, one of which was headed PAUL GUYOT, the other, WENDY DUREN.

When Amanda was done, she joined the others, who were standing at the kitchen table and staring at the boards in amazement and horror, as if they were studying four particularly disturbing paintings.

They were looking at four abstract portraits of murder.

The two columns that Amanda wrote read:

Paul Guyot
Gary Betz
Andrew Kosterman
Emilia Ortega
Oliver Pritchard
Melinda Soper

Wendy Duren
Hammett Aidman
John Eames
Dave Grayson
Dorothy Myack
Patricia Ohanian

"These are the patients they cared for who died in the last twelve months," Amanda said.

"My God," Jesse said.

As Steve's gaze shifted between the two columns and the connections made on the other three boards, a clear picture began to emerge.

"Okay, here's what we know," Steve said. "Wendy Duren and Paul Guyot worked together in the critical-care unit at Beckman Hospital in Torrance. During their time there, a number of sudden deaths occurred that officials now believe were murders."

"Duren and Guyot left Beckman," Tanis said, picking up the story. "She joined Appleby Nursing Services, and he went to work in the ICU at John Muir Hospital in West Hills. The fun begins again."

"And the number of deaths of recently hospitalized people with critical health issues reaches epidemic proportions," Amanda said. "Then they find out that Mark is onto them."

"How?" Jesse asked.

"Guyot works at John Muir," Steve said. "Dad was over there talking with Dr. Barnes and Dr. Dalton. Maybe Guyot saw Dad and got scared."

"Mark's face has been in the papers and on the air a lot lately," Tanis said. "Between the Lacey McClure case and the Nick Stryker scandal, he's had more exposure than Pamela Anderson's breasts."

Steve gave her a look. "I'm sure he'd love the comparison."

"I'm just saying he's known in LA for his work with the LAPD," Tanis said. "Guyot must have wet himself when he saw Mark Sloan way out there in the armpit of the San Fernando Valley. Mark certainly wasn't there to see the sights."

"So Guyot went looking in the neighborhood for an old, fast car with tinted windows and found one parked on a street in nearby Canoga Park," Steve said. "He stole it and tried to run over Dad with it the next morning."

"But Mark *wasn't* onto him," Amanda said. "Take a look at the two lists. Only one of the patient deaths he was investigating is among their victims."

"Guyot tried to kill him for nothing," Tanis said.

But Steve wasn't paying attention anymore. Something else on the board had captured his attention.

"All Guyot succeeded in doing was drawing attention to himself when nobody had even noticed him before," Jesse said. "Kind of ironic, isn't it?"

"This can't be a coincidence," Steve said, still staring at the two columns of names.

"It's not," Amanda said. "Mark's instincts were right. He just wasn't onto Guyot and Duren yet."

"I'm not talking about that," Steve said. "Look at the names in those two columns. Those two nurses have each killed five people."

"Maybe they have a list and split it in half," Jesse said.

"Or they are taking turns killing," Amanda said.

"If you're right," Tanis said grimly, "it's time for one of them to kill again."

"Not if we arrest them first," Steve said.

CHAPTER FIFTEEN

It was like preparing for a final exam. After Amanda, Jesse, and Tanis left, Steve spent the next several hours transcribing everything from the boards onto his laptop as a way of memorizing the information. Then he printed out his notes, highlighted the key points, and thought about the best way to present the case to the district attorney.

The next morning, he went for a jog on the foggy beach, going over all the facts again in his mind, making sure the connections were tight and that his conclusions were solid. He called the hospital to check on his dad as soon as he got back. Susan assured him that his father was doing fine and that there was no reason to be worried. As if it was completely normal for someone to be unconscious for three days and then have a hole drilled in his skull.

But Steve could not afford to be distracted by his concern for his father right now. He had to focus on making his case.

He had a quick breakfast of Cocoa Pebbles and coffee, showered, and made the long drive downtown in rush-hour traffic, listening to news radio on the way.

He met with assistant district attorney Karen Cross in her office. She was white but had the distinctive eyes and delicate features of a Japanese woman. She compensated for that delicacy with a penetrating gaze and an aggressive attitude that made her both alluring and a little frightening, especially for anyone on the witness stand.

Steve had good reason to be uncomfortable around her. Their last experience together had been a complex, high-profile celebrity murder investigation and trial that nearly cost both of them their careers. During the course of the trial, the police department and the prosecutors were humiliated on national television for weaknesses in their case. Although the authorities were ultimately proved correct and the killer was convicted, the public had a selective memory. The cloud of disgrace remained over the department and the DA's office despite their eventual vindication.

He would have preferred to work with any other assistant district attorney in the building, but fate, and perhaps a vindictive district attorney, wasn't on Steve's side that morning. Karen was assigned to hear his case, whatever it happened to be.

She didn't seem any more pleased to see him than he was to see her. She looked at him as if he were a sewage leak that was spilling into her office.

Her office had two guest chairs, both occupied by stacks of bulging files. Steve knew better than to move them and disrupt her filing system. So he stood awkwardly at the door, his notes in hand, while she irritably cleared a place for him to sit.

While she moved her files around, he began laying out his case. It wasn't the optimal way for him to present his facts, but at least they could avoid looking at each other while he did it.

He told her about Mark's initial investigation into the deaths of people who had recently recovered from critical illnesses or injuries and his father's discovery that the number of such cases had reached epidemic proportions.

By the time Steve got to the attempt on Mark's life, and the investigation that followed, Karen had freed up one of the guest chairs, returned to her seat behind her desk, and was taking notes on a yellow legal pad.

Steve figured her note taking was a good sign. It showed she was already investing herself in the case. She also hadn't bothered to interrupt him with questions yet, which he took to mean that so far his case was solid.

So he continued on, explaining in detail how the investigation had led to nurse Wendy Duren, to the suspicious deaths at Beckman Hospital, and finally to Paul Guyot, a nurse now working at John Muir. And just to show he'd done his research, Steve even threw in how Wendy Duren's actions matched Dr. Hudson's sociological profile of a medical murderer in virtually every way. All of which led up to his big finish, the one and only conclusion that could be drawn from the facts.

"These two are serial killers responsible for at least ten deaths, and probably more," Steve said. "Give me the word, and I'll have them arrested and behind bars within the hour."

"You have got to be kidding," she said.

He wasn't quite sure how to interpret the comment. Was she talking about the heinous acts these two nurses had committed, undetected, for so long? Or was she talking about his case?

"I'm afraid I don't follow," Steve ventured.

"There is no way in hell you're arresting these two," she said. "I don't even want you talking to them."

"You have got to be kidding," he said.

Now it was her turn to try and figure out what he meant.

"What part don't you get?" she asked.

"These two are killers. They've been killing for at least a year and will probably continue unless we stop them. What possible reason could you have for letting them stay free?"

She met his gaze. "Because you don't have a shred of proof that they've committed any crimes at all, much less multiple murders."

"I just gave it to you," Steve said. "The only way it could

be any clearer is if the two of them walked in here and confessed."

"You have a theory, based on guesses, assumptions, and a creative reading of statistics, none of which would stand up to the slightest scrutiny in court," Karen said. "You don't have one piece of physical evidence."

"I will once we exhume the bodies of the ten people they've killed this year and the patients who died in the Beckman Hospital critical-care unit. I guarantee the medical examiner will find traces of the drugs used to kill them."

Karen laughed. "How do you expect me to convince a judge to issue all those exhumation orders?"

"You tell him what I just told you," Steve said evenly, trying hard not to lose his temper. "You walk him through the investigation step by step."

"I'll tell you what. Let's do that right now." Karen referred to her notes. "Let's start with Grover Dawson, the patient that got your father interested in these deaths in the first place. Mr. Dawson's name isn't on your list of alleged victims. Why is that?"

"Because Grover Dawson doesn't appear to be a murder victim at this time."

"'At this time'?" she said. "Do you have evidence to indicate it wasn't an accident?"

"No."

"Okay, so Dr. Sloan began his investigation based on an accidental death that, lo and behold, was an accident," she said. "The investigation was off to a great start already."

"Even if Dawson's death was an accident, that has nothing to do with the information we subsequently uncovered," Steve said. "The fact is, Dad's instincts were right. A respected epidemiologist analyzed the annual data and determined that the odds were one in a trillion that the staggering increase in these kinds of deaths was due to natural causes."

"That's the epidemiologist's interpretation after a cursory examination of the data," she said. "I'm sure I could get a dozen other experts, medical and otherwise, who could give me a dozen other explanations."

"It's your job to prosecute the murderers, not defend them and refute the evidence."

"My job is to make sure there actually *is* evidence, Detective. I need to be especially vigilant about that in cases where you and your father are concerned. I've been burned before."

"We were right before, and you got the conviction."

"After I was publicly humiliated and nearly lost my career in disgrace along the way," she said. "That's not how I prefer to do my job. You and your father have a habit of building cases out of circumstantial evidence that's shaky at best and information acquired through creative means. Which brings me to my next question: Where did you and Dr. Sloan get the confidential patient records? I don't recall you mentioning anything about obtaining a warrant to search through hospital files. You sure as hell didn't come to me."

Karen made a show of going through her notes, looking for the information she knew wasn't there, then looked at him judgmentally.

Steve shifted uncomfortably in his seat. "They came from a confidential source."

"Who broke the law and violated the privacy of the patients involved. Therefore, any information derived from those stolen records is inadmissible in court. In fact, you and your father could both end up facing criminal charges for theft, invasion of privacy, computer fraud, aiding and abetting—and that's just for starters."

"Fine. Forget those records. We can get the same information through other channels. Or we can obtain the necessary warrants now to look into the hospital files and get what we need," Steve said, ignoring her blustering about his own possible criminal culpability. She wouldn't dare prosecute him and risk embarrassing the LAPD. "But the facts aren't going to change. The patients are dead. Guyot and Duren were their nurses and their killers."

"Let's talk for a minute about Ms. Duren, shall we? You focused on her because you picked her car at random from footage taken by a traffic camera on the San Diego Freeway."

"She was following the Camaro that nearly ran over my father."

"There were thousands of cars on the freeway at the time. How could you possibly know whether or not she was following him? Maybe she was just going to work."

"He got on the freeway at Wilshire Boulevard and so did she—"

"So do hundreds of vehicles every hour," she interrupted.

"She stayed three car lengths behind him, matched his lane changes all the way into the Valley," Steve continued. "He merged onto the eastbound Ventura Freeway and so did she, three cars behind him. He got off at the Van Nuys exit and headed north, and so did she."

"I'm sure there are lots of people who got on the San Diego Freeway at Wilshire Boulevard, transitioned to the eastbound Ventura Freeway, and got off at the Van Nuys exit. Did you check?"

"No."

"So it could be a coincidence that a nurse who is connected in some way with some of the thousands of natural deaths that occur in Los Angeles each year happened to be driving behind the car that allegedly was involved in the attempt on your father's life."

"She is hardly some innocent stranger. My father was investigating suspicious patient deaths. She is a nurse suspected of killing patients at Beckman Hospital," Steve said, raising his voice, his frustration getting the better of him.

"Even the investigators at the hospital concede they have no proof that she is culpable in any patient's death."

As Steve got more agitated, her voice got lower, more patronizing.

"Because they were unwilling, like you, to exhume the bodies and get that proof," he said. "Thanks to their cowardice and inaction, ten more people are dead."

"Spare me the melodrama," she said. "You don't even know Guyot was in that Camaro. All you know is that his brother stole cars—and you don't even know that, at least not as far as the court is concerned. His brother was convicted as a juvenile, and those records are sealed and therefore inadmissible. I'm such a nice lady, I won't even ask how you broke into those restricted files."

Steve took a deep breath and spoke evenly, almost gritting his teeth to keep from yelling. "No, Counselor, we don't know for a fact that Guyot was driving that Camaro, but he works in the Valley, near where the car was stolen. He worked on the Beckman Hospital critical-care ward with Duren when patients were dying—"

"Imagine, patients dying on a critical-care ward," she interrupted. "I wonder how often that happens?"

Steve ignored the dig and pressed on, even though he knew it was futile. "Five of Guyot's patients died shortly after surviving near-death experiences, and so did five of Duren's. These aren't coincidences. This is a straight line from a pile of corpses to the two people who murdered them."

Karen sighed wearily. "I bet if we look hard enough, which you clearly haven't, we can find other doctors and nurses who live or work in the San Fernando Valley who were also employed at Beckman Hospital. We might even find a few who happened to be traveling on the San Diego Freeway, the main route into the San Fernando Valley, during morning rush hour on the day your father was nearly killed. We might even find some who've had five patients die this year. This isn't a case, Detective. It's a joke."

Steve rose from his seat. "They will kill again. I hope

you'll be able to live with yourself when the next corpse comes in."

"I'll sleep just fine," Karen said, tossing her notes into the trash. "I can't prosecute a case without evidence. If you really believe these two are murderers, prove it."

CHAPTER SIXTEEN

There were restaurants that paid consultants and designers a fortune to replicate the eclectic, beat-up, sawdust-covered-floor character that Barbeque Bob's came by naturally. The ramshackle rib shack was a neighborhood fixture decades before longtime customers Steve Sloan and Jesse Travis bought the place from the original owner and became the guardians of his secret recipes.

The two men met for lunch in one of the back booths, seated on the hard benches across the scratched wooden table from Tanis Archer and Amanda Bentley. A big platter of pork spareribs, slathered in sauce, was in the middle of the table, along with bowls of macaroni salad, potato salad, baked beans, and hot buttered cobbettes of corn.

The four of them were wearing Barbeque Bob's bibs, which was one reason they were sitting in the back booth. Being seen in a bib wouldn't enhance the reputations of either Steve or Tanis as tough cops. Jesse had enough trouble overcoming his boyish looks and instilling confidence in his patients without getting caught wearing a bib. The only one of the foursome who didn't mind the bib was Amanda. One of the pluses of working with corpses was that they didn't care if she looked tough or competent. They were past caring at all.

As they ate, Steve recounted his meeting with ADA

Karen Cross and her unwillingness to pursue the case against Duren and Guyot on the basis of the existing evidence they'd gathered.

"The gutless bitch," Tanis hissed.

That was pretty close to Steve's first reaction, too. But once he cooled down and was able to look at the situation objectively, he couldn't blame Karen for her reluctance, considering what he had brought her and the misery he'd inflicted on her in the past.

He recounted that, too.

"You're saying you think she's right?" Amanda asked incredulously. She didn't like the idea that all her research counted for nothing with the DA.

"I believe Wendy Duren and Paul Guyot killed ten people and will kill more if we don't stop them," Steve said. "But what I believe and what we can prove are two different things."

"We *did* prove it," Jesse said. "We found all the connections."

"All we're missing are signed confessions," Tanis said.

"We have no proof that any of those ten people were murdered. We have no physical evidence linking either Duren or Guyot to their deaths," Steve said. "All we have are statistics and a pattern of events that seem to suggest these two might be involved in the deaths. It's all circumstantial at best."

"My God, Cross really brainwashed you," Tanis said. "Are you two sleeping together now or what?"

Steve gave Tanis a sharp look. "We need solid, irrefutable evidence of their guilt. Karen is right. We don't have it yet."

"It's *Karen* now?" Tanis said.

"If we can't get a court order to exhume the bodies and test their tissues for the presence of drugs," Amanda said, "and if we can't get warrants to search the two nurses' homes, offices, and cars to find the drugs and syringes they've stolen, how are we supposed to prove our case any better than we already have?"

"We'll have to catch them in the act," Steve said.

"You mean walk in on them murdering somebody," Jesse said.

"Yes," Steve said. "Preferably before they actually get to the murdering part."

"How do you propose we do that?" Tanis said. "We don't have the resources or manpower to follow them twenty-four/seven and watch them everywhere they go."

"Which is why we have to know ahead of time where they are going to be," Steve said. "And who they are planning to kill."

"Have you developed amazing psychic powers we don't know about?" Amanda said.

"There's this cable TV cop show about an FBI agent who was hit by lightning and now has visions of missing persons," Jesse said. "She can find people just by taking a nap."

"A nap?" Tanis said. "That's one exciting show."

"It's on Lifetime," Jesse said. "Napping is a big part of its viewers' lives."

"I'm afraid it's going to take more than a good nap to take these killers down," Steve said. "Though we may all need one by the time this is over."

"I haven't been hit by lightning lately," Amanda said, "but I sense you're going to ask us to do a lot of tedious research for you."

"We call it detecting," Steve said.

"You keep saying that," Amanda said. "As if it makes the work somehow more glamorous and thrilling."

"We need to find out why these ten people are dead," Steve said. "How are Duren and Guyot picking their victims? Is it by age, race, medical condition, or who they voted for in the last election? Is it based on where they live, what they eat, or what they do for a living? Or is it entirely random? How often are the murders occurring? Where are the murders being committed? What time are they happening?

Somewhere there's a pattern or a motive, and we have to
find it."

"Good luck," Jesse said, sliding out of the booth and
reaching for his cane, which was propped against the wall.

"Where are you going?" Steve said.

"Back to work," Jesse said. "My shift is about to start.
But in between patients, I'll look into the hospital records on
those ten victims and see what medical commonalities I can
find."

"I'll give you a ride," Amanda said.

"Where are you going?" Steve said.

"If I don't do a few more autopsies this afternoon, the
bodies are going to start stacking up in the hallway, which is
bad for business in a hospital. I'll try to dig up the death cer-
tificates on the victims and see what I can determine about
how they were killed. Of course, that's all going to be guess-
work, since all the victims were in poor health to start with,
didn't appear to die of suspicious causes, and weren't autopsied."

"I'll appreciate whatever you can tell me," Steve said to
Amanda, then turned to Jesse. "Check in on Dad and let me
know how he's doing, okay?"

"Of course," Jesse said and hobbled out with Amanda.

Steve sighed and glanced across the table at Tanis. "I
guess that leaves just the two of us on this case."

"You mean the two actual police officers," Tanis said. "I
wonder if we can protect and serve without a couple of doctors to help us."

"We'll just have to try and muddle through."

"It's my professional opinion as a law enforcement offi-
cer that we're going to need a slice of pecan pie to fortify us
for this endeavor."

"I think you're right," Steve said and motioned to the
waitress.

*   *   *

After they had successfully fortified themselves, Steve asked Tanis to find out everything she could about Duren and Guyot. Where did they come from? How did they meet? Were they friends? lovers? competitors? members of some bizarre cult? How often did they see each other now? When and where did they get together?

"That's going to require some serious surveillance," Tanis said.

"I know," Steve said. "We'll start tonight. I'll take him, you take her."

"The two of 'em could be a cell of some international terrorist group experimenting with germ warfare," Tanis said as they headed for the door of Barbeque Bob's.

Steve raised an eyebrow. "You think the ten people they killed were guinea pigs for some kind of terrorist attack using a deadly virus?"

She shrugged. "It makes as much sense as any other theory."

"We don't have any other theories," he said, chewing on a toothpick.

"Now we have one," she said.

"A stupid one."

"But one that makes sense if anyone I work for asks me why I'm using my Patriot Act powers to invade privacy and civil rights to find information on two nurses for you."

"Since you put it that way, I think you may be onto something with this germ warfare thing."

They stepped out of Barbeque Bob's into the bright sunlight of a perfect LA afternoon. She took a couple of steps towards her unmarked Crown Vic sedan, then stopped and turned to him.

"You've done an amazing job delegating all your dreary legwork to Amanda, Jesse, and me and leaving nothing for yourself to do."

"That's not true," Steve said. "I'm going to be doing the heavy lifting."

"You better not be referring to lifting the beer from the ice chest to the recliner while you watch ESPN all afternoon."

"I'm going to be thinking deep thoughts," he said.

"Like what?"

"Like trying to find the pattern behind these killings," Steve said.

"Where are you going to look?"

"My house," Steve said. "We've already found the answer. We just don't know it yet. It's somewhere on those dry-erase boards."

She nodded. "If I come up with anything, I'll join you. We can think deep together."

When he got home, he brought in a map of Los Angeles County from his car, spread it out on the kitchen table, and began the process of marking where each of the ten deaths took place.

As he worked, he was reminded of an afternoon several years ago when his father took on a similar task, charting each of the bombings committed by the Sunny View Bomber. Mark saw something that no one else had seen. He literally connected the dots and discovered the bomber was actually writing his name across Los Angeles.

Steve doubted these two psychopaths were doing the same thing, but he wasn't ruling out any possibilities. The only way to find out how the victims were being picked was to examine the killings from every angle.

The locations of the murders were spread out all over Los Angeles. The only thing they had in common was that the deaths all occurred in the victims' homes.

Where they lived alone.

No roommates. No family. No full-time caretakers.

Well, he thought, there was something. But it wasn't exactly a big revelation. It made sense that Duren and Guyot would pick people who were alone and vulnerable. It meant fewer witnesses and no one to come to the victims' rescue.

When Steve was done charting the geography of the killings, he taped the marked-up map to the wall, took a few steps back, and squinted at it, connecting the dots, trying to discern any kind of pattern.

There were no names or dates etched across the landscape. No Satanic symbols. No incomplete geometric shapes. No caricatures of political figures. Not even a big **X** to mark the spot.

All Steve managed to do with his squinting was give himself a headache.

He went to the kitchen, got two Advils and dry-swallowed them, then reluctantly returned to face the dry-erase boards and his map again.

In that instant, he was overwhelmed by an emotion so strong he had to take a seat to ride it out.

It was a deep, crippling sadness.

No, that wasn't quite right. It was grief.

He missed his father.

Sure, everyone kept telling him his father was going to be fine, that being unconscious for days was no biggie. That having a hole drilled into his skull was perfectly normal.

There's nothing to worry about, Steve. That's what they all said. But sitting there in that house, *his father's house*, staring at an impenetrable mystery, he was worried.

The puzzle in front of him filled him with dread. But it was the kind of thing Mark Sloan lived for. His father thrived on the challenge and loved sorting through the morass of information until he found the truth. The best part was doing it with his son.

Steve enjoyed those times, too. Not so much for the task itself but for the opportunity to be with his father, to see Mark work his deductive magic.

But now in the empty house, facing the boards and all the facts in the case, Steve felt alone in a way he never had before.

He closed his eyes for a long moment, and when he

opened them again, he tried to pretend that his father was with him now, not lying in his bed unconscious with a hole in his skull.

What would Dad do? What would Dad say?

Bring order to disorder and the truth will reveal itself.

His father would keep going over and over and over the information in front of him until that magic moment when all the disparate facts fell into place in his mind.

Fine, Steve told himself. That's what I will do.

He got up, grabbed a dry-erase marker, and went to the last board, the one that listed all the victims.

Okay, now what?

He looked at the names on the board and, for lack of a better idea, began with the simplest task: listing the victims in chronological order according to when they died. He wrote their names in two columns, side by side, under the name of the nurse who killed them.

Paul Guyot
Gary Betz
Andrew Kosterman
Melinda Soper
Emilia Ortega
Oliver Pritchard

Wendy Duren
Dave Grayson
Hammett Aidman
Dorothy Myack
John Eames
Patricia Ohanian

Steve had hoped that in doing the task he would discover some clear timetable for the killings, like one every seven days or after the full moon. But no such pattern emerged.

The shortest period between killings was twenty-four hours, the longest a month.

He stepped back and looked at the names, scratching at an itch on the back of his neck. The scratching didn't do any good. Because the itch wasn't on his skin. It was in his head. It was a free-floating anxiety. A nervous twitch.

It was something about those names.

He looked at the first name on Guyot's list. *Gary Betz.* He looked at the first name on Duren's list. *Dave Grayson.* He looked at the second name on Guyot's list. *Andrew Kosterman.* He looked at the second name on Duren's list. *Hammett Aidman.* And so it went. Five victims each.

Guyot killed the first patient, then Duren jumped ahead with two kills in one week, then Guyot caught up. Then they each made a kill in the same week to end up neck and neck with five each.

Jumped ahead. Caught up. Neck and neck.

It was as if they were playing a game, keeping score with corpses.

Yes, a game.

It felt right. But what kind of game was it? What were the rules?

Steve stared at the names of the first four victims in both columns and tried to think of them in terms of players or points in a game.

Gary Betz. Dave Grayson.

Andrew Kosterman. Hammett Aidman.

And there it was, finally. Right in front of his face. The pattern. It was so obvious in its crude simplicity, he couldn't imagine how he'd missed it before.

But he had. Everyone had.

Steve Sloan knew how they would pick their next victim. The *how* was easy.

The *who* was going to be a lot harder. If he wasn't too late already.

CHAPTER SEVENTEEN

Jesse finished his rounds and went to check up on Mark again in the ICU. He reviewed Mark's chart and took a seat in the guest chair beside the bed. His leg was aching and he was tired. It had already been a very long day, and it was far from over.

This wasn't the first time Jesse had seen Mark in a hospital bed. All too often lately he'd been injured in the course of his investigations. Jesse didn't know whether Mark was getting careless or if his luck was simply running out. It was reaching the point that Mark's enemies were beginning to outnumber his friends.

Each time Mark got hurt, Jesse became more afraid that he could lose the man he'd come to consider his surrogate father. This time, he'd seen Mark almost get killed right in front of him.

Jesse couldn't imagine what his life would be like without Mark's guidance. If it wasn't for Mark's influence, what kind of man would he be today? What kind of doctor? Mark had helped shape Jesse's character in so many ways. Jesse strived to emulate Mark's best qualities and had even adopted his clearly dangerous fascination with homicide investigation, much to Susan's concern.

He studied Mark's face and wondered what was going on

in the doctor's mind. Was Mark dreaming? And if so, what about? How far was his imagination taking him?

As it turned out, Mark's dreams hadn't taken him far at all, just two floors down in the same hospital.

Mark opened his eyes. He was lying on his back in a bed in the ER.

"Dr. Sloan?"

He looked up to see Dr. Kozak leaning over him.

"What happened?" Mark asked.

"You fainted," Dr. Kozak replied. "You were only out for a few moments."

Mark sat up. "Where's Emily?"

"She's in the OR with Susan," Dr. Kozak said. "Just relax. We still need to run some tests."

"I'm okay," Mark said. "It was just the shock of seeing Susan like that. First Jesse, now her. It was too much for me to handle."

"For all of us," Kozak said softly.

This was a nightmare that kept getting worse. It was so bad, it was bordering on surreal. Mark had forgotten the last two years, but it was the last two days he wished he could erase.

"You suffered a head trauma," Dr. Kozak continued. "Your fainting spell could be a symptom of serious complications."

"It's not," Mark said. He abruptly got off the gurney and stood up without any dizziness or disorientation.

"I strongly advise you not to do this," Dr. Kozak said.

"Duly noted," Mark said. "Which OR is Emily in?"

"Number three."

Mark nodded and marched out of the ER, very much aware of Dr. Kozak's eyes on him, watching for any sign that he was off balance or faltering in any way.

He got into the empty elevator and turned to see Dr.

Kozak staring at him. The doors closed and Mark leaned back against the wall, shutting his eyes for a moment.

You've got to be strong, he told himself. You're the chief of internal medicine. Everyone will be watching you and following your example. Get a grip.

He opened his eyes, straightened up, and took a deep breath. When the elevator arrived, he strode out like a man on a mission. He went straight to the observation gallery above the operating room. The gallery was crammed full of surgical interns, but they weren't there to learn from the delicate procedure Dr. Noble was performing. Mostly, they were there, like Mark, because of their ties to Jesse and Susan.

When Mark entered, everyone turned to him, their eyes brimming with tears.

He nodded to acknowledge their unspoken concern but said nothing, shifting his gaze to the operation going on below. Emily's back was to him, her surgical team huddled around Susan, working intently.

This wouldn't be the first time a brain-dead mother had been kept alive until childbirth. It had been medically possible for decades. He'd done it himself twenty-five years ago.

But the operation that Emily was performing now was still relatively rare, and the risks were great. If Susan died on the table—a distinct possibility considering her injuries— her baby would die as well.

Mark didn't think he could take that. There had been too many deaths already. He wanted to curl up in a corner and cry over the losses.

But he had a stronger compulsion—to do something, anything, to gain some measure of control over this situation, to bring this unendurable misery to an end.

There wasn't anything he could do medically. That left only one way he could act.

He had to find the killer.

He left the observation gallery and went to his office, sat

down at his computer, and fumbled with his mouse to call up the medical records on Grover Dawson, Joyce Kling, and Hammond McNutchin, three of his dead patients.

He accidentally clicked the "About" page on the software, filling his screen with a movie-like scroll of credits for the software design team.

Frustrated, he clicked his way out of the pointless screen and searched for the records he needed. It didn't take long to find what he was looking for.

Grover Dawson's insurance carrier was First Fidelity Casualty, one of the companies that was on the handwritten notes Mark had found on his desk. A few clicks later, and Mark found that Joyce Kling was insured by First Fidelity, too.

Was the insurance carrier the common denominator between the victims? He felt a tinge of excitement, but it was short-lived. A moment later, he discovered that Hammond McNutchin was covered by Cal-Star Insurance, another company Mark had recorded in his notes.

He recalled that his notes mentioned one other company—Kemper-Carlson Pharmaceuticals.

On a hunch, Mark checked Grover Dawson's prescription drug policy. According to the records, his insurance company didn't authorize pharmacies to refill Dawson's regular prescriptions. Instead, the company required that all refills be processed by mail and delivered through Kemper-Carlson.

Mark checked Hammond McNutchin's records to see what Cal-Star's prescription drug policy was. Like First Fidelity, it processed the prescription drug program through Kemper-Carlson.

Was this how the killer gained access to the victims? By delivering their prescription drugs?

Mark printed out the information on the three patients, found his car keys in his desk drawer, and hurriedly left the office.

He wanted to get back to the beach house and go through

the patient records again, sorting out the dead patients who got their drugs delivered to them by Kemper-Carlson.

From there, he would call their families and see if any of them were missing a personal item like a wedding ring, a glass fish, or a set of dentures.

When he was done with those tasks, he would have a list of likely victims and would be able to make a convincing case to Steve, who, in turn, could take it to his superiors. With the LAPD on board, they would be able to zero in on the killer much faster than Mark could on his own.

Perhaps it was his impatience, his eagerness to get back to work, that made the slow drive back to Malibu in evening rush-hour traffic seem so agonizing. There was something about being stuck in the drab Ford sedan that he found incredibly irritating. It wasn't just the slow crawl towards Malibu, the smell of exhaust fumes, or the car's ridiculous faux-wood trim.

He felt imprisoned in the car, acutely aware of its cheap materials and oppressive blandness. It was as if the car was part of some evil conspiracy to keep him from finding the killer.

It took him nearly an hour to make the trip home. It felt like days. The sky was dark, the night deeper and blacker than usual. The moon was hidden by the clouds, and the streetlights had inexplicably failed to go on.

As soon as he entered the house, he started for the stairs to the first floor. He was halfway down when he paused, realizing that he was starving. It was impossible for him to think on an empty stomach. The only things that would be on his mind would be cheeseburgers, pizza, and fried chicken.

He went to the kitchen and opened the refrigerator to make himself a quick snack. The refrigerator was stuffed with lunch meat, cheese, fruit, and some leftovers—his famous seashell casserole in an aluminum foil pan, a couple of cartons of take-out Chinese food, and a few slices of birthday cake.

Mark stared at the food, feeling a growing uneasiness. No, that wasn't what it was. He had the distinct impression that he'd experienced this moment before. He could remember standing in front of the refrigerator and seeing the same leftovers.

That was certainly possible. He made seashell casserole a lot, they were regulars at the Chinese restaurant across the street, and the cake—

The cake.

Mark lifted the plastic wrap and tasted the white frosting on the cake. It was a typical cake, the kind you'd have at birthdays or other celebrations. His birthday and Steve's were still months off. So where had this cake come from? Was it Emily's?

When was the last time he remembered having a cake like this?

The only thing that came to mind was the party at Barbeque Bob's celebrating Jesse and Susan's wedding. The cake was huge, and there was so much left over that Jesse and Susan insisted that the guests all take some home. Steve, never one to refuse cake, took a double share for him and Mark.

But that was *two years ago.*

When was the last time he remembered making seashell casserole?

The day he got back from Las Vegas.

Two years ago.

Mark's heart began to race and his mouth went dry. He thought about the drive back from Vegas and, more recently, the trip he'd just made from the hospital.

He reached into his pocket and looked at the car keys in his hands. The key chain had the Hertz logo on it. On the other side of the key chain was the car's VIN and license plate information.

The Ford was a rental car. The same one he'd rented in Las Vegas.

Two years ago.

Why was he still driving it? It made no sense at all. Unless . . .

"Mark?"

He looked up and saw Emily standing there, still in her scrubs. There were specks of blood on the blue cotton fabric.

How long had she been standing there? Why hadn't he heard her come in? How had she gotten there so fast?

"Susan's baby is going to be fine," she said. "It's a girl. We're going to be able keep Susan alive until the baby is ready to be born."

Mark stared at Emily and nodded silently. There was something eerily familiar now about her and this horrible situation with Susan.

"I was surprised that you'd left, that you'd driven yourself home," she said. "What were you thinking? What if you'd fainted behind the wheel?"

Mark staggered back from the refrigerator, leaving the door wide open.

"That's the same food that was in the refrigerator two years ago," he said. "I'm driving the same car."

He glanced at the wedding album, which was still open on the kitchen table, and motioned to the honeymoon pictures.

"All the photos taken of you and me in Hawaii are in places I visited before with Steve," Mark said. "Why aren't there any pictures taken in places that I didn't go to before? Because I don't know what the other parts of Kauai look like."

She took a step towards him. "Mark, you're not making any sense."

"No, this is the first thing that's made sense in days,"

Mark said and tossed his car keys across the room. "None of this is real."

"Listen to me. You had a severe head injury. You've suffered a terrible emotional shock. You need help."

"You're right, and I'm not going to get it by staying here," Mark said. "It's time for me to leave."

He strode past her to the front door. Emily hurried after him.

"Where are you going?" she said.

"Home." Mark opened the door and rushed down the front walk towards the street.

Emily caught up with him and grabbed him by the arm. "You *are* home. I love you, Mark. Please come back inside with me."

Mark yanked his arm free and continued walking across the private road and up the embankment towards the Pacific Coast Highway, the lights of the passing cars flashing like lightning through the darkness.

"Please, Mark. Stop," she yelled.

He stopped at the corner of Trancas Canyon Road and the highway. Trancas Market was across the street, and beyond it in the blackness, the Santa Monica Mountains. Cars and trucks sped by him in a blur, kicking up a speed-driven wind that shrieked like a dying animal.

Mark looked over his shoulder at Emily and smiled. "You're the only part of my life that wasn't a nightmare."

A look of horror washed across her face and she began to run towards him.

"No!" she screamed.

Mark glanced to his right. There was a bus speeding towards him. He took a deep breath and stepped into the highway right in front of it.

The next scream he heard was his own.

Chapter Eighteen

Mark opened his eyes and saw a young Asian woman staring down at him. It was that ER nurse again. He couldn't remember her name.

Déjà vu.

"Welcome back, Dr. Sloan," she said. "We've missed you."

He blinked hard, licked his dry lips, and tried to speak. His voice was raw. "How long have I been out?"

"Three days," she said. "I'll go get the doctor."

The nurse left before he could ask her any more questions. He looked around the room, seeing the same equipment he'd seen before, feeling that same sense of déjà vu even more intensely.

Mark checked to see if there was a copy of the novel *A Prayer for Owen Meany* on the guest chair and was relieved, and a little saddened, not to see it there. There wasn't a wedding ring on his finger either.

He reached up and felt the bandage on his head and the rubber tube underneath it that ran down to a bag below the bed. From that, and a quick glance at his IV and the equipment around his bed, he was able to confidently determine his medical condition and the procedures that had likely been done to stabilize him.

Next, Mark tested his ability to move and did the same neurological self-exam he'd done before.

Or at least that he'd imagined doing in the alternate universe he'd been living in for three days.

Someone spoke. "If you like, I can give you the file and you can write up the report on your condition."

Mark looked up and saw Dr. Jesse Travis hobbling in on a cane, a big smile on his face.

"You're alive," Mark said with a broad smile.

"I think that's supposed to be my line," Jesse said. "Do you know who you are and where you are?"

"I'm Dr. Mark Sloan and I'm in Community General Hospital," he said. "Would you like to know which room and on which floor?"

"Show-off," Jesse said. "What's the last thing you remember?"

Mark almost replied that it was looking at his wife, Emily, and then stepping in front of a speeding bus. The dream was still fresh in his mind, every detail as vivid as if he'd just lived it. But he tried to think beyond that, to his last true memory.

"I remember a car coming at me in the parking garage," Mark said. "And someone tackling me out of its path."

Jesse raised his hand hesitantly. "That would be me. I'm afraid I'm the reason you're lying there."

"Better here than in the morgue."

"You can say that again," Amanda said, arriving as if on cue, in her medical examiner Windbreaker. "It's so good to see your smile."

She gave him a hug.

"Yours too," Mark said. "I'm not married, am I?"

Amanda gave him a quizzical look, then glanced at Jesse. "Have you checked him out?"

"I was just getting to that," Jesse said.

Mark laughed. "Don't let my question worry you. It's not brain damage. There's a story behind it."

"I can't wait to hear it," Amanda said.

"Later, I promise," Mark said. "What happened to your leg, Jesse?"

"The same thing that happened to your head," Jesse said. "A lousy tackle."

"Has Steve caught whoever it was who tried to run me over?"

"Yes and no, but we'll leave that to Steve to explain," Amanda said, giving Jesse a stern look. "Won't we, Jesse?"

"Sure. We won't tell Mark how we're this close to nailing the killers." Jesse pinched his index finger and thumb nearly together to illustrate his point.

"Killers?" Mark asked. "There's more than one?"

Amanda swatted Jesse's shoulder. "Stop it. Do you want Mark to bolt out of this bed right now to get on the case?"

"You have a point, medically speaking." Jesse glanced back at Mark. "Forget what I said."

Mark thought that it was nice to be asked to forget something rather than being told that he'd lost two years of memories. He was glad he'd stepped in front of that bus.

Amanda gave Mark a kiss on the cheek. "I'll call Steve, and then I'll come by to check up on you later."

"If I'm still here." Mark grinned.

"You better be." She glared at him, then at Jesse, before walking out.

Jesse turned to Mark. "Okay, boss. You know the drill. Can you stick your tongue out at me?"

Mark could and did.

Steve used the DMV database to find out the make, model, and license plate number of the car Paul Guyot drove, and then he went to the John Muir Hospital parking structure to find it. Unfortunately, there were no syringes, stolen drugs, files on the dead patients, or signed confessions in clear view inside the ten-year-old Acura.

So he returned to his Ford pickup, found a parking spot

where he could see the parking structure exit, and settled in for a long wait.

Next to writing reports, stakeouts were the dullest part of Steve's job. They were also hard on his lower back, legs, and bladder.

If he was alone on a stakeout, which he preferred to being saddled with a talkative partner, he passed the time by listening to Dr. Laura or enjoying a detective novel on CD. His favorite reader was actor Joe Mantegna. Steve wondered what it would be like listening to Joe read an account of one of his investigations, but he decided that even the acclaimed actor couldn't make sitting in a car eating potato chips and relieving yourself in a Porta Potti sound exciting.

Bladder control was a serious issue in a stakeout. Steve had learned that early on. He'd learned to go without drinking as long as he could and, when he did drink, to have only a few sips.

Guyot left the structure at about six o'clock and then drove a few miles to the Trader Joe's market at Fallbrook Center. It wasn't until Guyot got out of the car to go into the market that Steve got his first good look at the killer nurse. The man was still in surgical scrubs, his hair curly and askew, which was a contrast to his neatly trimmed goatee. He wore wire-rimmed glasses that gave him the studious, scholarly look of a graduate student.

Guyot was about six feet tall and a little soft in the middle, though not enough to be called fat. Steve judged him to be in his mid-thirties.

There was nothing even slightly menacing about him, nothing in his manner or body language that betrayed the fact that he'd killed at least five people.

Steve had to restrain himself from beating the crap out of the man or, at the very least, placing him under arrest. Not that anyone in the store was in danger. Guyot killed only people who were weak, vulnerable, and defenseless.

Paul Guyot wasn't just a sociopath. He was a coward.

Steve waited outside, watching the customers go to their cars with their grocery carts full of organic this and free-range that. Was a chicken who ran free, eating whatever crap he could stick in his beak, really any healthier to eat than one that was given a controlled diet of chemically rich nutrition? Who knew what a free-range chicken was consuming? It could be toxic waste.

That's why Steve preferred to eat Kentucky Fried Chicken. Whether those chickens ran wild, crowing the theme from *Born Free* or not, he was confident that whatever poisons they had in them got pressure-cooked and irradiated into oblivion and rendered impotent by the Colonel's secret blend of eleven herbs and spices.

Guyot came out ten minutes later with a single grocery bag and two bottles of wine. He put them in the trunk of his car and drove off. Steve stayed a couple of car lengths behind him, careful not to get too close.

It didn't seem as if the nurse knew he was being followed. Guyot didn't try any switchbacks, sudden turns, or abrupt lane changes to flush out a pursuer.

Guyot drove south on Topanga Canyon Boulevard into Woodland Hills, crossing Ventura Boulevard and then making a right into one of the side streets that carried him into a tree-lined community of tiny ranch-style homes. He pulled into the driveway of a blue house.

Steve drove slowly past, noting Wendy Duren's Honda on the street and, at the corner, Tanis Archer's black Mercury Marauder sedan, which looked like a police car without the insignia, antennas, and flashing lights.

Steve pulled up beside her parked car, and they rolled down their driver's side windows simultaneously.

"Subtle," Steve said, tipping his head towards her car. "Why don't you just drive a black-and-white and turn on your siren?"

"Is this how you encourage people like me to help you on

your unauthorized investigations for no salary, no credit, and the risk of complete career ruination?"

"I'm relying on my winning smile," Steve said, offering her one. She didn't seem impressed.

"I think we know what Guyot and Duren's relationship is," Tanis said. "She let herself into his house with her own key. I wonder if these killings are some kind of kinky sex game."

"Funny you should put it that way," Steve said. But before he could finish the thought, his cell phone rang. It was Amanda.

"I have some good news," she said.

"You've got that list of former critical-care patients or Appleby clients whose first or last names begin with the letter *V*."

"Better than that," Amanda said. "Mark is awake."

The four of them—Steve, Amanda, Jesse, and Susan—were gathered around Mark's bed as if it were a campfire. He was sitting up and was about to tell them about how he'd spent the last three days.

"We know what you were doing," Steve said. "You were lying right there unconscious."

"I was doing more than that," Mark said. "I was dreaming."

"About what?" Steve asked.

"The investigation I was conducting before someone tried to run me over," Mark said.

"Of course you were," Steve said. "What a dumb question."

"Well, to be honest, there was also some romance involved," Mark said.

"There was?" Susan said, raising her eyebrows.

"Now you want to hear the story, don't you?" Jesse said.

"I'm not sure that *I* do," Steve said. "How romantic was it and how much detail are you going to get into?"

"Don't worry. It's nothing that's going to make you or me uncomfortable," Mark said. "But I suspect it's going to turn out to have some important symbolic value."

"Symbolic?" Jesse said.

"Something that is one thing but actually represents something else," Amanda explained.

"I know what it means, thank you," Jesse said. "But sometimes three Hawaiian Tropic swimsuit models wrestling in Cool Whip are just three Hawaiian Tropic swimsuit models wrestling in Cool Whip."

Susan gave him a look. "You dream about swimsuit models wrestling in whipped cream?"

"No, of course not," Jesse said. "It was only an example of a typical dream that some desperately lonely person who isn't me and isn't happily married to the most beautiful woman on earth might have. Someone like Steve."

"Gee, thanks," Steve said. "But I believe we were talking about my father and his dreams. So you're saying he's a desperately lonely person?"

Mark hadn't thought of himself as lonely. And yet he missed Emily, a woman who existed only in his dreams. He figured he wasn't the first man haunted by a fantasy.

"No," Jesse stammered. "What I meant was—"

Mark interrupted him. "I can assure you that no one was wearing swimsuits in my dream."

"They were *naked*?" Jesse said.

Susan swatted Jesse's shoulder. "Please go on, Dr. Sloan."

"In my dream, I was still looking into the sudden, often accidental deaths of individuals who'd recently survived life-threatening illnesses or injuries," Mark said. "Like Grover Dawson."

"It *was* an accident—" Steve began, but Mark cut him off.

"It was murder," Mark said. "I found the key to proving it during the last couple of days."

"While you were unconscious," Amanda said.

"Yes, and I believe if we can correctly interpret the symbolic elements of my dreams, it will lead us to the identity of the killer."

"You want our help analyzing your dream so we can solve a murder," Steve said.

"More than one," Mark said. "I think we're dealing with a serial killer."

Steve sighed. "It's not enough that you're a better detective than half of the LAPD combined. If word gets out that you can solve murders in your sleep, a whole bunch of us homicide detectives are going to be looking for new jobs. Me included."

CHAPTER NINETEEN

Mark could tell by the way they were looking at him that they thought he was crazy.

"Are you saying that slamming your head against concrete has made you psychic?" Jesse said. "Because if you are, there could be a TV series in this."

"I'm not psychic, but solving the mystery in my dream is not as ridiculous as it sounds," Mark said. "I'd already completed most of my investigation before I got hurt. All those facts and observations were swirling around in my subconscious. The dream was simply my subconscious working it all out."

"You call that simple?" Steve said.

"How do you know the facts and observations you were using in your dream weren't imaginary?" Susan asked.

"That's why you're all here," Mark said. "I'm going to tell you what I discovered and you're going to tell me if I based it on imaginary facts."

"This is a first," Amanda said.

"I can just imagine how this is going to play out in the courtroom when I'm on the witness stand," Steve said. "The defense attorney will say, 'Tell me, Detective, how did you discover the so-called connection between my client and the alleged murder?' And I'll reply, 'My father saw it in a dream while he was in a coma.'"

"Everything I'm going to tell you can be independently corroborated by data I assembled before I hit my head," Mark said.

"We've been doing some investigating of our own while you've been unconscious," Steve said. "We went back over a lot of ground you covered and questioned many of the same people. We came to a few conclusions of our own."

"Let me tell you what I discovered first while it's all still fresh in my mind," Mark said.

"Besides, I want to hear about this romance," Susan said. "Go ahead, Dr. Sloan. Tell us the story."

And with that, Mark began his tale. He told them how, in his dream, he woke up in Community General in much the same condition as he was now, only he'd suffered severe amnesia and Jesse had been killed saving his life.

"See," Jesse said. "Deep down, you *do* resent me for causing your injury."

"I don't think that's what it is," Mark said.

"My heroic death was definitely symbolic," Jesse said.

"It's going to be literal if you don't shut up and let Mark go on with his story," Amanda said.

Jesse turned to Susan. "Are you going to let her talk to your man that way?"

Susan nodded. "It saves me the trouble."

Mark explained that in his dream the last thing he remembered was Jesse and Susan's wedding, which, he'd been told by Dr. Emily Noble, had occurred two years earlier.

"Who is Dr. Noble?" Susan asked.

"A pediatric surgeon," Mark said.

"Then why were you her patient?" Jesse asked.

"She was my wife," Mark said.

"Your *wife*?" Steve said.

"I have a hunch that's one of the symbolic things we need to figure out," Amanda said.

"Clearly, she represents something important, but I can't

figure out what it is," Mark said. "Is it her name? Is she someone I know? Is it her medical specialty?"

"Maybe it just means you were married to the case," Susan said. "That the victims were all connected to you."

"Could be," Mark said. "But I have a hunch that if we figure out why she was in my dream, we'll find out the identity of the killer."

He described how he promptly resumed his investigation into the deaths of his patients Grover Dawson, Joyce Kling, and Hammond McNutchin, among others. He started by going over notes he'd left in his office at Community General. There was a list that included two insurance companies, a pharmaceutical company, and several odd items like dentures, a glass fish, and a pearl necklace.

"You must have a photographic memory," Steve said. "I found those same notes, and they mentioned the items you just listed."

"That's reassuring," Mark said, and continued with the rest of his story. He went home, where he'd converted the first floor of the beach house into an office that was dominated by dry-erase boards that were covered with details culled from the research conducted by Amanda and Jesse.

"I can explain what that means," Jesse said, raising his hand. "You'd like Steve to move out sometime before he turns fifty."

Susan shot him a look and Jesse swatted himself on the shoulder, saving her the trouble.

"You've got him well trained," Amanda said approvingly.

Mark talked in detail about his meetings with the epidemiologist and the cardiac specialist, as well as his encounter with Grover Dawson's daughter.

"I can vouch for your account of what you got from those doctors," Steve said. "I spoke to them and the sociologist, too. But I don't know if you really spoke to Dawson's daughter."

"I did," Mark said. "In my dream, I was reliving the real

meeting I had with Mallory Dawson the day before I nearly got run over. Only in reality, of course, my wife wasn't with me. The important discovery in both my real and my fantasy lives was that Grover Dawson had lost his wedding ring."

"Maybe he took it off before his hot date," Amanda said.

"I don't think he had a date," Mark said. "I think either someone swapped his regular meds with Viagra or forced him to take those pills."

"Can you prove it?" Steve asked.

"It's all in their medical files. All the victims lived alone, died sudden or accidental deaths, and had their prescription drugs delivered by Kemper-Carlson Pharmaceuticals," Mark said. "But the clincher is that they were all missing a personal item. Grover Dawson's wedding ring was gone. Sandy Sechrest's glass fish disappeared. Joyce Kling's pearl necklace was lost. You'll find that Leila Pevney and Chadwick Saxelid were missing things, too."

"You think the killer took those things as trophies," Amanda said.

"I'm convinced of it," Mark said. "If we backtrack through the files, using the pharmaceutical company link as our guide, I'm afraid we'll find more victims. But we'll also find the murderer."

There was silence as everyone mulled over what Mark had told them. Steve studied his father's face. Mark's brow was furrowed and he was frowning.

"Is there something else?" Steve asked.

"I'm not sure what it means, but it must be significant," Mark said, glancing at Susan. "In my dream, you were pregnant."

Susan blushed. "I can assure you that I'm not."

"There was more to it than that," Mark said. "You were hit by a drunk driver and left brain-dead. We were going to keep you alive until you could give birth."

"How awful," Susan said softly.

Jesse put his arm around his wife's shoulders. "It was only a dream."

"More like a nightmare," Susan said.

"Emily had to perform in utero surgery to save your unborn child's life," Mark said. "Your accident and your pregnancy mean something."

"I'm afraid I didn't study dream analysis in any of my college psych courses," Amanda said.

"This is more like English lit," Susan said, "Analyzing a writer's symbols and metaphors for the deeper, thematic meaning."

"Care to make some guesses?" Mark asked.

Susan bit her lower lip and thought about it. "Well, me and my unborn child could represent your patients and the almost parental way you protect and care for them. If you don't find this killer soon, another one of your patients, your surrogate children, could die."

"Maybe Emily Noble is the killer," Jesse said. "We ought to run a check on her name."

"Or maybe she represents the fact that the murderer is a mirror image of you, your evil twin of sorts. A medical professional who doesn't save lives but takes them," Amanda said. "Perhaps her name refers to our 'noble' profession, which the murderer has warped."

"But Emily didn't kill anyone in my dream," Mark said.

"Since when do dreams have to make sense?" Jesse said. "Why did Cap'n Crunch show up in the hot tub with the Hawaiian Tropic models?"

Everyone stared at Jesse, who shrugged.

"Hypothetically speaking, of course," he said.

"I wouldn't worry too much about what it all means, Dad. You did good work in your coma, but—" Steve stopped himself. "Now there's a sentence I never imagined myself saying."

"Go on," Mark said.

"But the thing is, you went in the wrong direction," Steve

said. "We know who the killers are. We've already solved the case."

"You have?" Mark said. "Who have you arrested?"

"Nobody yet," Steve said. "There's this little technicality we have to deal with first."

"All we have to do is prove they're guilty to the satisfaction of the district attorney," Amanda said.

"And that's going to be tricky," Steve said. "But I think I've got a way to do it."

"Tell me everything," Mark said. "Start at the beginning."

Before Steve could say anything, Jesse stood up and spoke. "I hate to behave like the responsible doctor around here, but this is enough for one night. Mark needs his rest."

"I've been resting for three days," Mark protested.

"You've been unconscious and you have a hole in your head," Jesse said. "You could have died."

"Now you tell me," Steve said pointedly to Jesse.

"It's time for everyone to go home and for Mark to get some sleep," Jesse said, ignoring Steve's comment. "We can pick this up tomorrow."

Susan, Amanda, and Steve got obediently to their feet. The fact was, they were pretty tired and looked it. The last few days had been hard on them all.

"Sit down," Mark said. "You can't leave me hanging like this."

"You're lucky I extended your visiting hours this long," Jesse said. "Don't push your luck."

"Listen to Jesse, Mark," Amanda said. "I don't want you to become one of *my* patients."

"I'm the senior doctor here, and I say I'm fine," Mark said.

Susan turned to Jesse. "Would you like me to give the patient a sedative, Doctor, or put him in restraints?"

"I don't know," Jesse said, looking past her and narrowing his eyes at Mark. "Would I?"

"Okay, okay, I get the point," Mark sighed, giving in. "I'll see you all tomorrow, bright and early."

Steve leaned down and surprised Mark by kissing him on the forehead. "Good night, Dad."

Mark watched his son and his friends go. There was no way he could rest now, not while there was so much to ponder. What did Steve mean when he said Mark had gone in the wrong direction? Steve himself had gone from arguing against foul play to accepting that a killer was at work. So why was he still maintaining that Grover Dawson's death was an accident? And why was Steve talking about *killers*? How many were there?

Mark kept asking himself unanswerable questions, which for him was like counting sheep, and within a few moments he was lulled into a deep, dreamless slumber.

CHAPTER TWENTY

Steve got up at dawn, put on shorts, a T-shirt, and running shoes, and headed out onto the chilly, fogged-shrouded beach for a jog.

He had the sand to himself. Anybody with any sense was still asleep in a warm bed, especially the people who lived on this stretch of Malibu, most of whom were so rich they paid people to jog for them. There didn't even seem to be as many seagulls as usual. The Malibu gulls were probably smart enough to sun themselves in the Valley until the fog cleared.

Steve couldn't blame them. He was freezing, so he pushed himself a little harder, hoping to quickly work up a sweat and warm himself against the cold.

The air was misty and the salt spray off the sea stung his eyes. Or perhaps what was irritating his eyes was the pollution, all those cancer-causing particles clinging to the wisps of fog as if they were cobwebs.

But, like most Los Angelenos, he consciously tried not to think about the air he was breathing, and so he immediately changed his train of thought.

Instead, he puzzled over the killer nurses and what it would take to nail them. He had only one option, and it meant gambling with the lives of innocent people.

He had to let the nurses come close to killing their next

victim and try to catch them in the act before they succeeded.

It was a hell of a risk.

Then again, if he didn't take the risk, those same innocent
people would surely be killed anyway, only without him sitting outside their door trying to guess the right moment to
come storming in to the rescue.

The only way his dangerous plan could work was if he
accurately predicted who the next target would be. Then it
would all come down to surveillance, timing, and luck.

But he wasn't at that point yet. Tanis was watching
Wendy Duren, while Amanda and Jesse were going through
confidential medical records, compiling a list of potential
victims in the nurses' sick game.

Steve was hoping for a short list. Even if there were only
a few possible targets, he didn't have the manpower or the
resources to protect them all or to follow Guyot and Duren
around the clock.

He would have to go with his gut.

The prospect of relying on his instincts made him uneasy.
His hunches hadn't proven to be all that dependable over the
years, certainly not as often as his father's. It was his father's
hunch that had brought these homicides to light.

Then again, Mark's investigation had gone astray. He
identified the wrong patients as homicide victims and the
pattern he'd discovered, of missing items and a shared pharmaceutical provider, were just simple coincidences.

It was Steve who'd managed to find the killers. Thanks to
solid, by-the-book police work. No smoke and mirrors. No
hunches. Just dogged determination, following the facts
where they led.

He was keenly aware that this would be the first time he'd
solved a crime on his own that his father was also investigating. Of course, Mark was operating at a slight disadvantage—he'd done most of his detective work while in a coma.

Even so, the victory was sweet. Not that it was a competition. It was simply nice for his self-esteem to best his old man once in a while.

Or even once.

Just once.

It was about seven o'clock by the time Steve, drenched in sweat, returned to the house. He was tired and yet at the same time he felt invigorated—the contradiction that was the miracle of endorphins. He knew it was nature's way of ensuring that humans would get off their butts. The more exertion, the more feel-good chemicals the body releases into the bloodstream. But nature didn't foresee satellite television, the Internet, and the Xbox. Mere endorphins couldn't compete.

Steve was planning on a quick shower, an even quicker breakfast, and then a meeting with Amanda, Jesse, and Tanis to go over their list. He would stop in to brief his dad, but he hoped to have the case solved before Mark was well enough to get involved again.

But he scrapped those plans when he heard footsteps upstairs. He grabbed his gun from his holster, which was draped over a chair, and cautiously crept up the stairs to the main floor. There was a chill in the entry hall, indicating to him that the front door had recently been opened.

Who the hell was in the house?

He eased carefully across the entry hall to the living room, where the dry-erase boards were laid out. Someone was sitting on the couch, his head swathed in bandages, like some kind of mummy. A folding walker was propped within reach.

"Dad?" Steve said incredulously, lowering his gun.

Mark turned his head and smiled. He was wearing a bathrobe and surgical scrubs. His skin was wan, his cheeks hollow, his eyes red.

"Good morning, Steve," Mark said jovially, but the effort showed in his expression. "How was your run?"

Steve set his gun on the end table and sat down beside his father on the couch. "How did you get here?"

"I checked myself out of the hospital and ordered a medical transport service to bring me home."

"Are you out of your mind?" Steve said.

"I'll recuperate better here with the peace and quiet and the sea air than I will at the hospital," Mark said. "Besides, I'll be under a doctor's constant care."

"You mean your own."

"You don't have faith in my medical abilities?"

"Dad," Steve said, "you've got a hole in your skull. What are you going to do, just put a cork in it?"

"I'll go back to the hospital next week when I'm stronger, and we'll seal it with a bone graft taken from my hip or from a cadaver," Mark said. "In the meantime, I will stay here and rest."

Steve gave him a skeptical look. "You're going to rest."

"I'm going to stay right here."

"You mean like the way you stayed in the hospital?" Steve asked.

"I'm going to lie in bed, sit on this couch, or relax in a chair on the deck, taking it easy and avoiding any kind of exertion."

"What about your meds?"

"You can pick them up for me at the pharmacy or I can have them delivered," Mark said. "I'll drink lots of fluids and we've got plenty of food. My leftover seashell casserole has proven medicinal powers. I'm sure Jesse, Susan, and Amanda will stop in to check on me, too."

"What about the case?" Steve said. "You're going to let that go?"

"Why not?" Mark smiled. "You said you've got it solved."

"I do." Steve motioned to the boards. "It's all right there."

Mark nodded. "I felt this sense of déjà vu the moment I saw those boards. It was like a moment from my dream, only the boards are up here instead of downstairs and the information on them is very different."

"I'll walk you through it—" Steve began.

"You don't have to," Mark interrupted. "I've had a few minutes to look it over."

"It's pretty complicated," Steve said.

"'Game Over,'" Mark said.

Steve stared at him.

"What did you say?"

"'Game Over,'" Mark repeated. "That's what Guyot and Duren are doing. They are competing to see who can spell those two words first using the names of their victims. Guyot is using the first letter of first names, Duren is using the first letter of last names."

"It took me days to figure that out and you spotted it in five minutes?"

"The pattern is pretty obvious when it's laid out side by side in columns like that," Mark said, pointing to the board. "The two nurses are tied, with five names each. Guyot has Gary, Andrew, Melinda, Emilia, and Oliver, to spell 'Game O.' Duren has Grayson, Aidman, Myack, Eames, Ohanian, to spell 'Game O.' Your next step is finding people who fit the profile of the other victims and who have either a first name or a last name that begins with *V*."

"How did you know that?" Steve couldn't hide his astonishment and, with it, his irritation. As much as he loved and admired his father, Mark's feats of deductive reasoning often made Steve feel useless and stupid. This was one of those times.

"Mostly it was just seeing the lists. But it's also similar to a well-known case of medical murder committed about twenty-five years ago by two nurses at a nursing home," Mark said. "The two women were lovers and, as foreplay, they took turns smothering their patients, whose initials, it turned out, spelled 'murder.' They thought it was cute."

"Do you think Guyot and Duren are committing copycat crimes?"

"No, I think they just enjoy killing," Mark said. "So tell me what you've got."

Steve laid out his case the same way he had for ADA Karen Cross, only this time he didn't have to dance around how he got his hands on confidential medical records, since Mark was the one who had started Amanda and Jesse on that research.

He told Mark all about how he found Wendy Duren and her employment at Appleby Nursing Services and her suspected involvement in a string of unexplained deaths in the Beckman critical-care unit. Steve explained how that led to the discovery that several patients who'd recently overcome critical afflictions were using Appleby Nursing Services at the time of their deaths. All of which led to another Beckman nurse, Paul Guyot, who worked at John Muir, where Mark had visited Dr. Barnes and Dr. Dalton.

"Your theory is that Guyot saw me there, assumed I was onto him, and then tried to run me over," Mark said.

"Pretty much," Steve said. "The locations where the Camaro was stolen and where it was later abandoned were both close to his home and workplace."

Mark motioned to the two lists on the board. "Were any of their victims missing personal items?"

"I don't know. I haven't checked. I suppose I could, but it's really not necessary at this point."

"Yes, it is. If Wendy Duren or Paul Guyot have any of those items it will connect them to the murders of Grover Dawson, Hammond McNutchin, Sandy Sechrest, and Joyce Kling for starters," Mark said. "What about Kemper-Carlson Pharmaceuticals? Did these ten victims have that in common, too?"

"Again, I don't know. We could check." Steve tried to hide his frustration, but he didn't do a very good job of it, and it seeped out in the tone of his voice. "But that's not the connection."

"How do you know?" Mark said. "Posing as someone delivering prescriptions could be how Guyot got into the homes of the patients he killed."

Steve took a deep breath and let it out slowly. "The nurses are lovers. They were killing at Beckman and they are killing now. He's picking victims that came through John Muir. She's targeting Appleby clients. It's a game."

"But Leila Pevney and Chadwick Saxelid were both patients at John Muir. They don't fit the 'Game Over' pattern, since the first letters of their names can't be used to spell the phrase."

"Because they weren't murdered," Steve said in exasperation.

"Of course they were."

"Dad, you said it yourself. 'Game Over.' That's the pattern, not drug deliveries or trophies."

Mark waved his hand dismissively at the boards. "None of this matches my dream."

Steve got to his feet and looked down at his father. "Because it was a *dream*. This is real. This is happening now."

"The dream made sense," Mark said.

"You were married in the dream. Does that mean your wife is going to walk through the front door? Or that Susan is pregnant?"

"Maybe Dawson, McNutchin, Sechrest, and the others were killed first and *then* the nurses began the game."

Steve shook his head. "The dates don't work. Grover Dawson, for instance, died while the game was going on and Guyot had already scored his *G*."

Mark was silent for a long moment, then drew his bathrobe tight around himself, as if he was feeling a chill.

"I suppose you're right," he said.

But it was a lie. Mark wasn't going to let go, and they both knew it. And that truth infuriated Steve. He wanted to lash out at his father. There were a lot of things Steve could have said, things that had gone *unsaid* for too long, and perhaps he would have if Mark hadn't been ill. But Steve realized this wasn't the time.

Dad's got a hole in his skull, for God's sake.

Instead, Steve choked back everything he wanted to say and decided the best thing he could do for both of them was to leave.

You mean run away, don't you, Stevie?

"I've got to go to work," Steve said. "Are you sure you're going to be all right here?"

"Positive," Mark said.

"I'll make sure someone stops in to check on you," Steve said. "And I'll give you a call, too."

"I don't need a babysitter," Mark said.

"You're right," Steve said. "What you need is a nurse."

"Maybe we should call Appleby Nursing Services and have them send someone over," Mark said with a mischievous grin.

Steve glared at him. "Don't even think about it."

CHAPTER TWENTY-ONE

For Dr. Mark Sloan, being left alone with the files, the reports, and the data on the boards was bliss. It was intriguing, challenging, and occupied his mind far more than being in a hospital bed watching TV or reading magazines.

While coming home had its risks, infection being chief among them, the dangers were outweighed by his belief that being in a comfortable environment and engaging his mind and spirit with research would have genuine recuperative value.

Of course, if one of his patients had tried to use those rationalizations on him as a reason to check out early from the hospital, he would have vehemently argued against it. He hoped his hypocrisy never got back to his patients.

The truth was, Mark simply wanted out, which was why he'd slipped away at dawn before Jesse, Amanda, or anyone else could block his escape.

He knew that Steve was frustrated and upset with him. But Mark was frustrated, too. There were still important pieces of the puzzle missing, and the answers were in this room.

Why couldn't Steve see that?

Mark was convinced that there was an overarching motivation or pattern to these killings beyond merely a sick game. His approach to the problem would be to examine each victim's profile, cataloging the commonalities and differences between them. He would use the ten victims Steve had identified as well as the ones who emerged from his dream.

As silly as it sounded, even to Mark, he didn't think of his dream as a dream. It was simply another form of concentration. The drama in his dream wasn't real, but the facts were. And yet the dramatic elements had investigative value, too. He was sure that the events, characters, and interactions held symbolic significance. All he had to do was interpret them and find the hidden meaning.

Yep, he thought. That was all he had to do.

Who was he kidding?

He barely had the energy to keep his eyes open, much less analyze the many possible meanings behind why he was married to a pediatric surgeon named Emily Noble or why Susan was pregnant and left brain-dead.

It was as if his own mind was taunting him.

Why couldn't his subconscious have just told him the important stuff flat-out without going to all the effort of symbolizing it?

To answer that, Mark would have to discover why people dream at all.

He decided to begin his toil by familiarizing himself with Guyot's victims. After barely an hour or so, he had to stop, unable to fight his growing fatigue, made worse by the soothing, rhythmic sound of the surf outside, which acted like a natural sedative.

Reluctantly, Mark cleared the files from the couch, stretched out, and took a nap.

Steve stopped by Krispy Kreme in Van Nuys, picked up a dozen glazed donuts and two cups of coffee, and headed east to Studio City, where Tanis Archer was parked outside of a condo complex off of Coldwater Canyon Boulevard, just north of the Ventura Freeway.

He got out of his truck and climbed into the front passenger seat of her car, setting the box of donuts between them and handing her a cup of coffee.

Tanis looked like she'd been sleeping in her clothes, though he knew she hadn't slept at all. Her eyes were red and ringed with dark circles. There were junk food containers piled on the backseat.

"Duren is inside the building, caring for a senile old lady," Tanis said, taking a donut and practically jamming the whole thing into her mouth.

"Does her first or last name start with *V*?"

"Clara Corn," she said, her mouth full. Steve thought he might have misunderstood her.

"Corn?"

"That's the name," Tanis said, while possibly setting a world record for the fastest consumption of a single original glazed donut. "Corn."

"Okay," Steve said. "I'll take over the surveillance from here."

"What about Guyot?" She reached for another donut, devouring half of it in one bite.

"He's at the hospital most of the day and she's on the move. So I picked her to keep an eye on, since we don't have the manpower to cover them both."

"Sure we do," Tanis said. "I'll stick with her while you cover Guyot."

"But who is going to relieve us? It's not going to look very good if Guyot and Duren kill someone and it turns out that one of us was sleeping outside while it happened."

"If I eat a couple more donuts, I'll have a sugar high that will carry me into next month," she said, reaching for a third donut. "I'll be wide awake."

"How can you eat donuts like that and stay so thin?"

"Tantric sex."

Steve gave her a look. She gave it right back to him.

"You're imagining me naked now, aren't you?" she said.

"No," Steve said. "I'm wondering if you're really going to eat that donut."

"How about calling in some favors with other cops, get them to help us in their free time?" She stuffed the donut into her mouth, meeting Steve's gaze as she did it.

"I have," Steve said.

"When are they starting?"

"You're it."

"How about recruiting some retired cops? They would probably jump at the chance to leave their mobile homes and security guard shacks." Tanis licked her sugary fingers, then reached for her cup of coffee.

"We've got enough civilians on this investigation as it is."

"Two of those civilians are going to find the next victim," Tanis said. "And your dad just might solve this case."

"It's solved," Steve snapped sharply.

Tanis made a show of recoiling. "Whoa. Have a donut. Raise your blood sugar before you shoot someone."

"Sorry," Steve said and remembered that he hadn't eaten breakfast yet. His blood sugar probably was low, especially after his run. He reached for a donut. "It's just that my dad can't accept that I solved this case before he could. He has more faith in a dream than he does in me."

Steve took a bite of his donut. It was incredibly sweet. He felt an immediate rush, as if the sugar was entering his bloodstream before he'd even swallowed his bite.

Tanis sipped her coffee like it was a fine wine. "He believes in you. But he's got a compulsive disorder. He's obsessed with puzzles and can't let go until *he* solves them. What you, me, or anybody else does won't change that. He's got to do it himself."

"Even if the puzzle is already finished?" Steve licked the frosting off his lips and took another bite.

Tanis nodded. "That's my cheap psychological insight of the day."

"Maybe you're right," Steve said. "Or maybe it terrifies him that I might be pretty good at this on my own."

Tanis set her coffee in a cup holder on the floor. "Of course it does, you moron. Mark's father abandoned him when he was a kid. His wife is dead. And he's made his home so cushy that you're in your forties and still haven't left the nest. Did it ever occur to you that he's afraid of being alone, that he solves crimes so you two have one more reason to stick together? If you don't need him anymore, you might abandon him."

Steve dropped the half-eaten donut back into the box. "More cheap insights?"

She shook her head. "Painfully obvious facts."

Steve's cell phone trilled. He reached into his jacket for his phone and Tanis reached for his half-eaten donut.

"Sloan," he answered.

It was Amanda and Jesse. They had a list.

They met in the morgue at Community General Hospital. Amanda and Jesse stood on one side of the autopsy table, facing Steve, their paperwork spread out in front of them like a corpse.

"Shouldn't Mark be here?" Amanda said.

"Yeah, in a hospital bed," Jesse said.

"Which is why we are going to keep him out of this," Steve said. "He's in no condition to be involved."

"He's not going to like it," Amanda said.

"It's for his own good," Steve said, glancing at Jesse for support.

"What Mark needs now is rest," Jesse said. "Susan is stopping by to check on him on his way home."

Steve could see Amanda wasn't happy about it. She sighed with resignation and directed her attention to the paperwork.

"Here's what we did. We didn't have access to the client records at Appleby Nursing Services," Amanda said, "but we were able to get into the systems at the various hospitals in the area."

"Because I have friends," Jesse said.

"So you've said," Steve replied.

"All the hospitals use the Enable software for their data-bases, so we knew how to find what we wanted once we got into their systems," Amanda said. "We got lists of patients who were in the intensive care or cardiac-care units of the hospitals over the last twelve months and who survived the experience."

"Then we just sifted out the people whose first or last names began with the letter *V*," Jesse said, handing Steve a sheet of paper. "As in, Voila."

Steve scanned the list. There were three people with first names—Vincent Kunz, Vivian Hemphill, and Victoria Sarnelle—and two with last names—Alan Vernon and Campbell Vroman—that began with *V*.

Jesse motioned to the other papers. "That's all their medical information, insurance providers, that kind of thing."

"It shouldn't be too hard to find out if Alan Vernon or Campbell Vroman is using private nursing care," Steve said.

"How do you pick who to put under surveillance?" Amanda asked.

"Anybody have a quarter I can flip?" Steve asked.

After two hours' sleep, Mark woke up dehydrated, his lips chapped and his mouth as dry as an old dishrag, probably with the smell to match.

He got to his feet, aching in every joint, leaning on his walker, and made his way to his bedroom. The journey seemed to take hours and all the strength he had. By the time he reached his bathroom, he was beginning to second-guess the wisdom of leaving the hospital.

But after brushing his teeth, drinking two large glasses of water, and putting some ChapStick on his lips, he felt human again and more or less revived.

He was making his way back to the living room, with a bit more speed and energy than his last trip down the hall, when Susan came in the front door carrying a take-out bag from Jerry's Famous Deli.

"Dr. Sloan, you scoundrel," she admonished him. "I should have put you in restraints after all."

"You really have to start calling me Mark, especially if you're going to scold me." He tipped his head towards her bag. The smell of hot food was making him salivate and his stomach growl. "What have you got there?"

"Chicken soup with matzo balls," she said.

"The perfect prescription for what ails me."

Susan went into the kitchen to prepare the food, and he followed slowly after her. When he got to the kitchen, with its spectacular view of the beach, she already had the bowls of soup set out, along with a platter of sliced cantaloupe and watermelon.

"Do you mind if I join you?" she asked, standing behind one of the chairs.

"I'd be upset if you didn't," Mark said, taking his seat.

While the two of them ate, they engaged in pleasant small talk about the weather, the remodeling of a local grocery store, and Susan's ongoing dispute with a mechanic about the repairs on her car.

Mark enjoyed their conversation immensely. Between her company and the hot soup, his spirits and his energy were buoyed considerably. He set his spoon down and looked her in the eye.

"Do you realize that in all the years I've known you, this is the first time we've been alone together outside of the hospital?"

Susan considered that for a moment. "To be honest, Doctor—" She caught herself. "Mark—you've always intimidated me. It was nothing you did or said. I just always felt like a tagalong, an outsider, even when I was helping in one of your investigations. But now that Jesse and I are married, I see you differently."

"Really? In what way?"

She shrugged. "Like a father-in-law."

Mark smiled, reached across the table and took her hand, giving it a squeeze. "Good, because that's exactly how I want it. This is your home now, too."

She squeezed his hand back. "Thank you. So, what's your plan for the day?"

"Nothing but rest."

"I'm family now, remember? What are you really going to be doing?"

He told her.

"Could you use an able-bodied assistant?"

He wasn't sure if she was offering to help because she was interested in the case or simply to have an excuse to stay and take care of him. Either way, it didn't really matter.

"Absolutely," he said.

CHAPTER TWENTY-TWO

Steve was quickly discovering the true benefits of the Patriot Act for law enforcement. For one thing, it meant that the Anti-Terrorism Strike Force had very little direct oversight of their activities and lots of high-tech toys that made it easy for them to invade people's privacy.

Tanis met Steve outside of Alan Vernon's bungalow in Santa Monica with a trunk full of tiny video surveillance devices. The cameras could send live audio and video feeds directly to a secure Web site, where they would be digitally stored and available for access anytime, anywhere by any cop with a high-speed connection and the right password.

The two detectives, as well as Amanda and Jesse, could have multiple live surveillance feeds playing in real time in separate windows on their laptops or desktop computers, allowing them to keep a protective eye on all the potential victims at once.

Steve was looking not just into a box of electronics but at the future of surveillance. No more Porta Pottis. Soon, he'd be able to sit in Starbucks with his laptop, enjoying a cup of coffee and cinnamon cake while keeping someone miles away under surveillance at the same time.

"Is this legal?" Steve asked they at stood at the back of Tanis's car, staring into the trunk.

"It is if each person gives us permission to install the equipment in their home."

That was the tricky part.

Steve couldn't tell the potential victims the real reason he wanted to put them under surveillance, not without panicking them. Instead he would have to come up with a convincing, but less than honest, explanation and hope it wouldn't undermine the cases against Duren and Guyot when they got to court.

"What kind of trouble are you going to get into for unofficially appropriating this equipment?" Steve asked.

"Let's just say I won't be getting a promotion when my bosses eventually find out about this."

"Even if using this equipment leads to the apprehension of two serial killers?"

"Catching the Silent Partner didn't send my career soaring to new heights."

"It might have if you'd played by the rules on your subsequent cases."

"If I'd played by the rules, we wouldn't be standing here having this conversation and I wouldn't have this stuff, which, I might add, you desperately need right now."

"Good point," Steve said.

Tanis hefted the box out of the trunk and they walked together to Alan Vernon's door. Vernon had been released from John Muir Hospital two months earlier after surviving a massive heart attack. It was his second coronary episode and, given his medical history, probably wouldn't be his last.

"How come I have to carry the stuff?" Tanis complained.

"You brought it. It's your responsibility," Steve said. "I'm the lead investigator. My hands need to be free to deal with situations."

"What situations?"

"Like this." Steve made a show of knocking on the door.

It took a few moments for Vernon to get to the door. Steve could hear him slowly approach. He was tempted to knock again impatiently, but it wouldn't get the man to the door any faster.

Finally, after what seemed like hours, the door was opened by a paunchy, balding man in his sixties with a thin black mustache. He leaned on a cane, wore a Nautica pullover and leather loafers with Velcro straps, and chewed mint gum with a flavor so strong that both Steve and Tanis could taste it.

"Mr. Vernon?" Steve said.

"Yes, that's me, Alan Vernon." The man had the baritone voice of an anchorman and replied as if he was facing a camera instead of two cops.

Steve half expected Vernon to continue with, "Reporting live from Santa Monica."

Soon, with any luck, he would be.

"I'm Lieutenant Steve Sloan, LAPD." He flashed his badge, and so did Tanis. "This is Detective Archer. May we come in?"

Vernon stepped aside. "Is this regarding my gardener?"

"Why is that?" Steve asked as they entered his modest home.

"I think he's an illegal, from one of those Latin American countries. A lot of them sneak over the border with drugs packed in their rectums. Or worse."

Steve couldn't imagine what that other contraband might be, nor did he want to.

"We aren't with immigration or the DEA," Steve said, taking a quick glance at the decor. Most of the furniture was twenty years old. He made a mental note to himself never to buy contemporary furniture. "We're investigating a crime involving nursing services."

"I'm not surprised," Vernon said, standing in place. "What are they stealing? Cash? Jewelry? Credit cards?"

"That's what we hope to find out," Steve said. "I understand you're a client of Appleby Nursing Services."

"Not for much longer," Vernon said. "I'm almost back to

peak shape. My friends call me Mount Vernon. Get it? That's how sturdy I am."

But Vernon hadn't moved from where he stood, so as not to show his guests he was weak. He seemed to be the kind of man who found it humiliating to reveal such vulnerability. Steve understood that failing all too well.

"How do you feel about being on camera?" Steve asked.

"Radio news was my game for thirty-five years, but I always felt I would have made a fine on-camera personality," Vernon said.

Tanis took one of the tiny cameras out of the box and held it up beside her face as if she was advertising a tube of toothpaste.

"Now is your chance," she said.

Victoria Sarnelle was a woman who lived alone and craved company. She'd nearly died after her quadruple bypass surgery, but there was nothing frail about her now. She was a formidable and astonishingly talkative person who did everything in her power to keep Steve and Tanis from leaving after they installed the surveillance cameras. Steve was afraid he might have to shoot his way out of captivity. But they managed to escape without bloodshed.

Vincent Kunz was worried that the police would use the cameras to spy on him having sex, even though his last erotic encounter had been during the Reagan administration. That was when his ex-wife, Rhonda, used cameras to catch him cheating on her with her best friend. Steve assured Mr. Kunz that they weren't interested in his love life and talked him into granting them permission to install the equipment. Tanis predicted that the cameras would give Kunz a thrill, that they would actually motivate him to take a lover just so he could show off. Steve prayed she was wrong because he didn't want to have to watch that.

There was no answer when they pressed Vivian Hemphill's buzzer outside her apartment building in

Tarzana. Steve buzzed the manager's apartment, and after a moment he heard a woman's voice crackling over the speaker.

"Yes?" Her voice was like a bark. She obviously didn't like to be bothered.

Steve looked up and addressed the large security camera positioned in a corner above the front doors. The camera was gigantic by today's standards but probably was cutting edge back in the eighties.

"I'm Lieutenant Steve Sloan, LAPD, and this is Detective Tanis Archer." He held his badge up to the camera. "We're here to see Vivian Hemphill. She doesn't seem to be answering her buzzer, and we were wondering if you knew where she might be."

"Sure do," the woman said. "Hartley and Hartley Mortuary."

Steve and Tanis shared a glance. They were too late.

"She's dead?" he said.

"Viv isn't laying in the coffin because it's more comfortable for her back."

Score one point for Paul Guyot, Steve thought.

"When did she die?" Tanis asked.

"Yesterday," the voice said. "I hear she had another heart attack. Are either of you looking for a place to live? Viv has a corner apartment with spectacular city views."

There was no such thing as a spectacular view in the flats of Tarzana, but Steve wanted a look around the apartment.

"That would be delightful," he said.

"Did you just say delightful?" Tanis whispered.

The manager buzzed them through and was waiting in the lobby when they came in. An elderly woman with a bee-hive hairdo, she was wearing a housedress and a string of fake pearls the size of hard-boiled eggs. She introduced herself as Mabel Folkner and took them to the fourth floor and down a long corridor to the corner apartment.

Many of the apartment doors that they passed were ajar,

affording Steve a peek inside the units. Almost all of the apartments were occupied by senior citizens sitting in recliners watching Dr. Phil.

Mabel unlocked the door to Vivian Hemphill's apartment. Steve and Tanis slipped on rubber gloves. Mabel cocked an eyebrow.

"Viv had heart disease," she said. "It's not contagious."

"Force of habit," Steve said. "We'd appreciate it if you didn't touch anything once we're inside."

"Why?" she asked. "Has there been a crime?"

"You never know," Tanis said, letting her voice trail off mysteriously.

"We're suspicious by nature," Steve said. "It's an occupational hazard."

The front door opened directly into the combination kitchen and living room. A short hallway led to the bathroom and the one bedroom. The place smelled of antiseptic and air freshener and age. Every inch of wall space was covered with family photos of all sizes.

The central feature of the living room was the recliner, of course, which faced a TV in a wooden cabinet from an era when they were considered pieces of furniture. A hand-knit blanket was draped over the back of the recliner and a TV tray was positioned beside it, the latest issues of *TV Guide*, *Soap Opera Digest* and the *National Examiner* laid out beside the remote control.

"She died right there in her favorite chair," Mabel said.

"Who found her?" Tanis asked.

"Her son Norman," she said. "He came by to deliver her weekly allowance for groceries and things."

Steve noticed that there were no signs of forced entry or a break-in. "Do you have tapes of the visitors who came and went over the last forty-eight hours?"

"No," Mabel said.

"You don't keep the tapes?"

"Our camera doesn't record," she said. "We use it to see

who is ringing the buzzer. No one gets in who doesn't belong."

So whoever killed Vivian Hemphill was someone she either knew or was expecting. Like a nurse she'd met at the hospital, coming to check on how she was doing.

"Isn't that an incredible view?" Mabel held both her hands up to the window, as if she was one of those models presenting the showcase prizes on *The Price Is Right*. She was a little old even for Bob Barker.

Steve looked out at the other apartment buildings on White Oak Boulevard, the traffic on the Ventura Freeway, and the open Dumpsters behind Valu-Rite Oil and Lube.

"Charming," he said.

"There's more. We have a potluck dinner the last Friday of every month down by the pool," she said. "You haven't lived until you've tasted my marshmallow salad. I know you'd be very happy here."

"I don't think we're old enough," Tanis said.

"To be honest," Mabel said conspiratorially, "we're trying to attract a younger demographic."

Steve met Norman Hemphill, the late Vivian Hemphill's forty-seven-year-old son, at the mortuary in Burbank and asked for permission to have his mother moved to the morgue for an autopsy. Tanis was in the car on the phone, arranging for the transfer of the body on the assumption that Norman would agree.

Norman Hemphill was turnip-shaped, with the basset-hound face of a man continually suffering all of life's woes.

"I don't understand," he whined. "Dr. Endicott said she died of natural causes. She was done in by old age, a weak ticker, and a pack-a-day cigarette habit."

"We have reason to believe that she met with foul play," Steve said.

"What reason?" Norman asked.

"I wish I could tell you, but I can't, not without jeopardizing an ongoing homicide investigation."

"But I already invited everyone to the funeral," Norman said.

"I'm sure they will understand."

Norman frowned. "Will this cost me extra?"

"Excuse me?" Steve asked.

"Am I going to have to pay for the autopsy?"

"No," Steve said.

"Will there be any associated costs related to the autopsy?" Norman said. "You know, in terms of making her presentable for an open-casket funeral."

"I don't think so, but if there are, we'll work something out with the mortuary."

"If she was murdered, does that mean I don't have to pay for the funeral?"

"No," Steve said. "You still have to pay for it."

"Shouldn't the murderer have to pay the bill, since it's his fault she's dead?"

"You'd think so," Steve said. "But sadly, that isn't the case."

"Then what good will it do me to have her autopsied?"

Steve stared at him. "Because if she was murdered, the autopsy will help us gather the evidence we need to put whoever did it behind bars for life."

"And if she wasn't murdered?"

"Then no harm done," Steve said.

Norman considered it for a moment and then nodded his head with a world-weary, life-weary, and all-around-weary sigh.

"I can't imagine who would want to kill her," Norman said. "It's not like there was anything to inherit."

"I guess that rules you out, then," Steve said.

*   *   *

After several hours of going through the medical files with Susan, Mark was no closer to understanding what was going on than he was before.

The one thing that became clear very quickly was that his son was right about the "game over" pattern and that the deaths Mark was investigating had occurred before, and during, the time frame of those ten murders.

Mark was trying to determine if the deaths that he found suspicious were actually moves in another game, one that was being played at the same time but under a different set of rules.

If so, what were those rules?

He made a list of the victims he'd identified so far:

> Grover Dawson
> Sandy Sechrest
> Hammond McNutchin
> Joyce Kling
> Leila Pevney
> Chadwick Saxelid

There were probably others, Mark feared, but these were the only names he had at the moment. He organized the victims alphabetically by first and last names, and then chronologically by date of death as well as date of birth, trying to see if another word was spelled out by the first letters of their given names or their surnames.

There wasn't.

Susan ran the names through several anagram programs that she'd found on the Web, to see if the names alone or in pairs or all together spelled anything interesting.

They didn't.

Mark tried integrating his list of names with those of the other ten victims, rearranging them alphabetically and chronologically again. Still, nothing came of it. The anagram program gave them hundreds of awkward sentences.

So Mark and Susan examined the causes of death.

The ten cases that Steve investigated all seemed to be deaths by natural causes.

The six deaths that Mark was examining appeared, at least on the surface, to be a mix of natural causes, fatal drug interactions, and tragic accidents. Joyce Kling was a lupus patient who died of respiratory failure. Chadwick Saxelid took his nitro tablets when he shouldn't have. Leila Pevney succumbed to an overdose of sinus medication. Sandy Sechrest was electrocuted when her hair dryer fell in the bathtub. And so it went.

What those six victims had in common was that they had all survived previous brushes with death, they were all missing personal items, and they all got their prescriptions filled by Kemper-Carlson.

What about the other ten victims?

Only two of the ten were covered by insurance companies that required them to use Kemper-Carlson to deliver their medications. Unfortunately, there was no way for Mark and Susan to determine if the victims were missing anything unless they went out and interviewed their next of kin or close friends.

By nightfall, both he and Susan were exhausted and their efforts had accomplished nothing. But he was glad to have had the opportunity to spend the day working with her. She was conscientious, thorough, and single-minded. And yet, there was never a moment during the day when Mark wasn't aware of her keeping a watchful eye on him, attuned to the slightest change in his comfort or level of energy.

She brought him food, coffee, and medication before he was even aware he needed or wanted it. There was a reason she was such a good nurse.

The affection that Mark felt for Susan was undoubtedly heightened by the memory of nearly losing her. Although it was just a bad dream, he still felt the lingering sadness and fear. He wanted her to know how much he appreciated her, especially since he'd obviously been remiss in showing it before.

He felt as if he'd lived his own personal version of *It's a Wonderful Life* and now had a chance to recognize the wrongs he'd done and right them before it was too late.

Mark thanked her for coming and made a point of telling her how much he'd enjoyed their time together, even though much of it was spent hunched over files and laptop computer screens.

"I enjoyed it, too, Dr. Sloan," she said, then added, "I mean, Mark."

Susan had to go home and get some sleep before her next shift, but she didn't leave until she'd changed Mark's bandages and got him to promise he'd call her if he needed anything at all.

Mark kept working on the files for a while after she left, looking for that elusive pattern, but it didn't emerge—and even if it had, he would have been too tired to see it.

It was there, though, right in front of his face. He was convinced of it.

He trudged off to bed.

CHAPTER TWENTY-THREE

Susan was alive but dead.

Mark knew it was her even though her head injuries were so bad it looked as if her face had been attacked with a machete.

Her body was laid out on a bed in the ICU. She wasn't a human being anymore. She was an incubator. All kinds of tubes ran between her and the life-support equipment, sustaining her body so that the unborn child in her swollen belly might live. But the machines were covered with dust and cobwebs, dragged out of the hospital basement, where they had apparently been rotting for at least twenty-five years. It was amazing that they still worked.

Susan was wearing a bloodstained wedding dress, which was bizarre, since she wasn't wearing it when she had her accident. But that wasn't the only weird thing about it. She was wearing Emily Noble's wedding dress, the one Emily had worn when she married Mark.

Emily was standing right there beside the bed, but she didn't seem to care about the wedding dress or the woefully outdated equipment. She looked over to Mark.

"There isn't going to be a problem keeping her alive until the baby comes to term," Emily said.

"What will happen to the baby after that?" Mark asked, much to his own surprise. There were lots of other, more

pressing questions on his mind. He wasn't exactly sure what those questions were, but he knew they had to be a lot more important than the one he'd asked.

"That's for social services to decide," Emily said. "I'm sure she'll go to a good family."

"She?"

"It's a girl," Emily said.

Mark awoke with a jolt, instantly alert, the bizarre dream still fresh in his mind. He was in his bed at the beach house, the morning light leaking between the closed slats of the shutters on his windows.

He reviewed the dream. Once again, he'd been married to Emily Noble and Susan was brain-dead and pregnant.

What was the meaning of Susan's tragic fate? Why was Susan wearing Emily's wedding dress? Why was it bloody? Why was all the life-support equipment so old? Why was Mark married to Emily Noble and what did she represent?

As weird as the dream was, there was something unsettlingly familiar about it.

Was it because it harked back to the dreams he had had while he was at Community General? Or was there something else about it that was tugging at his memory?

What the hell was his subconscious trying to tell him?

He wouldn't find out by lying in bed.

Mark threw off his sheets, put on his bathrobe, and using his walker for support, went down the hall to the living room. He was still weak and light-headed, but his strength was returning fast. With luck, he would be able to ditch the walker and rely on a cane for support before the day was out.

He found Steve, already dressed for work, adding another name to the list of Guyot's victims on the dry-erase board. Steve wasn't telling Mark about it; he was just adding a note to a board, as if the information wasn't worth sharing. It felt to Mark like a betrayal.

"There was another murder?" Mark said, trying hard to mask his feelings.

Steve turned to his father. "Not that we can prove yet. But yes, there was another one. How are you feeling this morning?"

"Like someone drilled a hole in my head." And stabbed me in the back, Mark thought. He read the name on the board: Vivian Hemphill. "How did you find out about her death?"

"She was one of the names on the list," Steve said. "We just didn't get to her in time."

"What list?" Mark said. There was no disguising the edge in his voice anymore.

Steve grimaced. This was clearly a conversation he wanted to avoid, at least for now.

So why did Steve add the name to the list at all? Mark wondered. It certainly wasn't for Mark's benefit.

Steve had done it for himself, so he could get a clear picture of the crime, to see if actually looking at the facts in front of him jogged any new conclusions.

"A list of potential victims," Steve said. "People with first or last names that begin with *V*. Amanda and Jesse put it together for us yesterday."

Mark felt his face flushing with anger, but he tried to keep his voice steady. Steve would get sullen and defensive in response to anger, and Mark knew he would get more attitude and even less information from him if that happened.

"Why wasn't I told about this list?" Mark asked.

"Because it didn't involve you."

"They tried to kill me. I had to have a hole drilled in my skull to save my life," Mark said evenly. "That makes me involved."

"You were in no condition to go down to the morgue for a briefing."

"So you could have had it here," Mark said. "Or you could have simply called me up and put me on the speaker."

"Why? We know who the killers are. What difference would it have made telling you about the list?" Steve said, the color rising in his face now, too. "Vivian Hemphill would still be dead. Nothing would have changed."

"I could have helped you."

"How?" Steve snapped. "What could you have done that would have made any difference at all?"

"We'll never know now, will we?"

"You're supposed to be in a hospital bed. The last thing you should be doing is trying to help anyone. You need to take care of yourself and leave the police work to me."

Mark glared at him defiantly. "Were there any personal items missing from the victim? Did she get her drugs from Kemper-Carlson?"

"I don't know. Her name began with a *V*. That's all that matters right now."

"Did anyone see Guyot or Duren at the scene?"

Steve had a decision to make. He could walk away now and end this conversation for the time being or give his father the answers he wanted and hope that would mollify him rather than provoke him into action.

Mark knew the alternatives his son was weighing and waited for him to decide.

Steve sighed, giving in. When he spoke, the anger was gone from his voice, replaced by weariness. "No. She lived in an apartment building. There's a closed-circuit security camera at the door so residents can see who is ringing their buzzers. But the camera isn't hooked to any recording device. The camera is so old, it probably only records to kinescope anyway."

"What about fingerprints and other forensic evidence in the apartment?"

"Until we have some proof that Vivian Hemphill didn't die of natural causes I can't bring in a CSI unit," Steve said. "Even if I could, I'm pretty certain we wouldn't find anything useful. These nurses are pretty slick about covering their tracks."

"There's always the body."

Steve gave his dad a withering look, as if Mark had reminded him that it was necessary to breathe. "I talked the
victim's son into letting Amanda do an autopsy. I'm waiting
on the results."

"Let me know when they come in."

"Dad, there is no mystery here," Steve said firmly. "We
know who the killers are. All the autopsy will do is confirm
what we already know is going on."

Mark moved closer to his son and looked him in the eye.
When he spoke, he tried to do so without bitterness. "Why
are you shutting me out of this investigation?"

"I'm not," Steve said. "I'm trying to keep you healthy.
The investigation is over. All that is left now is the
endgame."

"You haven't caught them yet," Mark said. "So where
does that leave the other potential victims? What are you
doing for them?"

"We have them under constant surveillance."

"I thought you didn't have any manpower besides Tanis
Archer," Mark said.

"I don't even have *her* officially. I have the targets under
electronic surveillance."

Steve motioned to a laptop that was open and running on
the kitchen table. He explained that the screen was divided
into four windows, each showing a wide-angle live video
and audio feed from a target's home.

"Meanwhile, we're watching the two psycho nurses the
old-fashioned way," Steve continued. "Tanis is parked outside of Paul Guyot's house, which is where Duren spent the
night. They're still there. I just came back for a shower and
a fresh set of clothes."

Mark glanced at the laptop, then back to his son with a
look of disapproval. "You're using those innocent people as
bait."

"I didn't pick them," Steve said. "The killers did."

"You could place them all in protective custody," Mark said.

"No, I can't. I don't have the evidence." Steve went to the kitchen table and started packing his laptop and cables into a leather carrying case.

"You could warn them," Mark insisted, hobbling after him. "Let them know that Guyot and Duren are dangerous."

"I can't do that either, for the same reason. No evidence."

"Better safe than sorry."

"It's not that simple, Dad. If we warn these people and Guyot or Duren finds out, the two of them could disappear tomorrow, show up somewhere else with new names and start their killing game all over again. Or they could stick around and sue the department for spreading career-damaging lies about them, which would cost me my badge and the city millions of dollars. Or—"

"I get the point," Mark interrupted. "But there has to be a better way."

"When you think of one, let me know." Steve grabbed his laptop case and walked to the door.

"I thought you didn't need my help," Mark said to his back.

Steve stopped, let out a deep breath, then turned back to face Mark. "Please try to rest, Dad. If you have your heart set on solving crimes today, do me and yourself a big favor and watch some *Murder, She Wrote* reruns instead."

He turned and walked out, slamming the door behind him.

Amanda called Steve on his cell phone five minutes after he left the house. He was in his car, heading south on the Pacific Coast Highway and already regretting his argument with his father—not that there was any way he could have avoided it. They would patch things up when the case was closed and Mark was himself again.

"I've just finished the autopsy," Amanda said. "I thought you'd like the headlines before I write up my report."

"Give me the front-page headline," Steve said.

"I'm calling it murder," Amanda said.

Steve thought that was an unusual way of putting it, an equivocation of sorts. "What would someone else call it?"

"Natural causes."

"But you're the medical examiner," Steve said. "It's what you say that counts."

"Until we get into court. Then what counts is whatever the jury believes."

"Tell me what you believe."

"Vivian Hemphill's doctor determined, based on her age, past medical history, and external evidence, that she died from cardiac arrest," Amanda said. "He was right. She did. But I found what I consider to be unusually high levels of epinephrine in her blood. The drug can cause a lethal change in the heart rate, especially for someone her age and with advanced coronary disease."

"You found the drug in her system," Steve said. "Sounds open and shut to me."

Amanda let out a deep breath. "In the final moments before death, your body releases large amounts of epinephrine from the adrenal glands in a last-ditch effort to survive. Think of it as your internal cardiologist trying to jolt you back to life. So finding high levels of epinephrine in the blood after death isn't unusual. That's what makes epinephrine poisoning very difficult to prove."

"Even if the level of epinephrine in her blood is higher than normal?"

"That's the problem. Unless the level of epinephrine is outrageously high, it's hard to know how much of it is endogenous, from within the body, and how much was introduced exogenously, from outside the body," Amanda said. "It's a subjective determination. I'm saying that based on my experience, Vivian Hemphill's epinephrine level was too high. Another ME might disagree."

And Steve was sure that whoever defended Guyot and Duren in court would find at least one expert witness who would convincingly dispute Amanda's findings.

Steve swore to himself.

Guyot and Duren weren't simply thrill killers. They were *careful* thrill killers. It took cunning to choose a drug that the body produces naturally and inject just enough into the victims to kill them but not enough to clearly indicate murder.

"She wasn't on an IV," Steve said. "So if she was injected with epinephrine, there must be a puncture mark somewhere on her body."

"There was," Amanda said.

Steve smiled to himself. Even the most clever killers have to make a mistake sometime. "Well, isn't that all the proof we need that she was injected with epinephrine?"

"It would be, except—"

He interrupted her. "Oh no, please don't say 'except.' I don't want to hear 'except.'"

"Vivian Hemphill saw her doctor the morning of her death and was given a blood test. The puncture wound could be from that."

Guyot knew she'd gone in to John Muir for an exam. He planned the murder to coincide with her visit. And he gave her the deadly injection in the same spot where the doctor had drawn blood.

Oh, they're clever all right, Steve thought.

"If we were to exhume the other victims," he asked, "would you be able to detect if they also had high levels of epinephrine in their tissues?"

"If the bodies are still mostly intact, probably," she said. "But if the bodies are severely decayed, embalmed, or only skeletal remains exist, no."

Steve slammed his fist against the dashboard in fury. "So we're back where we started."

"Not quite," Amanda said. "I'm saying that Vivian Hemphill was murdered. That makes this an official homicide investigation now."

"But I still can't arrest Guyot or Duren," Steve said. "I don't have anything."

"Now you have a corpse," Amanda said.

"No," Steve said grimly. "Now I have eleven of them. This is just the only one that hasn't been buried yet."

CHAPTER TWENTY-FOUR

Steve met Tanis in her car, which was parked up the street from Guyot's house. Her laptop was open on the passenger seat. Her cell phone was plugged into the computer, giving her an Internet connection. On the screen, she had the four surveillance feeds up and running.

"You're really multitasking," Steve said.

"I figure if Guyot or Duren were to slip past me, which is entirely possible given how tired I am, I'd better keep an eye on our targets, too."

"You just want to see if Vincent Kunz has sex."

"I've got twenty bucks riding on that bet," she said. "The old man is going to get lucky. You'll see."

"I don't want to see," Steve said. "Go home. I'll take over watching Wendy Duren. Get some sleep and a shower. Especially a shower."

"Who is going to watch Guyot?"

"Jesse will follow him until you've rested up," Steve said. "Guyot is working in the hospital all day anyway. He won't make his move, if he's going to make one, until nightfall."

"Are you willing to gamble one of their lives on that?" Tanis said, gesturing to the live feeds on the laptop. The four targets all seemed to have forgotten the cameras were there; they were going about their business without so much as a glance at the lens.

"I may not have to for much longer," Steve said. "Amanda says that Vivian Hemphill was murdered. We can get some more detectives on this stakeout detail."

"Based on what?" Tanis said. "Until you've got real evidence that can link Guyot and Duren to her death, the captain will never okay the overtime for surveillance."

"Since when are you the voice of reason?"

"Fatigue makes me reasonable. I lose the energy to delude myself," Tanis said, punctuating her comment with a yawn. "How's your dad?"

"Mad," Steve said. "He thinks he's being excluded from the investigation."

"He is."

"The man should be in a hospital," Steve said irritably. "He's in no shape to be involved."

"Is that the reason?"

"Yeah," Steve said. "What the hell else do you think it is?"

"Why don't you the hell tell me?" she said.

"Sweet dreams." Steve got out, slammed the door, and marched back to his own car.

"Gee," Tanis said to herself. "I wonder if I touched a nerve."

Jesse stopped by the beach house on his way to John Muir Hospital. He was going to take Malibu Canyon into the Valley, thus avoiding the gridlock and misery of the northbound San Diego Freeway.

"What are you going to the Valley for?" Mark asked while Jesse changed his bandages and examined the burr hole in his skull.

"Steve didn't tell you?"

"I'm out of the loop," Mark said.

Jesse hesitated. "I'm following Paul Guyot while Tanis rests up."

"I'd like to tag along," Mark said casually.

"This is a twist," Jesse said. "Usually I'm the one begging to be included."

"Now you finally have the chance to return the favor."

"I wish I could."

"You can," Mark said.

"You shouldn't even be home, much less sitting in a car on a stakeout."

"I'll just be sitting in your car instead of on this couch," Mark said. "Plus I'll be under a physician's observation at all times."

"I can't," Jesse said. "I'm saying that as your doctor and as your friend."

"If you were my friend, you'd bring me along."

"You're not really missing anything, anyway. The case is all but over."

"What did Amanda find in her autopsy on Vivian Hemphill?"

Jesse told him. Mark raised an eyebrow. "That doesn't make any sense."

"It's how they made the deaths look like natural causes," Jesse said.

"Not Grover Dawson, not Joyce Kling, not Chadwick Saxelid," Mark said. "The MO isn't consistent."

"Maybe because they weren't murdered."

Mark looked Jesse in the eye. "You're doubting me now, too?"

Jesse shifted his gaze. "No, it's just that—"

"What?" Mark prodded. "Say it."

"You did your investigation in a coma. Are you really surprised that what you discovered doesn't fit perfectly with the real-world investigation?"

"I didn't dream up the facts," Mark said.

"Epinephrine could have been used to kill the patients at Beckman Hospital, couldn't it?"

"Yes," Mark said.

"And those murders didn't spell 'Game Over,' did they?"

"No."

"And those deaths didn't appear to be accidents or fatal drug interactions, did they?"

"No."

"So the only cases that aren't consistent with epinephrine poisoning are the ones you pulled out of your dream."

Jesse had never challenged Mark like this before. Mark didn't particularly like it. The defiance especially irritated him since he knew that Jesse wouldn't be challenging him unless the young doctor felt he had a strong argument and his mentor was obviously in the wrong.

"Those were the cases I was investigating before I hit my head," Mark said. "I didn't imagine them."

"Do you think Paul Guyot and Wendy Duren are killers?"

"Yes," Mark said.

"Do you believe that between them they've killed at least eleven people?"

"Yes."

"Then why are you arguing with Steve?"

Mark sighed. "Because something doesn't fit. We're missing something."

"All the pieces will fall into place after those two nurses are arrested."

"And if they don't?"

"At least two killers will be off the street and in prison." Jesse finished bandaging Mark's head and admired his handiwork. "I'd like to schedule the bone graft for early next week."

Mark shrugged. "You're the doctor."

"You have to be very careful. The risk of infection is high. And if you were to trip and fall, your head could crack open like an egg."

"I won't wear my roller skates today."

"Good idea. I'll see you tomorrow."

Jesse smiled and hurried off to play detective, leaving Mark alone and on the sidelines of the investigation.

But the more Mark thought about it, the less angry he became. So what if he wasn't on the street? So what if he wasn't included in the briefings? If he could solve most of the mystery while in a coma in a hospital bed, he could certainly figure out the rest while conscious in his living room.

After all, the missing pieces were right here, hidden in the patient files and in the images in his dreams.

All he had to do was figure it out.

How hard could it be?

Mark sat himself down with the files again and went to work. He wasn't sure what he was looking for, but he hoped he'd know it when he saw it.

Paul Guyot left the house first, bouncing to the beat of whatever he was listening to on his iPod. Steve called ahead to Jesse, who was just arriving in front of the John Muir Hospital parking structure. He told Jesse to call him the moment Guyot showed up.

Ten minutes after Guyot drove off, Wendy Duren emerged from the house in her Appleby nurse's uniform, her hair still wet from her shower. She got into her car and drove to the Starbucks on Ventura Boulevard. Steve was tempted to follow her inside, if only to get himself a fresh coffee.

She emerged carrying a cup of coffee and a paper bag, got into her car, and drove east on Ventura Boulevard. He stayed a couple of car lengths behind her as she took the onramp and merged onto the eastbound Ventura Freeway.

Duren stayed in the far right lane. Steve moved one lane over, and as the traffic ebbed and flowed, he found himself at times either a car length or two in front of her or behind her.

Steve didn't dare glance at her when he passed her car for fear of catching her eye. They were transitioning to the southbound San Diego Freeway when Jesse called Steve to report that Guyot had arrived at John Muir Hospital.

"Stay on him until Tanis shows up," Steve said. "If he leaves, call me right away."

"You got it," Jesse said excitedly. "This is fun."

"Let's see how fun you think it is after you've been sitting there for a few hours, you back is aching, your legs are stiff, and your bladder is about to burst."

"I've got my laptop tuned in to the four possible targets."

"See anything?"

"Vincent Kunz is picking his nose and reading the sports section."

"Detective work doesn't get much more exciting than that," Steve said and hung up.

Wendy Duren took the westbound Santa Monica Boulevard exit off the San Diego Freeway. On a hunch, Steve dialed Appleby Nursing Services and got the receptionist.

"Hello, my name is Phil Bevnic. I'm Wendy Duren's brother-in-law," Steve said. "Her sister has had a little accident. Nothing too serious, just a broken arm, but I thought she should know. I called over to Clara Corn's place, but they said she wasn't working there today."

"She was there yesterday," the receptionist said. "Have you tried her cell?"

"Yeah," Steve said. "I couldn't reach her. She must be in a bad zone. The Sepulveda Pass or one of the canyons."

"Do you have Roberta Karsch's phone number?"

"Is she the one in Santa Monica?"

"No, Mrs. Karsch lives in North Hollywood," the receptionist said. "Wendy should be there around noon. You could try her there."

The receptionist gave Steve the number, but he didn't pay any attention to it. His heart was pounding so hard the sound of it drowned out her words. He thanked her and ended the call.

It looked like Wendy Duren might be in a big hurry to catch up with her lover by scoring a kill and a *V* of her own.

The endgame could be coming sooner than Steve had thought.

He had a pretty good idea where Duren was going.

Steve broke off his tail, made a hard left off the boulevard, and took a shortcut, putting his bubble light on the top of his truck as soon as he was out of Duren's sight. He weaved at high speed around cars and roared through intersections to gain time on his adversary.

He was parked in front of Alan Vernon's house, with his laptop powered up and already streaming the live audio and visual feed when Wendy Duren drove past him and disappeared around the corner.

Steve wasn't worried about losing her. He figured she was parking away from the house so no one would take note of her car and license plate.

Sure enough, she appeared on foot a few moments later, carrying her Starbucks bag and with her nursing uniform unbuttoned just enough to show a tantalizing hint of cleavage.

As she walked up to Vernon's front door, Steve opened his glove box, took out a handheld TV that was about the size of an iPod, and tuned it to the short-range signal emitted from the surveillance cameras.

He got the earpiece in place just as Vernon opened the front door. The sound and picture were crisp and clear on the tiny screen.

"Mr. Vernon?" Duren asked.

"Alan Vernon," he said boldly, as if introducing himself to her and a television audience, which, as it turned out, he was. "What can I do for you, young lady?"

"I'm Wendy Duren from Appleby Nursing Services."

"That would explain the nurse's uniform," he said with a grin. "I wasn't expecting anyone from the agency until this afternoon."

Steve got out of his truck, closed the door quietly, and made his way towards the house, crouching and using the row of parked cars for concealment. He kept his eyes on the tiny TV screen.

"Your doctor called us this morning. He says you need a shot and he didn't want you to have to schlep all the way to his office in your condition, not for the two seconds it will take to get the injection." She held up the Starbucks bag and flashed her best smile. "I have some sweets to make up for the sting."

Steve wondered if she was referring to her pastries or her open shirt or both. Whatever enticements she was offering, they worked. Vernon stepped aside and welcomed death into his home.

CHAPTER TWENTY-FIVE

It was the most gripping drama Jesse had ever seen. One of the killer nurses was in Alan Vernon's house. And, incredibly, Jesse could see and hear it all as he sat in his parked car in the San Fernando Valley. But he wasn't watching a DVD of a TV show or a movie on his laptop. This was real life. There were no immunity idols or tribal councils. The loser of this reality show was going either to prison or to the grave.

From the day they were born, Alan Vernon, Wendy Duren, and Steve Sloan had been following an inexorable trajectory to the next few moments.

This was too compelling to miss. Jesse couldn't have stopped watching even if he'd wanted to.

And he didn't.

So he stared at his screen in stunned fascination as the deadly scene unfolded. Meanwhile, people walked by on the sidewalk outside, completely unaware of him or the violent forces of fate that were converging like three runaway trains on a tiny bungalow in Santa Monica.

Wendy Duren opened the bag of pastries and set them out for Alan Vernon on the living room table, then helped him to his seat, pressing his arm against her side so he could feel her breast against his skin.

"I hope you like cinnamon coffee cake and blueberry muffins, Mr. Vernon."

"I love them," Vernon said, sitting carefully in his seat, facing the front door. "You didn't have to go to all this trouble for me."

"It was the least I could do," she said behind him, opening her purse and pulling out a syringe and a tiny vial.

"Sort of like a last meal?" He chuckled in that boisterous, insincere manner that had been perfected by anchormen, evangelists, and salesmen over the ages.

"You could say that," Duren said lightheartedly as she plunged the needle into the vial and drew out the drug.

"I'm not afraid of shots. I've had so many lately, I don't even feel them anymore." Vernon started rolling up the sleeve over his pale right arm.

"This will be your last shot," Duren said, turning around and approaching him.

"Do you promise?" Vernon asked, propping his arm on the armrest of the chair for her. A big vein pulsed in the crook of his elbow, just under his thin skin. She dabbed his skin with an antiseptic wipe.

"On your life," she said, tossing the wipe on the table and bringing the needle down to his skin, her thumb on the plunger.

"Mine?" he said with another chuckle. "Isn't it supposed to be *yours*?"

Things were happening too fast. Steve wasn't even at the front door yet. He tossed the TV set on the ground, drew his gun, and charged towards the house.

As he ran, Steve wondered if Vernon had set the dead bolt. He doubted it. Vernon probably hadn't even bothered to lock the door. The only thing holding the door in place would be a weak little doorknob.

Not that it mattered now. Steve was committed to action. There was no stopping, even if it meant breaking bones. He turned his left shoulder to the door, braced himself for the pain, and threw his entire body weight against it, propelled by the momentum of his run.

The door blasted open, splintering the wood of the doorframe, and Steve spun inside, landing in a firing stance, his gun aimed directly at Alan Vernon.

Wendy was behind Vernon, her left arm across his throat, her hand gripping his right shoulder, pinning him in his seat. Her right hand held the syringe, the needle tip already breaking his skin, a rivulet of blood rolling down his arm.

Alan Vernon was her hostage.

"LAPD. Game over, Wendy," Steve said. "You lose."

She licked her lips, her eyes darting around, as if she expected more cops to come crashing through the windows into the room.

"We know all about the game you've been playing with Paul Guyot and the bodies you left behind at Beckman Hospital," Steve said. "We also know about the epinephrine in that syringe."

"One move and he's dead," she said. "I'll empty this into his veins."

"Go ahead." Steve shrugged as if he didn't care, which allowed him to adjust his aim without drawing attention to it. "The paramedics are on the way."

"You better do what I tell you," she said, almost shrieking as her panic grew. "Once I inject this, there's nothing they can do to save him."

"The paramedics aren't for him," Steve said. "They're for you."

He fired in the same instant that he saw the meaning of his words register in her eyes.

The bullet slammed into her right shoulder, the force of the impact throwing her back. As she fell, she pulled Vernon and his chair down with her.

Steve was on her as she hit the floor, kicking the syringe away from her quivering, blood-splattered right hand. She wailed in agony and fury, kicking her feet and squirming like a child having a tantrum, knocking Vernon's chair away.

"You're under arrest for murder," Steve said, keeping his gun trained on her as he quickly read her her rights. When he was done, he glanced at Vernon, who lay on the floor by her feet. Vernon was making strange gasping sounds. "Are you all right, Mr. Vernon?"

"Were you telling the truth about those paramedics?" Vernon asked between gasps.

"No," Steve said.

"Then you better hurry up and call them."

Steve took another look at Vernon, a longer one this time. Vernon was clutching his left arm and grimacing in pain.

"I think I'm having a heart attack," Vernon said.

Mark Sloan sat exhausted on the couch, surrounded by papers, his head swimming with patient names and medical details, none of it gelling into anything substantial. Not only did all the database printouts look the same, but the cases themselves were beginning to blur into one. He was so tired, *everything* was blurring.

He set aside the files and closed his eyes, sliding down and letting his head rest on the top of the couch cushion behind him.

Forget the files, he told himself. Concentrate on the dream for a while instead.

Which dream?

The most recent, Mark decided, the one he'd had last night.

He deconstructed the dream into its most dramatic images. The brain-dead, pregnant nurse in the wedding dress. The twenty-five-year-old medical equipment. His wife, Emily, the pediatric surgeon.

The images were references to, and elaborations upon, similar moments from his coma dream. The new elements were the wedding dress and the twenty-five-year-old equipment.

Twenty-five. Where had that number come from?

Nowhere.

He'd simply assumed the equipment was twenty-five years old.

But why *that* number? Why not eighteen or twenty? Why not twenty-two or twenty-seven?

He tried to recall if the number twenty-five had ever come up in his coma dream.

It had.

It was when he went to see Emily performing the operation to save Susan's unborn child. What was it he'd thought in his dream?

This wouldn't be the first time a brain-dead mother had been kept alive until childbirth. It had been medically possible for decades. He'd done it himself twenty-five years ago.

He remembered the case now. A seven-months-pregnant medical student was seriously injured in a car accident on her honeymoon. Her husband was killed instantly, but she suffered massive head injuries that left her brain-dead.

The parallels to Susan in his dream were obvious. Susan was hit by a car, she was a nurse, and she was recently married. Jesse was dead, and she was left brain-dead.

In the real case, Mark made the difficult decision to keep the newlywed woman alive until the baby came to term.

Just like Emily did with Susan in his dream.

The baby girl survived and was taken by child services. Mark had no idea what had become of her.

Now that he thought about it, he recalled what the medical student was studying at the time of her accident.

Pediatrics.

Emily Noble's area of expertise.

It was obvious to him that his dreams were all about that incident twenty-five years ago. Mark couldn't remember the patient's name, but it wasn't Emily Noble, that much he knew.

So what was the significance of that case?

What was his subconscious trying to tell him?

How did it relate to the murders that Guyot and Duren were committing today?   .

Or was that memory also symbolic, a clue meant to lead him to yet another conclusion?

The answers weren't yet in his grasp. Even if they had been, by the time he asked himself those questions he was already drifting into sleep.

Jesse couldn't believe what he'd seen on his laptop. When it was over, he wanted to rush straight to the hospital. Instead, he unplugged his cell phone from the laptop and called 911 to get paramedics to the scene. And then he called Tanis Archer at home.

When she got done swearing at him for waking her up, he filled her in on what had happened. She told him to stay put until she arrived.

Within thirty minutes Tanis and half a dozen police officers took over the surveillance of Paul Guyot, freeing Jesse to break several traffic laws speeding back to Community General Hospital, where both Wendy Duren and Alan Vernon were being treated.

When Jesse arrived in the ER, he saw Steve in the middle of a heated discussion with ADA Karen Cross and decided to steer clear of them. He went straight to Susan, gave her a kiss on the cheek, and asked for a full update on the status of Alan Vernon and Wendy Duren.

Steve held his ground with Karen Cross, who was livid.

"You're telling me you bugged the homes of four individuals without a warrant?"

"There was no need for warrants. We got their permission and complete cooperation in writing," Steve said. "They were aware that they were under constant audio and video observation by the police."

"Did they know *why* they were under observation?" she asked pointedly.

"They were informed that we were conducting an investigation involving their nursing care."

"Did they know they could get killed?"

Steve was getting tired of dancing with Karen Cross on this issue. "Would you really have wanted us to tell them we suspected that Paul Guyot and Wendy Duren were murderers? What if we'd been wrong? What lecture would you have given me after Guyot and Duren found out what we'd been telling people? How many lawsuits would that have exposed us to?"

"That's your excuse?" Karen said, putting her hands on her hips.

"You pushed me into this."

"I didn't tell you to set up civilians to be killed."

"If I'd listened to you and done nothing, they'd be dead anyway," Steve said. "You didn't believe anyone was in danger."

"I didn't say that," Karen said. "I said you had no proof."

"This was the only way to get it."

"The *only* way?" she repeated, shaking her head. "Alan Vernon had a heart attack. He may die, and if he does, it will be your fault, Detective."

"Excuse me," Jesse said as he walked over, now wearing his lab coat and stethoscope. "It wasn't a heart attack."

"What was it then?" Steve asked.

"A panic attack," Jesse said. "Similar to the one I experienced watching the whole thing go down."

"He was watching it?" Karen said, looking at Steve and motioning to Jesse with a tip of her head. "Why didn't you just sell the feed as a pay-per-view program?"

"Mr. Vernon is going to be fine," Jesse said.

"And very wealthy after he sues the LAPD and wins," Karen said.

"He thinks Steve is a hero," Jesse said.

"Until his lawyer talks some sense into him," Karen said.

"I don't give a damn. If that happens, dealing with it will be your job, not mine," Steve said. "I'm done arguing with you, Counselor. I only want to know one thing. Do we have enough to charge Wendy Duren with murder and make it stick?"

Karen glared angrily at Steve, her cheeks red, her lips practically in a snarl. But she nodded.

"Then you can stand here stammering about my actions all you want. I have a murderer to interrogate."

And with that Steve marched off, leaving Karen Cross behind. He knew she had the power to get him suspended, knocked down a pay grade, or even thrown off the force, but right now all that mattered to him was closing this case and taking those two nurses down.

There were worse ways to end a career.

CHAPTER TWENTY-SIX

Steve flashed his ID to the two uniformed officers posted outside the door of Wendy Duren's room and went in to see her.

Her right shoulder was wrapped in bandages. An IV line ran into her left arm, which was handcuffed to the rail of her bed. She stared at Steve with hatred. Steve smiled back at her, knowing it would infuriate her even more.

"Here's the situation, Wendy. We had a camera in Alan Vernon's living room," Steve said. "It should make quite a show for the jury. We might even sell it on the Internet and make a few dollars."

"If you've got such a good case," she sneered, "why are you in here talking to me?"

"Because you have one opportunity to save yourself from getting a lethal injection of your own," Steve said. "You can give us Paul Guyot."

"I've never heard of him."

Steve shook his head, pulled a chair over, and sat down with a weary sigh. "You spent the night with him. You walked out his front door, drove to Starbucks, and then went straight to Alan Vernon's house. I know. I was following you."

"Were you looking in the bedroom window, too?" Duren asked. "Did you get off watching us make love? Did you wish you were him? That I was doing all those incredible things to you? I bet you want me right now, don't you?"

She blew him a kiss and laughed.

"I didn't see it, but I'm sure you two couldn't keep your hands off each other. Paul had just killed Vivian Hemphill and that's what makes you both hot. Killing people is your idea of foreplay," Steve said. "I wonder what he'll do for foreplay with his new lover, the one he'll be with while you're in prison."

Wendy's smug smile immediately faded, her face hardening with anger.

"Oh, come on." Steve looked at her with mock bewilderment. "You thought he'd take a vow of celibacy because you're on death row? He'll find someone else to play games with."

"Good," she said. "I want him to be happy."

"He'll be happy, all right. Delirious with joy. Because you'll be on death row for his mistake while he's setting the sheets on fire with some other lucky lady."

"What mistake?"

He had Wendy Duren then and he knew it. She'd taken the bait. She had to know what had tripped her up.

"We would never have known what the two of you were doing if it wasn't for him," Steve said. "The truth is, we didn't even know there were any murders, or that you two even existed, until Paul tried to run my father down."

Wendy looked confused.

"I know what you're thinking," Steve said, and it was true. It was all over her face. "'But Paul saw Dr. Sloan at John Muir. He was on to us.' That's what Paul told you, isn't it? Well, Wendy, Paul was wrong. It was a coincidence that my dad was there. See, my dad had no evidence of murder. He wasn't even looking at the right patients."

"That isn't true," she said.

"We didn't believe my father. We weren't going to do a thing. You were completely in the clear and you would have stayed that way—if it wasn't for Paul's brilliant idea to kill my dad."

Steve studied her face. For a moment he felt the heat of her anger shift from him and radiate in another direction. It was an opening, and he moved in for the kill.

"It *was* Paul's idea, wasn't it, Wendy? You knew it was wrong from the start. You tried to talk him out of it, but he just wouldn't listen," Steve said. "Now you're going to die for his stupid mistake—and all you want is for him to be happy."

Steve got up and shook his head. "You know something? What you said about me before was right. I do wish I had a woman like you, someone willing to sacrifice everything for her man. But I guess the women I end up with are too damn selfish. See you at your execution."

He sighed, turned his back to Wendy Duren, and headed for the door.

"Wait," she said.

Mark was startled awake by the ringing of his phone. He reached for it, knocking over the files stacked on the coffee table and spraying papers all over the floor.

He cursed, something he didn't often do, and picked up the receiver.

"Yes?" he said irritably.

"It's me, Dad," Steve said. "You sound angry."

He was, but it was the fleeting kind of anger he got when his alarm woke him too early, or he burned himself cooking, or a car cut him off on the road. It wasn't what his son thought it was, that he was still bitter about their argument that morning.

"I'm not angry at you. It's just that I was sleeping and knocked a whole bunch of papers on the floor. It's going to take me forever putting the files back together."

"You can take your time," Steve said. "In fact, you can forget all about it. The case is closed."

"What do you mean?"

"I'm calling from Community General. We caught Wendy Duren attempting to murder a patient," Steve said. "She's just given up Paul Guyot in exchange for taking the death penalty off the table in her case."

"That's terrific," Mark said. "Congratulations."

"It feels good to get those two off the street," Steve said.

"What are you doing at the hospital?"

"There was an altercation during her arrest," Steve said. "She got hurt."

"Did you?"

"My career might have taken a hit," he said, "but otherwise I'm unscathed."

"Did she confess to all the murders?"

"That was part of the deal," Steve said. "She has to admit to everything, going back to Beckman or wherever her killing spree actually started. There's no reason for her not to confess. She's going to prison anyway."

"Did she admit to Grover Dawson, Sandy Sechrest, and the others?"

"No," Steve said. "I don't think they were killed."

"Maybe it was Guyot who did them," Mark said.

"Maybe. I'll let you know," Steve said.

Mark knew he was being patronized, but he didn't say anything about it.

"We've still got to arrest Guyot and bring him in for interrogation," Steve continued. "Then I've got to write up all my reports. It's going to be a long night. Don't wait up for me. I'll fill you in on everything in the morning."

"I'll be eager to hear all about it," Mark said. "Good work, son."

"Thanks, Dad."

Steve hung up. Mark held the receiver for a long moment. Something still didn't feel right.

He set the receiver back in the cradle and regarded the mess on his floor. It was going to be hell reconstructing the

files. The papers all looked the same, mostly pages and
pages of Enable database printouts. They all looked alike.
Figuring out which page belonged in which file would take
forever.

He froze.

There were Enable printouts everywhere.

All the victims were listed in the Enable system. *That*
was something they *all* had in common. How could he have
missed that before?

Enable.

He said it aloud. "Enable."

There was something about that word that bothered him.
He repeated it aloud again.

"Enable," he said. "E-nable."

It sounded to him a lot like . . .

E. Noble.

Emily Noble.

*His subconscious was telling him to remember the soft-
ware!*

He thought back to his coma dream. When and how did
he use the Enable software?

That's when he recalled the coma dream moment when
he'd sat in front of his office computer at Community General. He'd inadvertently clicked on the "About" tab and all
the names of all the software designers scrolled by like
movie credits.

Why was that in his dream?

Because he'd made the same fumble before, in real life,
sometime in the days before his head injury.

Mark got to his feet and went to his laptop, which he'd
set on the kitchen table. He booted up and remotely accessed
the Enable medical records database at Community General.
He clicked the "About" link on the "Help" menu and
watched the names as they scrolled past.

And everything suddenly made sense. He knew why the

deaths he was investigating didn't match the "Game Over" pattern.

But he had no evidence to prove it.

So he decided he would follow Steve's lead.

He would use the next target as bait.

Steve's cell phone rang only a moment or two after he ended his call with Mark. It was Tanis Archer, calling from John Muir Hospital. He figured she was simply notifying him that they had Paul Guyot in custody.

She wasn't.

"We've lost him," she said. "Paul Guyot is gone."

He tightened his grip on the phone as if it might try to escape before he got the rest of the bad news.

"How did his car get past you?"

"His car is still in the parking structure," Tanis said. "He left on foot."

"Or he stole another car," Steve said.

"Damn," Tanis hissed.

"Tell me what happened."

"He walked out of the cardiac-care ward a couple of minutes before we got there. At least that's what the nurses up here tell us," she said. "Was there any way Wendy Duren could have warned him we were coming?"

"No, but maybe she didn't have to. The fact that she hasn't talked to him or didn't show up where she was supposed to this afternoon may have tipped him off that something was wrong," Steve said. "He could still be in the building. Are you covering all the exits?"

"We're trying," Tanis said. "But there are a hundred ways in and out of this place, including the sky bridge between the hospital and the office building next door."

The implications of Guyot's disappearance were deadly. It was one thing if he'd simply fled. But what if he'd slipped away to murder his next victim in the game, to snag the *E* in "Over"?

Steve didn't have a list of possible targets with a first name that began with the letter *E*. Whoever they were, they were totally unprotected.

They had to catch Guyot fast.

"Pull the security camera tapes for the hospital, the parking structure, and the office building next door," Steve said. "I'm on my way down."

Steve flipped his cell phone shut, put it in his pocket, and was hurrying down the hall when Amanda cut him off, the smile on her face evaporating when she saw his expression.

"I was about to congratulate you on catching Wendy Duren," Amanda said. "What's gone wrong?"

"I need you to put together a list of potential victims whose first names begin with *E*."

"How much time do I have?" she asked.

"We've already run out," Steve said and kept on going down the hall.

Mark awoke in bed from a dreamless sleep, his heart racing, his eyes staring into the darkness. He could hear the crashing surf, the creak of the house settling, the rustling of the leaves in the gentle ocean breeze.

But he could feel something else, a ripple in the air that brought chills to his skin.

It wasn't a cold draft.

He knew this feeling, this fear.

There was another presence in the room. He could almost smell the impending violence, like the scent of rain as storm clouds gathered in the sky.

The killer was out there, and not as an abstract concept in Mark's mind.

No, the killer was there. *In the bedroom.*

Mark remained very still. "I know you're here, Kristen. I'm going to turn on the lamp on my nightstand so we can see each other."

"Slowly," she whispered.

The voice raised goose bumps on his skin.

Mark reached out and turned on the lamp. He was startled to see Emily Noble standing at the foot of his bed.

She was the woman from his dreams, only in her early twenties and dressed entirely in black, including her gloves. Instead of looking at Mark with affection, as Emily had in his imagination, Kristen radiated hatred and pity.

"You look just like your mother," Mark said, sitting up against his pillows, his hands under the sheets.

If Kristen was startled by his remark, she didn't show it. "You remember her?"

"I do now," Mark said.

On some deep, subconscious level he'd remembered her at least a week ago, when he accidentally clicked "About" on the Enable software "Help" menu and saw Kristen Nash's name flicker quickly past in the scroll of software designers' credits. His mind began making the connections amidst the minutiae of his buried memories, serving them up to him as an elaborate dream while he was in a coma.

"Have you come to kill me?" Mark asked, his heart thundering in his chest.

She nodded.

"Why?"

"The same reason I killed the others," Kristen said. "You're supposed to be dead."

"Like you?"

Kristen nodded again. "You kept me alive in my mother's corpse. I should have died with her. But you didn't let that happen. For twenty-five years, I've been tortured for living a life I wasn't supposed to have, for the mistake *you* made."

"What makes you think you were punished?"

"After I was born, I was discarded into the child welfare system. I was given to a couple who used me as their slave. My so-called parents only wanted me and their four other foster children for the support checks from the state and the work we could do," Kristen said, speaking in a cold monotone, as if describing someone else's life instead of her own. "They used us for their pleasure, to gratify their sick physical desires, and then they rented us to others by the hour. I was nothing but a body to be used. I wasn't human anymore. I wasn't alive."

"I'm sorry," Mark said. The apology seemed ridiculously insufficient and her sneer confirmed it. "If you believed I was responsible for your suffering, why didn't you just kill me? Why kill the others?"

"I'm not a murderer, Dr. Sloan. This isn't about revenge," she said. "It's about doing what's right."

"How many people have you killed?"

"I haven't really killed anyone," she said. "I've freed them."

"How many?" Mark insisted.

"Fifteen, twenty. I don't know. But not enough," she said. "Not nearly enough. There are so many who need to be saved."

Mark shuddered to think of all the killing she'd done and the murders she had yet to commit. "How can you say you're not a murderer?"

"Because you can't kill someone who is already dead," she said. "They weren't living any more than I am. They were doomed to purgatory because of doctors like you. It took me a long time, but I finally realized that the only way I could truly free myself was to save others from my fate, from being punished the way I was. I'm only making sure that the people God has chosen to die actually do."

Mark could envision the rest of her story now as if he'd written it himself. In her mind, he probably had.

Kristen learned computer programming. She used her programming skills to get a job with a company that made database software for hospitals. While working on the program, she created a "back door" for herself so she could access the medical records of any hospital and find people who'd been saved from seemingly certain death.

She approached her victims by posing as someone from Kemper-Carlson Pharmaceuticals. Once she was alone with them, she found a way to engineer their accidental deaths, by overdose, drug interactions, or other means.

Mark didn't become one of her targets until he'd narrowly escaped death himself. If Jesse hadn't tackled him out of the path of that car and then later drilled the burr hole in his skull to relieve the fluid buildup, he would have surely died.

"How did you get Chadwick Saxelid into the hot tub?" Mark asked.

"I took off my shirt and got in first," she said. "He practically dove in to join me. Men like to see me naked. I learned that very young from my foster father."

"You encouraged Chadwick to drink some beers."

She shrugged. "He was thirsty."

"You knew what the combination of that hot water and the alcohol would do to him."

"Of course. I did my research."

"What about Grover Dawson? How did you get him to take the Viagra?"

"I switched his meds," she said. "He thought he was taking his prescription drugs."

"You used the same method to murder Leila Pevney, only in her case you swapped her pills with pseudoephedrine," Mark said. "Then after she died, you staged the scene with crumpled tissues and empty cold tablet packages to make it look like she'd been suffering from a cold."

"You make what I did sound evil," she said. "It wasn't. I was doing them a favor."

"Do you think that's what Sandy Sechrest thought you were doing when you tossed the hair dryer into her bathtub and electrocuted her?" Mark said. "Tell me you didn't see terror in her eyes."

"Everyone is afraid of death, Dr. Sloan. But we all have

to die. There is no escaping it. That is why I am here tonight. That is the mission God has given me. I saved them."

"But they weren't suffering," Mark said. "They didn't think their second chance at life was punishment. They weren't like you. They were happy. They didn't want to die."

"You don't know that," Kristen said.

"I know that I don't want to die," Mark said.

"It's not up to you or me," she said. "It's God's will."

"Isn't it God's will that I was saved? That the others all got a second chance, too?"

She shook her head. "There is a natural balance. There is life and there is death. Both are absolutes. You want to know what true evil is? It's doctors who prevent souls from passing on, who doom them to a living death in a slow-rotting corpse."

Mark might have felt some sympathy for Kristen, for all the unspeakable horrors she'd endured, if not for the lives she'd taken. There was no forgiving that or the careful premeditation with which she carried out her executions.

When she described her killings, Mark detected a pride in her work, maybe even a tinge of sadistic pleasure. There was a reason she took something personal from each victim besides their lives. She wanted trophies, souvenirs so she could relive the experience of killing again and again.

Kristen was wrong about herself.

She was human. She just didn't possess any humanity.

This wasn't about doing God's work. This was about lashing out at the world for her suffering, relieving her pain by inflicting pain on others.

"What's my accident going to be?" Mark asked.

"You're going to take a bad fall down the stairs and break your skull open."

"What makes you think I'll cooperate?"

"All you have to do is lie there," she said. "I'll smother you into unconsciousness, then drag you to the stairs and give you a little nudge."

"You're not worried about me putting up a fight?"

"You're a weak old man," she said. "I can take you."

"You probably could," Mark said. "But I was expecting you. That's why I went to bed tonight with a gun."

He pulled back the sheet with his free hand to show her that he wasn't bluffing. One of Steve's guns was in his hand, aimed squarely at her.

Kristen seemed no more surprised by the gun than she'd been by the fact that he'd known who she was.

"I've been watching you for years." She casually picked out one of the throw pillows on a chair, held it between both of her hands, and advanced on him. "You won't shoot me."

"Only in self-defense. So please, turn around and walk away," he said. "Don't force me to pull the trigger."

She shook her head. "You'd rather die yourself than take someone's life. Hell, you kept a dead woman alive just to birth me."

"Are you willing to bet your life on it?"

"I'm dead already."

She lunged. Mark fired. The bullet blasted through the pillow in her hands in an explosion of tiny feathers. She staggered three steps back, stood for a moment in bewilderment, and dropped the mangled pillow.

Kristen looked down and regarded the wound in her side as if she'd merely dribbled some food on herself.

"It's over, Kristen," Mark said softly, his voice shaking as much as he was. "Sit down or walk away, but don't come a step closer."

She looked up at Mark, her eyes glinting with furious intent. "I can still take you."

She lunged for him again, hands outstretched like talons, and he fired once more, the bullet catching her in the chest and spinning her around. Her body banged off the edge of the bed and she hit the floor on her back, her legs curled underneath her.

Mark got out of bed and went to her side. He saw blood

seeping from her chest wound. She was wheezing, trying to speak.

"Stay still," Mark said. "I'll call for an ambulance."

She shook her head, grabbed him by the collar of his pajama top, and pulled him close.

"You delivered me twice," she whispered. "First into life and now into—"

Kristen seemed to run out of air before she could finish, her mouth agape, her eyes unseeing.

She was dead.

CHAPTER TWENTY-SEVEN

It was just after daybreak. Mark sat on a sand dune, his back to his house and everything that was going on there.

The private road in front of the beach house was crammed with patrol cars, unmarked detective sedans, vans from the crime scene investigation unit, and a morgue wagon from the medical examiner's office. Reporters and satellite broadcast trucks jammed the parking lot of the Trancas Market across the Pacific Coast Highway.

This kind of activity wasn't new to Mark's wealthy, publicity-shy neighbors, who were virtually prisoners in their beachfront homes that morning and were probably simmering with anger about it.

Over the years, Mark had brought a lot of unwanted law enforcement and media attention to the street. Not so long ago, a corpse dressed as a mermaid washed up in front of Mark's house, a notorious serial killer was arrested in Mark's living room, and Mark's next-door neighbor was gunned down in bed with a naked starlet.

Most of the residents on the street were still bitter about the time Mark's house was quarantined because he took in a sick man who'd been infected with genetically altered smallpox. The entire block had to be evacuated and people prevented at gunpoint from returning to their homes.

That isn't the sort of thing that happens in most communities, he thought ruefully, unless Dr. Mark Sloan happens to be your neighbor.

Mark wouldn't have been surprised if soon his neighbors gathered with torches outside his door to burn his house to the ground and drive him away.

That was assuming, of course, that some mad arsonist or bomber didn't beat them to it. There were already a few people matching those descriptions rotting in prison cells, nursing their grudges against Mark, the man who put them there.

He'd be hell on real estate values wherever he went.

But the way Mark was feeling now, he might just move on his own anyway, saving his neighbors, the mad arsonists, and the bombers the trouble of forcing him out.

He wasn't sure he could live in the same house, and sleep in the same room, where he'd killed a woman.

His hands stung. He didn't know whether it was a physical consequence of firing the gun or an emotional reaction to what he'd done.

It didn't really matter, though.

He would be feeling what happened last night, in one form or another, for the rest of his life.

One thing he *wouldn't* be feeling was guilt. He knew he'd had no choice except to shoot Kristen. If he hadn't, he would have been killed. It was unquestionably an act of self-defense. Yet he still felt an overall queasiness that went beyond shock or revulsion. It was deeper than that. It was an uneasiness in his soul.

Kristen had been right when she said he'd rather die than take a life. But what he had discovered last night was that his will to survive was much stronger than any of his ethical and moral reservations about killing.

It made him wonder what else he didn't really know about himself.

Mark was so lost in thought that he wasn't aware of Steve approaching until his son sat down beside him on the sand.

"How are you holding up?" Steve asked.

Mark shrugged. "I don't regret what I did, but I'm not feeling very good about myself right now." That was an understatement and he figured his son probably knew it. "Any word on Paul Guyot?"

"He was arrested trying to hot-wire a car last night about a mile from John Muir Hospital," Steve said. "A civilian saw him and called the police. We were already patrolling the area, so we got there within a minute or two of the call."

"What made Guyot run?"

"A bad feeling," Steve said. "He tried to call Wendy on her cell. When she didn't answer, he called Appleby Nursing Services and they told him they hadn't heard from her and she hadn't shown up to see her assigned patient. That spooked him."

"Is he talking?"

Steve laughed. "We can't shut him up. The instant he sat down in the interrogation room he offered to testify against Wendy in return for a lesser sentence."

"The two of them were certainly made for each other," Mark said. "Where do I stand?"

"What do you mean?"

"On the shooting," Mark said. "Despite the obvious signs of forced entry, the crime scene doesn't necessarily support my claim that I shot Kristen Nash in self-defense. For one thing, she wasn't carrying a weapon."

"You have nothing to worry about. I just got a call from Tanis. She tossed Kristen Nash's place and found the trophies she took from her victims. That pretty much confirms your theory about the killings. We'll get a computer crime forensics expert to check her computer and see if she left a trail when she accessed the medical records."

Mark was relieved. He wasn't relishing the prospect of having to defend himself in either a court of law or the court of public opinion.

"How did you figure out there was another killer at work?" Steve asked.

"I knew Grover Dawson and the others were murdered," Mark said. "It wasn't until I dropped those files that I finally realized there was a reason I couldn't link their deaths to Guyot and Duren. It was because there was another killer, someone else with an entirely different motive."

"But like Guyot and Duren, she got away with it unnoticed for so long because she picked people who were expected to die."

"Kristen Nash killed them because they'd nearly died before. That was her motive," Mark said. "Guyot and Duren picked them because their deaths were less likely to be investigated."

"Why didn't you tell me about Kristen?"

"It was still a series of guesses on my part. I didn't have any real evidence," Mark said. "I thought it could wait until morning and we could argue about it then."

Mark regretted the dig at his son the moment he said it.

Steve looked his father in the eye, acknowledging that his comment had hit home. "But you went downstairs and got yourself one of my guns anyway."

The accusation in the remark was clear to Mark. Steve didn't think his father was being honest with him, that Mark had other motivations for not informing his son about what he knew.

"If you think I wanted the glory of capturing Kristen all by myself, you're wrong," Mark said. "I'd cheated death and I was alone. I realized that I fit the victim profile perfectly and, given what I knew, I had to assume she wouldn't be able to resist killing me. I was afraid, that's all."

"Not enough to call me. Not enough to call someone, *anyone*, to stay with you so you wouldn't be alone," Steve said. "You set yourself up as bait."

"I didn't have to set myself up. I was a target no matter what I did," Mark said. If that sounded familiar to Steve, it was meant to.

"How did you know she was going to come for you last night?"

"I didn't," Mark said. "I thought I'd have some time to prepare the trap, so that you and a squad of police officers would be there when it was sprung. I never intended to be alone when it happened."

"So you took a gun to bed just in case."

"Better safe than dead," Mark said.

It sounded to him like something his son might say. Tough and cynical—two adjectives Mark had never thought of as applying to himself. He hadn't enjoyed shooting Kristen Nash, not one bit.

However, as frightened as he'd been last night, even with the gun for protection, he'd felt a thrill of victory, like a gambler scoring a blackjack, when he turned on the light and saw Kristen Nash standing in his bedroom.

In that chilling moment, he had still been able to take some satisfaction in having figured out the solution to the puzzle. But he had taken no pleasure from squeezing the trigger. It made him feel sick.

Steve looked out at the water, and Mark followed his gaze. The sky was surprisingly clear and blue for so early in the morning. Sailboats were already out in the bay. In the distance Mark could see a freighter or oil tanker. The ship seemed still, but he knew it was moving, just too slowly to notice from afar.

"You could have been killed last night and all because you were angry at me for keeping you out of the investigation," Steve said. "I did it for you. I didn't want you ending up in the ICU."

"You just wanted to solve the case on your own," Mark said.

"So did you," Steve snapped back.

"Well, we both succeeded," Mark said. "And look at what we risked to do it."

"I gambled with Alan Vernon's life and you gambled your own."

"Like father, like son," Mark said.

"Yeah," Steve replied, a smiling growing on his face. "I suppose you're right."

Mark smiled back at him. "What are we going to do?"

Steve shrugged. "We could become private eyes."

They shared a laugh and then were silent for a long moment. Finally, Mark sighed and said what needed to be said.

"I don't want to compete with you."

"You don't have to," Steve said. "We both know you'd always win."

"That wasn't the point I was trying to make," Mark said. "I'm proud of you and I want you to succeed. I'm not trying to outdo you at your profession."

"You do whether you try to or not."

"Do you want me to stop investigating homicides?"

"You couldn't stop if you wanted to, much less if I wanted you to," Steve said. "And I don't."

"Do you hate me?" Mark asked.

"No, but sometimes I wonder if I'll ever be able to step out from under your shadow and prove myself."

"I think you just did," Mark said. "You solved a serial murder case on your own. I wouldn't have discovered those murders. I would have missed Paul Guyot and Wendy Duren."

"I would have missed Kristen Nash."

"So, I guess we need each other after all."

"Was there ever any doubt?" Steve asked.

"No," Mark said. "Never."

Mark spent the next few days in a hotel, then checked himself into Community General Hospital for the bone graft surgery.

While Mark was hospitalized, Dr. Amanda Bentley

arranged for a crime-scene cleaning service to remove any signs that a shooting had ever occurred at the beach house.

Every inch of the room was cleaned and disinfected. The soiled bedroom carpet was pulled up and replaced with something new. The blood-spattered walls were repainted a different color.

Steve took the cleanup one step further than that. He bought Mark a new bedroom set and rearranged the room so it looked entirely different than it had before.

Although Mark hadn't said anything about being reluctant to come home, Steve couldn't imagine his father would be comfortable returning to a place where he'd killed someone.

But Steve wasn't going to let some insane killer drive him and his father from their home. That would be giving the killer too much satisfaction, even if she was dead and couldn't enjoy the manipulation.

It was the principle that mattered to Steve.

He couldn't tolerate the ugly precedent that moving away would set, the message it would send. He couldn't let the killers they pursued think they held any power over their personal lives.

The question that remained was whether his father felt the same way.

The morning Mark was released, Steve picked him up and drove him back to Malibu. On the way, Mark didn't voice any hesitation about returning home. He didn't talk much at all.

For the first time since Mark Sloan began investigating murders, he was dreading revisiting the scene of a homicide. But when Mark stood in the doorway of his remodeled bedroom, he felt tears well up in his eyes. His son had done exactly the right thing. It was a new room, and a fresh start, yet in a warm and familiar place.

"Thank you," Mark said, wiping his eyes.

Steve pretended not to notice the tears.

"There's more," he said, leading his dad back to the kitchen.

The table was set for two. Steve opened the refrigerator and started taking out items. First out was a cheesy noodle casserole.

"Homemade seashell casserole," Steve said.

"You made it?" Mark asked incredulously.

"It's not like I had to split the atom to do it," Steve said. "But that was the easy part."

He reached into the refrigerator and took out an amazing chocolate cake, layered with nuts and several different kinds of chocolate.

"Chocolate Decadence à la Sloan," Steve said proudly.

Mark smiled broadly. "I don't believe it. What did I do to deserve all this?"

"We're celebrating your return to health and the end of your sadness."

"What sadness?"

"Over killing Kristen Nash."

"I don't think a slice of cake, not even Chocolate Decadence à la Sloan, can cure that."

"You didn't save just your life that night, Dad."

Mark nodded. "I know. I saved all the people she might have killed. That doesn't make me feel much better."

"You saved me." Steve reached into his pocket and pulled out a sheet of paper, handing it to his father.

"What's this?"

"We found it on her computer," Steve said. "It was her kill list. I was on it."

Mark stared at the names. Hammond McNutchin, Joyce Kling, and Leila Pevney were on it, of course. And so was Steve. Not because Steve was his son, but because he'd once cheated death.

Several years ago, Steve had been shot by a would-be assassin during an early-morning breakfast with Tanis Archer and police chief Masters. He nearly died on the operating table, and even afterward his prognosis wasn't good. But luck was on his side. Apparently, it still was.

Mark had no reservations about killing to save his son. None at all.

Back then, when his son was shot, he'd been ready to kill to avenge him. The anger he felt even now, just at seeing Steve's name on that list, burned away the lingering sadness that had plagued him for days.

"Let's have some of that cake," Mark said, crumpling up the paper and tossing it away.

Steve started to slice into the cake. "I'm warning you, this is so rich and chocolaty, it could kill you."

"What a way to go," Mark said.

It was good to be home.

Read on for a preview
of Mark Sloan's adventures in the next
Diagnosis Murder novel

THE LAST WORD

Coming from Signet in May 2007

Carter Sweeney was a pale, slight man with a receding hair-line and a meticulously groomed goatee. He wore a loose-fitting bright orange jumpsuit and sat in a stiff-backed stainless steel chair. His wrists and ankles were in irons, which were looped around his waist and strung through an eyebolt in the concrete floor.

Despite these restrictions, Sweeney was completely re-laxed, as if he were lounging on a beach instead of sitting in the chilly, sterile visitation room at Sunrise Valley State Prison for extremely violent offenders. The visitation room was a luxury suite compared to solitary confinement in his twelve-by-seven-foot cell, where his bed, writing shelf, and stool were all made of poured concrete.

During his first year at Sunrise Valley, Sweeney was al-lowed outdoors for only one hour per day, by himself, in a concrete cavern known as the Dog Run. After three years of incarceration, he was allowed three hours per day in the Dog Run with two other prisoners. With continued good behav-ior, that was the most sunlight and social interaction he could expect to enjoy until his execution.

So the opportunity to spend time in the visitation room with someone from the outside world was truly an experi-ence to be savored for as long as possible. Unfortunately for

Sweeney, his reluctant guest didn't share his eagerness to prolong the visit.

"You don't call. You don't write. I was beginning to wonder if you still cared about me," Sweeney said in the smooth, calming voice that had once made him a Los Angeles talk radio star.

Dr. Mark Sloan sat across from Sweeney in a stainless steel chair that felt as if it had been carved from a block of solid ice. He was shivering from the cold, but he couldn't let Sweeney see it. Sweeney would interpret the shaking as fear and use it as a psychological weapon against him.

Mark knew it would be foolhardy to underestimate Sweeney simply because he was chained and imprisoned. Sweeney was the most dangerous man Mark had encountered in his forty years as a homicide consultant to the LAPD.

It wasn't that Sweeney was a violent man, at least not physically. As far as Mark knew, Sweeney had never hurt anyone with his bare hands. His preferred method of killing was explosives encased in ornately crafted, hand-carved wooden boxes. Sweeney and his younger sister Caitlin learned their bomb making and wood carving skills from their father, Regan, a furniture maker who set off bombs all over Los Angeles after his store was condemned by the city to build a new freeway.

But Carter Sweeney's true weapon was his mind, which Mark was sure the years of near-solitary confinement hadn't broken. He was a brilliant analytical thinker with the frightening ability to manipulate others into doing exactly what he wanted, often without their ever being aware of it.

"I didn't come here to play games with you," Mark said, knowing full well that he was deluding himself. Simply by showing up, he was already playing whatever game Sweeney had begun.

"Of course not," Sweeney said. "We both know how much you dislike games—unless there's a corpse involved."

"You kill people," Mark said. "I don't."

"So that must have been a different Dr. Mark Sloan I read about a few months ago," Sweeney said. "*That* Mark Sloan gunned down a woman in his own home."

"It was self-defense," Mark said. "Not premeditated murder."

For an instant, that horrible moment played out again in front of Mark's eyes. He was in bed, helpless, recovering from a head injury. She was going to smother him with a pillow. He had to shoot. But the first shot didn't stop her. *She just kept coming—*

He blinked hard, willing the image away, but he knew it was a temporary reprieve. The memory of that blood-soaked night would haunt him for the rest of his life.

"But you knew she would show up," Sweeney said. "If you didn't intend to kill her, why were you waiting for her with a loaded gun?"

"I tried to reason with her," Mark said. "I didn't want her to die."

"Sure you didn't." Sweeney winked.

So was *that* what this visit was about? Mark wondered. Did Sweeney want to revel in Mark's deadly misfortune? If it was, Mark wasn't going to play along.

"You're in no position to judge me or anybody else," Mark said. "You're a mass murderer. You blew up a hospital, maiming and killing dozens of innocent people."

"Come now, Mark. You know I didn't do that. My poor, disturbed sister Caitlin planted those bombs. You saw her there yourself, right before the hospital fell on top of you."

"She was acting on your orders," Mark said. "You wanted revenge against me for sending your father here."

"You killed him."

"I *caught* him," Mark said. "The state of California executed him."

Within days of Regan Sweeney's execution, Carter Sweeney had embarked on a copycat bombing campaign to make it appear that Mark had framed an innocent man. Sweeney also used his popular radio program to expertly turn the public opinion against Mark, the LAPD, and the district attorney's office. But Carter ultimately failed, undone by his own arrogance, which Mark used to trick him into incriminating himself in the bombings.

But Mark hadn't known that Carter's sister was also involved in the plot. She remained free and blew up Community General Hospital, trapping Mark, his son Steve, and many of his closest friends in the flaming rubble.

That was just the beginning of the nightmare for Mark Sloan.

Caitlin joined the Revolutionary Order for Armed Rebellion, a white supremacist group, using them to hijack the bus that was taking her brother to prison. Together, Carter and Caitlin kidnapped Mark and forced him to help them steal one hundred million dollars from the Federal Reserve.

But Mark outsmarted them once again. Now the Sweeneys were finally imprisoned, and Carter was sentenced to death by lethal injection. Like father, like son.

"As much as I enjoy reliving your downfall," Mark said, "I'm sure you didn't invite me here to rehash your history of violence."

"I'm an innocent man," Sweeney said.

"Oh, spare me," Mark said.

"I couldn't possibly do that," Sweeney said, a gleam in his eye. "I wanted you to hear the good news directly from me. I'll be out of here in a few weeks."

"The only way you're leaving prison is in a coffin," Mark said. "All your appeals have been denied."

"Not all," Sweeney said. "The court has granted my writ of habeas corpus. There's going to be a hearing soon. I have a feeling it's going to go very well. I might even be freed in time to cast my vote for mayor. But it's such a difficult choice. Do I vote for Police Chief John Masters, whose department unjustly arrested me? Or District Attorney Neal Burnside, who railroaded me into this hellhole?"

"The evidence against you is overwhelming and irrefutable. No court will ever overturn your conviction," Mark said. "But go ahead, enjoy your fantasy. I'm sure it makes the hours pass more swiftly in your cell."

"I won't be the second innocent Sweeney wrongly put to death because of you."

"You're wasting your act on me," Mark said. "We both know the truth."

Sweeney broke into a broad grin. "Haven't you heard? Clinton never had sex with that woman and Iraq has weapons of mass destruction. The truth doesn't matter anymore. Truth is so last century. The new currency in our culture is perception. And everyone's perception of me is about to change."

"Not mine," Mark said.

"I'm counting on that," Sweeney said. "So, tell me, Mark, how's your health these days? I heard you took a nasty fall."

"I'll live."

"That's good, because I want you to enjoy a very long life."

"It's too short to waste any more of it here with you," Mark said. "Make your point already."

"I already have. Weren't you listening? Let's have lunch when I get out. How do you feel about Chinese food?"

"This is the last time we'll be seeing each other." Mark rose from his seat. "At least until your execution."

"Now *that's* more like the Mark Sloan I know," Sweeney said. "You never miss an opportunity to see someone die, do you?"

Mark went to the door and pounded on it a little too urgently.

"Guard, I'm ready to go."

"What's your hurry? There are so many of your friends in

here. You should really say hello to them before you leave. I know they'd love to see you."

"I'll pass," Mark said.

The serial killer known as the Silent Partner was here. So was former councilman Matt Watson, psychiatrist Gavin Reed, detective Harley Brule, mob accountant Malcolm Trainor, and many others Mark had helped capture. He didn't need to see how the years of incarceration had taken their toll on the minds and bodies of all those murderers.

He took no pleasure from their suffering, even though they deserved it. His investigations weren't about vengeance. Although it was about seeing that justice was served, he'd come to accept the fact that it wasn't his primary motivation. It was the chase. It was the intellectual challenge of the hunt, the methodical piecing together of the clues that led to the killer. *That's* what drove him.

Mark never again wanted to see the faces of the killers he'd caught, not in the flesh or in his memory. And yet here he was in a room with Carter Sweeney, the worst of them all.

What was he thinking, coming here?

What was taking so long for the damn door to open?

"Think of all the vacancies they'd have in here if not for your diligence, Mark. They should really have named this prison in your honor," Sweeney said. "Maybe they're just waiting until you die."

Finally Mark heard the electronic hiss of the locks opening automatically inside the thick steel door. A guard stepped in, eyed Sweeney warily, and escorted Mark out. The big door closed behind them, the locks sliding into place with a heavy, satisfying *thunk*.

Carter Sweeney was chained into place behind a steel door. He couldn't do Mark, or anybody else, any harm ever again. Even so, it took every ounce of self-control Mark possessed not to run all the way out of the prison.